Dream Seller

By

Amy Stephens

August 15, 2022

Dream Seller Foreword

The American South is filled with misconceptions, most of them formed from movies, television, magazines and books and just about every other medium including social media. Television shows like *The Dukes of Hazzard*, *The Beverly Hillbillies,* and *Hee Haw* suggest that we are all backward, ignorant, prone to drunkenness and intermarried if not incestuous.

Of course, *Gone with The Wind* has been an obvious stereotype of Southern women, a large dose of happy darkies, and the perpetuation of "The Lost Cause". And *Deliverance* further painted a picture of decadence. *Steel Magnolias* probably come closer than any movie to a realistic depiction of my South.

Every Southern writer has painted his own picture of his or her South. There is Faulkner's South, Eudora Welty's South, James Dickey's South and even Harper Lee's South. Even more modern writers like Pat Conroy, Lewis Grizzard, Willie Morris, James Lee Burke, Fannie Flagg, Ron Rash, and Rick Bragg tell their stories from their own unique perspective. That's what writers do. That old instruction still applies: "Write about what you know."

All of those portraits have some truth because The South is unique to each person's experience. One of the constants in every portrayal, accurate or not, is that Southern families are dysfunctional in some way. Faulkner's *Long Hot Summer* focuses on the Varner family with the patriarch of Big Daddy and Yoknapatawpha county full of Compsons and Snopes. Many a doctoral thesis has been written on the genealogy of that fictional county.

In all honesty, the members of the Southern family are much like any family members anywhere else. There are some who are extremely eccentric and some that have out-right mental problems; but we are not ashamed of them. As the old saying goes, "We don't hide them in an institution; we put them on the front porch with a glass of sweet tea and a rocking chair and listen to their stories."

The southeastern part of North Carolina has its own unique culture. That's where Amy Stephens and I grew up. It is a diverse culture, a diverse landscape, and it has a history that has created a people that are still tied to the land. Our origins are not so much the cotton fields and plantations like The Deep South as they are the small farms, woods and swamps, rivers and ever-changing seacoasts. Although the number of folks who make their living directly from the soil, the woods or the sea has diminished over the years, those who went away still cling to the hunting and fishing; they grow large gardens and give away produce; they form environmental groups to preserve their natural heritage and still come back to "the home place" long after they have moved to the city. I believe that you my move away, but you can never leave home.

For most of our history, the rivers and swamps separated communities. As a result, there were not many large cities. Small towns still dominate the landscape of the Tarheel state even as the big urban areas continue to expand and ingulf those communities where everybody knew their neighbors, those who lived next door and those who lived "down the road a piece", where food was the common denominator for funerals and weddings and solace (if not the cure) for every illness from measles to cholera. And they took that food to their neighbors even if the illness was contagious. That's just what we do.

I guess the most misunderstood element of our South is race. Certainly, there was an unseen line, a dichotomous line, that separated Black, White and Indian. We knew it existed and, in our hearts and even in our minds, we knew it was wrong. But it was a line that was sometimes ignored and sometimes moved depending on the individuals involved. Our vision of race was broad but our relations with individuals of other races tended to be personal and sometimes, even though we knew that line was there, we chose to ignore it.

A Southern writer can't write a real story of his home and ignore the race element. It is a part of us. Sometimes we are ashamed of the past--- and the present—but we have to acknowledge it as a part of who we are. All too often in trying to depict the reality of a story, a Southern writer will just make up what he wanted the past to be, not what it really was. Sometimes the reader won't believe the story because it doesn't meet their preconceived notion of what relations between races was really like. Although the weight of the historical depiction of race relations is heavy, it doesn't mean that it was all dark. I have always said that, "Every thing in the world is personal". And that applies to relationships among people regardless of their race. A good Southern writer adheres to that philosophy.

I hope the reader of this story, sees the uniqueness of the characters, the image of a time and place that was different from anywhere else, certainly different from what the media has presented. My South and Amy Stephens' South, is home. And there's no place like home.

--Bill Thompson--

Acknowledgements

Thank you to my friend Bill Thompson for the introduction, my son Wesley Stephens and my cousin Betsy Stafford for proofreading, and a huge thank you to all of my friends for listening to me talk about this project for years.

Dream Seller

Table of Contents

The Family

Iver Johnson Murphy—A sixteen-year-old boy from Donahoe Creek, Bladen County, North Carolina

Gene and Roy Murphy—younger twin brothers of Iver

Lauralee and Walter Scott Murphy----Iver, Gene and Roy's Mother and Father

Mariah McLean---Grandmother of Lauralee and one of the wives of Erastus Rembrandt Edwards

Erastus Rembrandt Edwards (Doc)—Grandfather of Iver, Gene and Roy

John McLean and Judith McArthur McLean (Big Judy and Big Jack)---Great Grandparents of Iver, Gene and Roy, Grandparents of Lauralee Murphy, and parents of Mariah McLean

Rudolph Hatcher—Works at the store and husband of Betsy Hatcher

Betsy Hatcher—Wife of Rudolph Hatcher and keeps house for Lauralee and Walter

T.R. (Theodore Roosevelt) Murphy—Walter Murphy's Brother

Naomi Lopez Murphy-T.R. Murphy's Wife

Daphney –T.R.'s ex-wife

Braddy—Cousin of Lauralee who is from Washington DC

Helen----Crazy cousin of Lauralee who escaped from Dix Hill in Raleigh

Girlie Carter—The daughter of Henrietta and Iver's great uncle George McArthur

Sissy (Celeste) Reynolds – The beautiful girl of Iver's dreams

Chapter 1

The Old Man and the Marvelous Machine

The sign hanging from the mailbox post said, "Dr. Erastus Rembrandt Edwards, MD, Masseuse and Artificial Blood Circulator." The words were in shiny gold on a black board with brass rings on top to hang. I sucked up all of the air around me and walked up to the front door.

There was a sign hanging on the inside of the front door that read, "Come in." I turned the doorknob and started to push the door open when I heard someone squall out, a kind of moan, some ooooo sounds and a grunt.

Then a quiet, firm voice said, "Now Mac, you are paying for an arthritis treatment. You want to get around better; let me loose those joints. Hold on to the handlebars."

There were panting sounds and then a sigh. "All right, Doc. I've pissed my britches. Let's finish."

Curiosity was raised. I eased open the front door and peeped through the crack. No one was in the front room. I slipped on in and sat down. I heard a man moaning. Curiosity was killing me now. I slipped over to the curtain that hung in a doorway and spied through the crack between the curtain and the doorframe. What I think had been the dining room was now full of what looked like Dr. Frankenstein's lab equipment. I was sure that a Hollywood director could make a movie there. I couldn't take my eyes off of the blinking yellow and red lights on a box about six feet high and three feet wide. The lights looked like taillights on a Cadillac. There were light switches, fuses and bare light bulbs. There were brass wing nuts holding what looked like jumper cables to the front of the machine and some of the switches had numbers. Across the top was written in bold red letters "Blood Circulator." And "Caution."

Standing in front of the lights and switches was an old man who had a big head of white hair, bald about halfway back--- brushed back, not slicked back. He was my Granddaddy, Momma's daddy, and my Grandma MaMariah's ex-husband, I thought. My brothers, Gene and Roy, and I called him Doc. Daddy called him Mr. Rastus. Momma called him "Your Granddaddy" when she was talking about him to us boys. He had great eyebrows, waxed out to look like the horns of an old Texas Longhorn, suspenders and a black string tie like cowboys' wear. His sleeves were pushed up with women's red garters. And to put the icing on the cake, he had a big white waxed mustache that looked like another set of horns hanging off his upper lip. Doc had a trademark look that no one else in the world could match. When I told Daddy, I wanted to be a doctor he said, "Go down in the morning and talk to Mr. 'Rastas." That was about a week ago. What actually got me down here to talk to Doc was a help wanted ad he put in the paper. The ad said "Doctor in need of assistant. Applicants need a driver's license and willingness to learn. Pays well." I wanted a car. I thought I wanted to be a doctor. I knew I wanted a car.

Back to the moaning. I knew the old bald-headed man that was moaning. It was Mr. McDonald, the barber. He was sitting on a black Western Auto bicycle that was mounted on a wooden frame contraption. There was more Hollywood magic. The bicycle didn't have a back tire but an electric motor to turn the pedals. The bicycle had a metal tractor seat and strap-on skates for the pedals. The wheels had been taken off the skates. The set of jumper cables coming off the front of the Blood Circulator were hooked with gear clamps to the handlebars. Mr. Mc-Donald wasn't wearing any socks and his bare feet were in the skate straps. Dr. Edwards flipped a light switch, and Mr. McDonald started pedaling the bicycle, or, more correctly, the bicycle started pumping Mr. McDonald's legs. Then Doc flipped another switch, and I heard a kind of sizzling sound. It dawned on me that a sizzling sound came off a Weed Chopper Electric Fencer. I had been on an electric fencer before, helping Mama get her hogs hemmed up. If you hit an electric fencer that pulses, it just kind of makes you mad, but if you grab a hold to a strand of electric fence wire hooked to a Weed Chopper Electric Fence, well you just clamp down and grind your teeth. A Weed Chopper doesn't pulse. It just stays on. It won't ground out. It will burn through weeds. It will burn through a frog if he gets hung across. It will set the woods on fire. I had heard and felt that sound before. I cringed all the way to my feet. This time, Mr. McDonald did not, or could not, say anything. Doc said, "I can hear those joints cracking loose. Satan is loosening his grip on your bones." Mr. McDonald's teeth were showing, and his eyes started to roll back in his head, and the motor kept the chain turning. His hands were clamped to the handlebars, and he was swaying. When the color of his eyes was nothing but white, Doc flipped the switch and caught Mr. McDonald as he was rolling off of the Bone Cracker Bicycle. Doc helped Mr. McDonald off the bike and stood him up.

Doc, the old man with white hair and waxed horned eyebrows said," Well, how do you feel?"

Mr. McDonald blinked slowly like his eyes were dry. He rolled his head around and started to march around in a circle. All he could say was "Praise God! The 'ritus is gone. Praise the Lord. Hot damn!" Over and over again in that order. Dr. Edwards slowed the march down long enough to get Mr. McDonald to put his socks and shoes on.

He said again, "Well, how do you feel?"

Mr. McDonald said, "Like a rabbit."

"You're going to be chasing the women again."

"I doubt that. After I catch one, I'm too old to play with her. "

"You need some of the Rooster Juice I perfected. I'm thinking about selling in the Farmer's Almanac. Want to try it?"

"Hell, yes!

I saw Mr. McDonald pass him a ten. "How much for the tonic?"

"First one's on me. Just don't tell anybody about my machine or the tonic. I can't take any more customers." I saw him wink. This old man was a good salesman; that was for sure. Mr. McDonald was going to tell it or bust. Everybody that knew him was going to see he's walking better and ask what he did. I'm not sure about the tonic. That might have been the same thing, I thought. O Lord. I knew what he and Mrs. McDonald were going to do. Old people getting frisky. I said to myself, 'No, Iver, just put that out of your mind.' I couldn't.

Mr. McDonald walked out past me, grinning as he put the blue bottle in his pocket; his pants smelled like piss. He knew his pants were wet and he had to go home like that, and he was still grinning. I guess he would go home and have to tell his wife why he was wet. I would have just slipped around to the machine and washed them myself. Maybe his wife won't mind him walking better. Maybe that blue bottle of Rooster Juice would make up for pissed drawers and trousers. What was I thinking? This sure wasn't any of my business.

The white haired, horned eyebrow man, the doctor, stepped into the parlor. He stepped close to me and looked hard into my eyes. I was startled, as always, because his eyes were the same sky blue as Mama's and mine. He put out his hand and introduced himself. "I am Doctor Erastus Rembrandt Edwards, M.D. Esquire, Teller of Truths and Master of My Destiny, Masseuse and Artificial Blood Circulator. What is it that I can do for you?"

Chapter 2

Granddaddy

I took a deep breath and started talking with all the stupidity of a typical teenage buck.

I said to Doc, "There is an ad in the paper that you might need some help in your office. I've got a driver's license."

Doc started nodding slowly and grinning at me, which I thought was strange, like he knew more than I did. And he did.

I went for broke and started talking. Words just kept coming out of my mouth.

"My name is Iver Johnson Murphy. Before you ask, yes, I was named for a gun company. Mama likes guns. By tradition, I should have had my daddy's name, but he didn't want a junior. So, I was named for a shotgun, which isn't too bad. Daddy says I was born like a shotgun blast. He said Mama stood up and I hit the floor hollering. He said he wanted to name me 'Oh Hell,' but Mama wouldn't discuss it.

"I am thinking about being a doctor. My daddy thought it might be a good idea to work for you. I saw the ad in the paper, and I would like a job. I want to buy a car. And of course, learn about being a doctor. I'm an awfully quick learner. I'm good with books."

I knew I was talking too much, but my mouth just kept spewing words. That old man didn't need me to tell him all of this and he was just grinning at me. If I was this far, I might as well finish my spiel and take my chances on getting this job. That grin on his face was getting a little unnerving.

"I know as much or more than the teachers know and the principal agrees--- so I was only going to school on Mondays till I turned sixteen. I'm not going to high school anymore. I've had enough of that. I'm going to see if I can apply to college anyway, when I decide which one. I think I told you that I want to be a doctor. I know how to keep books. I check behind Daddy at the store for mistakes. I have read a set of law books and a set of medical books that were in the barn. (I lied somewhat. I looked at the pictures in the medical books and turned pages in a law book looking for pictures.) I guess I am self-taught. I want to be a doctor, like I said. Daddy thought it would be a good idea to work away from the hardware store. Sorry, I didn't mean to repeat myself.

"The twins are eleven now and are stepping and fetching at the store like I do. Well, I need a job and I saw the ad in the paper. Well, Daddy saw it and brought it to my attention. I know about everybody in town from the store. I'm not sure what you would need me for, but I am a quick study of about anything.

"Doc, I hope you don't think I'm a smart behind teenager. I am just selling my skills."

Doc hadn't said a word during all of this spewing of sound from my tongue, just the grin, making his gold teeth show under the mustache.

"Iver," he said, "I need an apprentice and I think you may be just the fellow to learn the trade. Come on back with your good clothes if it is alright with your Ma and Pa. Ask your momma if you can bring those medical books and let me use them. And bring the law books. They will make the parlor look like a doctor's office."

Doc paused and looked past me, like he was looking out the window.

"Hold on, boy. Let me think. If you leave the store, who is going to do the heavy lifting? Your Pa can't keep the store and load. And your Ma hates to wait on customers. She still has chickens, in the egg business."

"Rudolph and his boy, Henry, keep the warehouse like always. They can get along without me."

"Just go home and talk to Lauralee and Walter. If it is alright with them, come on back and bring the books. Ask them first. Don't cause a problem for anybody. You understand, boy?"

He put out his hand to shake. I shook his hand and we both said, "Deal."

I had a job. Going to make some pocket money. Get me a car. Then I thought, oh hell, I didn't make a deal on the money. I really wanted some money to go courting. I really wanted to ask Sissy Reynolds for a date. She was the prettiest girl I had ever seen.

"Doc, we didn't talk about pay." Then I second guessed myself. That might have been rude to ask.

"I'll pay you fifteen dollars a day, five days to the week. I don't like to work on Thursdays."

I didn't know what to say. It was 1968 and I was going to be making seventy-five dollars a week. I thought, 'Granddaddy must be raking it in.' I was sixteen years old and going to be making seventy-five dollars a week. I was sure the angels were on my side.

I pushed out my chest and threw back my head and just about strutted like a Bantam rooster down the front steps. I got on my bicycle and rode back across the river to the store. It wasn't a hard ride, all flat land except for the bridge over the river. I wonder if there has always been a white side and a colored side of town. Dr. Edwards' office was on the edge of town, not on either side of town, in a two-story farmhouse with a long front porch with a screened in part at the end. It had a fresh coat of paint, and the yard was swept. Back then it was just a house to me; now I see it as the most wonderful house I have ever seen. I found out later that he owned that farm for years and it was in his and MaMariah's name. I am sure Momma didn't know until Doc and MaMariah died. He had tobacco barns, a packhouse and a tenant house. He must have rented out the tobacco. I was getting paid. As I was riding along, I thought, "Wonder if he treats negros 'rtheritus? Daddy always said if we skinned everybody, we couldn't tell the difference. I wondered what everybody would think of me working for a negro-treating doctor. And we were integrated now, so it wouldn't matter. I think riding that bicycle made me think. Riding over to the doctor's office didn't seem as far as riding back to the store.

There sat Rudolph on the porch of the store, on a stack of Golden Eagle 10-10-10. That was a kind of fertilizer people used on tobacco, the only kind in Donahoe Creek.

Rudolph was so dark; he looked a little blue. His hair was salt and pepper but even the black hair that was left was kind of bluish. When he had his shirt off, he looked like Atlas in Bulfinch's Mythology. Rudolph came with the store. He said he started living at the back of the store when he was six and he is sixty-five now. His mama was the colored cook for the man that originally opened the store. When Daddy got the store, he just came in the deal. Rudolph says every white man needs a negro and every negro needs a white man. He had been here his whole life except when he was drafted in WWII. Daddy said that in the agreement when he bought the store, Rudolph had to have a home and a job till he died. He thought or, more likely, he knew he was helping raise us boys. And Momma and Daddy needed help with three boys.

He said, "Where you been IV?" He didn't call me Iver; he said I V. At least he didn't call me Four.

"Oh, Sweet Jesus. Do you have to know everything I do? I am a man now. I'm 16."

"You ain't no man."

"I'm sixteen. I'll have you know I am a grown man."

"You ain't no grown man. You still got a gristle for a backbone."

I grunted.

Rudolph said, "Go on boy." I heard him laughing behind me.

Rudolph was good to me. He showed me a lot of the things I know that Momma and Daddy don't think I knew. He would give me a cold beer when I rode with him to Loris to get lumber.

He took me to a joint by Sugar Branch Church so I could learn to dance. Those colored girls just laughed at me. Said 'White people don't have no rhythm.' I guess I was rhythm-less, but they were afternoons to remember. Those girls holding me close trying to teach me to dance was wonderful. Their skin was so soft and smooth. I wondered if white girl's skin felt like that. I wondered if Sissy Reynolds' skin was that smooth.

I looked over my shoulder and he was pulling out a pouch from the pocket in front of his overalls. His white shirt looks like it is glowing against this black skin. He could roll a cigarette with one hand and not spill a bit. He taught me to roll when I was seven. I didn't smoke much but to keep the gnats off my face. Still don't. I don't know if all colored men have two tobacco pouches, but Rudolph did, one for Prince Albert and one for Abadaba.

One time when we went to Sugar Branch Church and bought Abadaba. White people called it marijuana. We rode past the church back to an old colored man's house. You wouldn't have known the house was there except for the little two-rut trail. He had the plants growing in the garden behind his house. Rudolph bought some of the stuff. It looked kind of like ground up tea leaves, Lipton. Rudolph took it and rolled a little cigarette with a twisted end and gave it a try, just to check the quality. Rudolph bought a one-pound paper sack about half full of the stuff from the old man. The old man rolled down the top of the bag and ran a string around it. He had done that before. Rudolph let me have a drag once, but he said 'White men's brains-es go when they smoke it. God had made it for Negros.'

I walked back to the counter and Daddy was propped up looking at the Monroe Hardware catalogue. The Monroe Hardware salesman came by once a month, and this is his week. The store had groceries, hardware, seeds, farm implements, fertilizer on the porch and in the warehouse, dust for your garden, a cold drink box, a Lance Jar, and a Merita shelf of bread and sweet cakes. Just about anything you could think of. He knew everybody in three counties. Daddy went to church every Sunday and sang in the choir. But let him get his sugar out of whack and he was a Hell on Square Wheels Crazy Man. He took the Lord's name in vain, said everyone was descended from canines and accused people of having incestuous relations with their mothers.

My first word was "damn". It was Daddy's fault. Momma said Daddy said "damn" to everything I did. My first word was spoken during a children's sermon at the Presbyterian Church. Mama carried me to the front so I could be with the other little children. You know how people like to show off their children. I supposedly uttered my first word after Preacher Jenkins had given a detailed account of Noah and the flood. "Damn." I spoke. Daddy piped up and said, "That was a damn good telling of the story, Preacher. You're right, Iver." Word was Momma stood up and swung me on her hip, walked out of church and sat in the car. Daddy continued to go to church every Sunday, as always. Momma and I did not go to church for the next year. No Bible School, no Christmas party, no Easter Egg Hunt until the deacons came to the house and asked her to come back and bring me too. We went back to church, but I never got to go down front for children's time again. All that said about Daddy, he was a good man. If there was an advertisement to buy in a high school yearbook or a Last Supper plate being sold by a Sunday School, Daddy would buy it. I think store owners just have that as a cost of doing business. If there was a house fire, he went through the store and got a "box of essentials" as he called it. He didn't give high school graduation gifts but if a child was going to college, white or black, he gave them $10 for gas or bus fare. Daddy says, "If you don't finish your freshman year, you have to work the $10 off with hard labor. Everybody will know you are a quitter."

"Well, Daddy. I got a job, away from the store. Doc said I could come and work for him at his doctor's office." I was trying to act grown, leaning on my elbow, feet crossed, cleaning my fingernails with my pocketknife.

"I don't know about that. You had better ask your Momma. I don't think that she is going to agree to that. You might have talked to Laura-lee first."

"Well Daddy, you suggested it." He just looked at me. I think Daddy might have been a little afraid of Momma sometimes. Maybe not afraid. He just never wanted Momma to get wound up. He valued a quiet life when his sugar diabetes was good.

"You said I needed a job, away from the store and I got one. He said to wear my good clothes. I told him I wanted to be a doctor. I told him I had read the set of medical books. He said he would like me to ask Momma if I could bring the books with me. He said they would make his office look better."

He looked up from the catalogue and said, "Those are your momma's books. I tried to get her to sell those books to the high school. But she said she wasn't finished with them. She said they were her library. You had better check with her. Did you talk much to Mr. 'Rastus?" Daddy never called him Erastus, just Mr. 'Rastus.

"A little bit. I didn't know the books were Momma's. Where did she get them?"

"They were her Daddy's, Mr. 'Rastus." Maybe Doc just wanted to borrow them back.

I walked with dread to the house to talk to Momma.

You had to ask Momma important questions very carefully. She could turn my words around so quick it would make me sick. I know she did it for my own good, but damn! She was good at it. I think Momma might have a little evil streak in her somewhere, or maybe she was what people called strong-willed. Hard-headed was what Daddy called her. I think she must have been a mean little girl. I was totally intimidated by my mother. Daddy was a brave man to live with her for all those years.

Momma and Daddy met at a club at the beach. Momma had slipped away with a bunch of her friends after her senior prom and went to Myrtle Beach. Daddy came to Myrtle Beach to go to the titty bars, but he didn't have enough money to touch one, so he left to go shagging. Shagging means dancing in the South, a slow jitterbug. Daddy got drafted, and when he got back, they got married. (That was the story they stuck to.)

Momma did not work in the store except at Christmas time. She put the orders together for the Christmas cooking. She said she only had enough "Nice" for December and Daddy was on his own for the rest of the year. Momma hated the store. She knew Daddy had a store when they married, and Daddy knew from the start she wasn't going to work in the store. But she has made sure the twins and I worked in the store. Momma had a farm: pigs and chickens. She raised Landrace hogs that she sold for breeding stock. She made them into pets, called them by name and scratched their ears. It was impressive to see a boar hog lay down for a piece of peppermint. Momma was slick about selling livestock. She went to the State Fair in Raleigh to show the hogs. She had color brochures printed with sows and pigs and boars, and just talked the talk. And then there was the laying house, 1000 laying hens in one long building. She got a new flock every other year. The old layers overlapped with the new layers, so sometimes she would have a thousand pullets and a thousand layers. Pullets won't lay till they are about five months. She sold some of the old layers to a cannery to make chicken soup. And she gave some away to whoever needed some layers. It worried me that she gave the layers to potential egg customers. She said the poor people she gave the layers to wouldn't be able to buy the eggs anyway. It all worked out. The old layers got gone. The eggs got gone. Momma was happy with her farm. Daddy thought it was wonderful. He says, "Happy wife, happy life." He just wanted a quiet, peaceful life.

I decided to ask Bet first, see how she said to ask Momma. Bet was standing in the kitchen working on dinner.

Bet and Rudolph were married. Her whole name is Betsy Louise Lacewell Hatcher. I guess she came with the store, too. I don't remember her not being here. Bet wasn't just the cook: she talked to us like Momma and MaMariah did. (MaMariah is Momma's mother.) And Bet listened to us, that was the most important part. She cooked dinner and left enough for supper. She did all of the laundry for the grown people. She made me and the twins do our own laundry and help with the cooking. She wanted to know what we were reading, and we told her about the stories in the books in detail. She wanted to know why the characters did what they did. Made us think. She had the twins read her the paper just like I did. And she quarreled about politics in the paper. Bet said when she and Rudolph finished raising the three of us, we were going to take care of them. Bet said so. I guessed that was the way it was going to be. And it was.

"Iver, you said you got a job with Dr. Edwards? Why?" Bet asked. "Daddy said it would do me good to get some experience working for someone else besides him. You know I want to be a doctor. And I saw an advertisement in the paper for an assistant. The ad said, 'Doctor needs assistant.' And besides, he has already hired me."

"Iver, you need to go back and tell Dr. Edwards that you have changed your mind. You don't need to go to work for him."

"But why? He's my granddaddy."

"You don't need to work for him. You don't need to mention to your momma about this. Just go down there and tell him you can't work for him. I mean it, Iver. This is serious."

I was kind of surprised that Bet was getting wound up. She never told me not to tell Momma something. Maybe I should have listened. Nope, I wanted a car. I wanted to get a date with Sissy Reynolds. I didn't care what Bet said. Seventy-five dollars a week, I knew I was going to keep that job. I just won't tell her where I have a job. Maybe I wouldn't tell her who I was working for. Yeah. I had gotten a job: I would just tell her I am working somewhere else. Let's see, the Colonial grocery store, the Shell gas station, the department store. No, I was going to tell her the truth. No, I wasn't going to lie about it. Why not tell her? I had to ask Bet why I didn't need to work for Dr. Edwards. "Bet, why can't I work for Dr. Edwards?"

"Iver, this is Missy and Miss Mariah's business. I don't have a dog in this fight. You need to talk to your momma first. I'm serious, Iver. Talk to your momma about this. She is going to tell you the same thing. You don't need to work for that man."

I was going to tell everybody at supper I got a job, a job working for a doctor. I have no idea why I thought that was a good time to break the news.

At supper I said to everybody at the table, "Did y'all know there is a Masseuse and Artificial Blood Circulator here in Donahoe Creek?"

Nothing in response from anybody. The grown people stopped eating.

I said, "Dr. Erastus Rembrandt Edwards, M.D. Esq., Masseuse and Artificial Blood Circulator. Yep, he's a doctor. He's got that M.D. and Esq. after his name. Right nice fellow. Y'all know, mine and the twin's granddaddy, Doc Edwards."

Momma looked up at me and just stared. I saw a little squint come in her eyes. I don't think I had ever seen her look at me like that. Bet might have been right.

Momma said, "Iver, did you talk to him?"

I nodded my head up and down.

"Why did you go to his office? I didn't send you or take you to see him. You aren't old enough to go to the doctor by yourself. And you are not going to see that doctor. We see the doctor in Clarkton." She said this in tight, clipped little sharp sounds.

I was stymied. I was shocked how her lips hadn't hardly moved when she said the words. Sharp and cold. And her eyes kind of pinched up, like slits.

"I answered an advertisement for a doctor's assistant, Momma. I told you I wanted to be a doctor. And working for my granddaddy would be O.K. MaMariah and he are just divorced. It's not like he is a criminal". Well, I was about to be schooled on the criminal aspect of my granddaddy.

I heard Daddy take a deep breath in through his nose. MaMariah sniffed. Bet was standing in the kitchen door fiddling with a drying towel.

Momma said, "Gene, Roy, go outside."

MaMariah said, "Let them stay. Iver will tell them anyway. Might as well hear the truth firsthand.

My twin brothers were twelve and they hadn't said a word. They were hunkered down in their seats, trying to be invisible, eating pie in little, tiny bites. Their eyeballs kind of stuck out a little, like they had pulled their eyelids back too far in wonder.

MaMariah started talking. "Be quiet Lauralee. I met Erastus in Charlotte, visiting my brother while he was in town. I fell in love with Erastus. He is the only man I have ever loved. My brother worked with the circus. And so did Erastus. Close your mouth, Iver. He really is a doctor and fashioned himself a veterinarian. His special interest was training acrobats and contortionists. I've some photos of his other children performing with him in nightclubs."

I gasped. The saliva went in my throat and I gave a little cough. "Other children? I thought Momma was an only child".

"Well, she is my only child. But Erastus has several families."

"So, he has been married more than one time? What's the problem with that?"

"Erastus never divorced; he just married women. They were in different places. He wasn't a bad father. He sent money and visited."

Momma started to say something and MaMariah gave her a squinty eyed look back. It was like dueling eyeballs of mean little girls. Then they both looked at Daddy like he was a villain. I was feeling kind of bad that Daddy had hung me out to dry, after all; he was the one that suggested the job, but Daddy was going to catch it, too.

This was better than the soap operas on television. No, Iver, worse than the soaps. This was real. We couldn't be like those crazy people on television. We were discussing our own family. Well, this was going to be one of those tragic soap operas.

Momma made some kind of noise like she wanted to say something, and it got caught in her throat.

MaMariah said, "Lauralee, just be quiet." She looked at me and said, "Iver, all this was a long time ago. I don't want you working for Erastus because you won't hear anything but hell from your momma. If she agrees not to rag you about it, I won't say anything."

MaMariah said, "Lauralee, just shut up and let it go. Past is past and you just keep it alive."

I have never heard MaMariah tell anybody to "shut up". And she told Momma, her only child, to shut up. I was thinking that

my momma was going to bring out some old, rusty nails to cruci-
fy somebody.

"Lauralee, this is the time to bring all of this out to the boys. Get
this old stuff out in the open."

MaMariah is the one that brought out the rusty nails.

"Why, MaMariah? This wasn't your fault, it was his. And you have
been embarrassed by him for how many years? Now, he's living right
here in town. You are going to agree with Iver so he can taint him with
his foolishness. He is just an old quack."

Momma and MaMariah were hot, at each other. I had never seen
them like this. MaMariah was standing up with her hands on her hips,
just about to stare a hole through Momma. Momma was on her feet, too,
with her hands on the table, like she was going to leap across the table
at MaMariah.

This was not good. Bet was at the kitchen door watching with a
look of horror on her face. Daddy had pushed his chair back from the
table, but he hadn't said a thing.

"Iver, my momma, your MaMariah, fell head over heels for the
doctor. Apparently, he talked a good game."

I was speechless. I was holding on to the edge of the table like there
was an explosion on the way.

"He told Momma he owned the circus and I guess he did. They got
married in the courthouse in Charlotte. He and my momma left with the
circus, me in her belly, incubating. Momma and I came home for me to
go to school when I was six. He came and stayed for a few weeks every
winter for years until your great-granddaddy, Big Jack, shot him." (Big
Jack and Big Judy were MaMariah's daddy and momma.)

I said, "Big Jack shot him?"

Momma said, "Yea, Big Jack was trying to get up with him to get
the tuition money for me for Agnes Scott where I graduated high school.

Big Jack got up with him in Richmond. A guy working for the circus told Big Jack that Dr. Edwards was with his wife on the train. Well obviously, it wasn't my mother, your grandmother, with him on the train."

MaMariah asked me, "Son, do you want to hear any more? It is kind of bad."

Now she asked me. If I had known any of this, I would have listened to Bet. I might have started another world war. All I could do was nod my head "yes". I really wanted to hear all of this.

Momma said, "I hoped the Old Bastard would leave town or die before I had to deal with him. I hate him."

"Momma, I've never heard you call anybody a bastard or hate anyone." I was shocked. Hell, shock didn't touch how I was feeling.

"He's the only one I know that fits the bill, and I'm the only white female bastard that I know."

I sat in silence with my head bent to the side. MaMariah had sat down now. Daddy had leaned back in his chair and was watching Momma.

"Do you know what a bastard is?"

"Yes, born on the wrong side of the sheets. Oh, Lord!", I uttered.

MaMariah sucked in a sob. I couldn't understand why Momma was keeping this up. MaMariah's heart was breaking, and Momma was still carrying on. "And what else does a bastard mean?"

"Someone of poor character?"

"Well, he has acted badly, and I was born a bastard. So, we are both bastards. Mariah McLean, my mama, was his fourth wife. He just never got a divorce from the other women. So, my momma and daddy were never legally married. I was born a bastard."

There was a long pause. Momma had a kind of a sad look. MaMariah let out a pitiful sob and stepped away from the table. She walked to the window and looked outside.

MaMariah said, "And he is the only man I have ever loved."

Yes, that's what she said. Like some fairytale princess would say. "The only man I have ever loved." Soap opera and fairy tale.

Momma said, "I am the shame of the family. Have you ever met any more of my family than Mariah, Big Jack and Big Judy? Ever thought about it?"

I said, "No. I've never thought about it. Well, there is Big Judy's brother, Uncle George McArthur, I've seen him a couple of times. I thought we just had a small family. What about Big Jack shooting Dr. Edwards—Granddaddy? Momma, MaMariah is crying. Don't you think you should just quit talking about it right now. We can wait."

Momma said to MaMariah, "Momma, quit crying. Your tears are not going to change anything. When Big Jack found Daddy with another woman, all he could do for the family honor was to shoot him. It was just a little .22 he used to carry in his pocket, and he hit him in the shoulder. So, they came to a gentleman's agreement. Erastus wouldn't press charges for Big Jack shooting him and Big Jack wouldn't make a stink about the bigamy, excuse me, polygamy. Big Jack paid for two years tuition, and Erastus paid for two years tuition. Big Jack said, 'She can't help who her daddy is but, Mariah could have picked somebody besides a Chautauqua Tent Carnie for her daddy.'"

Momma said, "Iver, he just did the whole family wrong. And he is living right here in Donahoe Creek, big as day. Everybody in town knows the facts. I don't know why you haven't heard this before from some busybody. All of us have been victimized by the old bastard."

Well, this put thing in a different light. He had wronged my whole family. He had embarrassed all three of the women in the family. Mama was born a bastard, MaMariah having a bastard child, not knowing Dr. Edwards was married, and Big Judy, MaMariah's mother, for having a daughter that had a bastard. Oh, Lord. This man had shamed all the women in the family.

This wasn't a soap opera. It was real and awfully sad. In 1968, it was scandalous.

Momma and Bet looked at each other and Bet turned back to the kitchen.

"Momma, I can't work for that man. I'll just do without that money. I don't need a car that bad."

"It is your call, son. I'm not going to stop you from making money off of him. Maybe getting some of his money will be a little more revenge for me. No, I… He is your granddaddy. I have such a hatred for him, I …. He has apologized to Momma and to me and to Big Judy a hundred times. Keeping you boys away from him is my way of revenge. And raising hell with MaMariah about him hasn't helped anything either. I'm just rubbing salt in the wound. I'm sorry, MaMariah. This seems to me to be the worst kind of revenge I could have been keeping the boys away from him. I'm trying to get revenge and I'm hurting the folks I love the best. Daddy has been back in the area for years. He set up his office in that old house a couple of months ago and treats people for free if they can't pay. He used to help people with polio. I think he still helps some of them. He just charges for his crazy machine that makes old people walk again."

I said, "MaMariah, what do you think? I don't want to do anything to hurt you. I didn't know all of this; I really didn't. I just wanted a job that wasn't at the store. Him being a doctor just made it even better."

It was like I got shocked into being grown-up.

MaMariah said, "Iver, go on and work for Erastus. Your momma doesn't understand this, and I don't understand either but I still love your granddaddy. (Momma gasped.) I have always loved him. I just can't get over being embarrassed here in town. It's been over 20 years since I found out I wasn't really married to him. And I still want to kill him. I had a bead on him a couple times right after Big Jack shot him, but I changed my mind. All these years and I still can't decide what to do.

Momma looks at me and says, "If you decide to work for him, take the medical and law books but leave the rest. They are Daddy's books anyway. The twins can read the novels. I know he won't mind. In the morning we will go to Spiro's and get you some new clothes. I want you to look good if you are going to work for him. He's a doctor and a lawyer. Maybe you can read the law under him."

Momma puts on a half a smile and says the jump rope song: "Rich man, Poor man, Beggar man, Thief, Doctor, Lawyer, Indian Chief."

I got Daddy's truck and went to the barn to get started loading the medical books. I knew it would take me a while to load them and put them in Dr. Edward's office. Loading the books in the truck and sweating, fanning gnats, I got to thinking about the seventy-five dollars a week, working inside.

About halfway through loading the truck, I walked from the barn to the house. I was standing on the back porch rinsing my hands and arms before I went in the house and heard Momma and Bet talking.

Momma said, "Bet, have you heard how my Daddy is getting along lately?"

Bet said, "Doc brought a turn of shirts to my sister Henrietta's for her to starch and press. She lined up her daughter, Girlie, to keep house for him. That last girl didn't work out. Henrietta said Judge McLean sent a nice package to Girlie. He's always sending packages to Henrietta and Girlie. I know he still wants Henrietta back in Columbia with him."

Momma said, "Uncle George looked good when Henrietta was taking care of him and his house. Maybe Henrietta will go back. Big Jack has said for years that Henrietta made him the good man he is."

Momma said, "I can't stop hating my daddy."

Bet said, "You need the Holy Spirit."

I stepped off the porch to the kitchen, walked to the Fridge and got the jar of water out and poured me a glass. The jar was a little orange tinted from the iron in the water, but it was still good water to drink. Everybody around there had iron water. That was why Henrietta did the white shirts, she had a really good well.

I got my courage up to ask Momma about this situation, now that she had cooled down.

"Momma, would it hurt you and MaMariah for me to go to work for Dr. Edwards? I don't think I'll find another job making that kind of money. I want to hate him for embarrassing MaMariah but I want the money. I know greed is a sin. Do you think I'll go to Hell for working for greed?"

"Iver, I hate him and I love him. I think I hate him more than I love him right now. MaMariah still loves him. I think he loves Ma Mariah and I think he loves me. He always sent MaMariah and I money to live on when I was growing up, generously. He sends me and you boys money for Christmas and birthdays. I just put it in the bank. If I really hated him that much, I would have sent it back. I don't know, Iver. Life is complicated."

"Wait a minute Momma, what about money in the bank? He sent money and we didn't get it? You kept it?" I was shocked. I wanted a car. "You kept gift money from us? Mama!"

"Whoa, Iver. The money is for you when you get grown. The money is yours and you boy's names are on the accounts."

"But there may be enough for me to get a car."

"You can forget that, boy. That money is in the bank for when you get grown."

I couldn't stand it. That old man that I wanted to hate had been sending me and the twins money. He did care for us. I had no idea things could be this stirred up. I just hated the old man for doing MaMariah that way. But I wanted a car.

I had carried the books to the office and put them on the shelves yesterday. Momma called Wallace Spiro last night and he opened the store at seven o'clock. Momma and I went to Spiro's and Mr. Wallace already had things picked out in my size, sport coat, shirts, pants, shoes, socks, underwear. It was like I had grown up, in my mind and had on a new skin. I guess like a snake shedding, same snake, just new skin. Maybe I shouldn't have compared myself to a snake, but I thought a butterfly and chrysalis was kind of girly. I had my pants hemmed and out of the store by eight-thirty. Mama drove me to the office and didn't look when I got out the truck. I got my bicycle out of the bed of the truck and pushed it to the front steps.

I still hadn't decided for sure if I'm going to work Granddaddy, Dr. Edwards, Doc, but I didn't want to carry the clothes back.

I went up the steps to Doc's office and tried to open the front door. The sign said open at nine o'clock. I figured he must be just eating breakfast, so I walked around the back to the kitchen and looked in the screen door. There was a colored girl sitting at the kitchen table reading a Harlequin Romance novel. That's a first. I have never seen a colored person reading a romance novel before.

I walked in and the girl at the table said, "My name is Girlie. I know your name is Iver. There are some biscuits in the stove and sausage in the skillet.

I hadn't thought about eating this old man's food. It sure smelled good. I was hungry. I might as well eat while I was deciding whether to work here or not.

I said, "You are the cook. You fix me a plate." I was a fool.

Girlie said, "Not for some snot-nosed, shirttail white boy like you. You're hired help, too. You are no better than me." And she said this with a sassy tone that, for some reason, I thought was wonderful.

I said, "How did a colored girl from Columbia get to go to college? Bet talks about you all the time."

Girlie said, "Your momma has to pick the right daddy for her babies."

I said, "Your momma must have picked a rich one."

Girlie said, "That's right." I reached for a plate. "I put some Pepsi Colas in the Frigidaire"

I got my plate and Pepsi Cola and stood at the table. Girlie looked up at me and said, "I'm not getting up so you can sit at the table. "

I didn't know what to say. Bet tells us all what to do, but she never sits at the table when we eat. I was still standing there. She was still sitting there. I sat at the table. She turned around and got an opener out of the drawer and laid it on the table. Times were changing. I decided right there I was just going to go with the flow.

She was awfully pretty for a colored girl. What was I saying? She was a colored girl and I thought she was pretty. Then lightning struck. I was looking at my cousin and thinking about…the things males think about. She looks like Big Judy, the same freckles. I was going to have to think on this.

I finished eating breakfast, put my dish in the sink and the bottle in the crate. No sense in being a pill. I was hired help, too.

I walked from the kitchen into the dining room where the Bone Cracker machine rested. The thing was amazing and kind of scary. I guessed everything medical was kind of scary. I thought, 'Iver, you need to get over this being scared.'

Doc was in the parlor waiting room reading the paper. I couldn't really get my mind around calling Dr. Edwards "Granddaddy". Maybe he wouldn't mind me calling him "Doc". I might as well say what I need to say. If I decided I was going to be working here, he needed to know what was on my mind.

"Morning, Doc."

"Morning, Iver. Have you eaten breakfast? Those were some good sausages. One of my customers gave me those. Excellent."

I thought I had to get things off my mind. It was like a sin: it is just as bad to think it as to do it. Well, this wasn't a sin, but it had to rate somewhere on the list of something. I didn't know what. If I had had any sense I would have just come to work and kept my mouth shut, but I was a stupid teenager that knew enough to be dangerous.

"Doc, I heard my momma use words talking about you that were kind of bad. Momma said you were never married to MaMariah."

Doc folded up the paper. I thought he was going to tell me to go home. He dropped his chin to his chest and sighed. He stayed that way so long I thought he was crying. When he raised his head there were tears in his eyes.

"Yes, and I came here to make something right."

"You can't change how Momma was born."

"I can change how she feels about me before I die."

"Are you dying soon?"

"Not that I know of. Look, boy, let me explain something to you. I am a man, an old one now. Women have always been a weakness to me. I loved women and I married them".

"What has you loving women got to do with my grandmother?"

"You're missing the point I'm trying to make. Do you have a girl-friend, boy?"

"What are you talking about, old man? And what does this have to do with my grandmother?"

"I love Mariah with all my heart. It is like I was looking for her when I was with my first wives. Mariah was the woman that took my heart. Love and lust control a man until the perfect woman comes in his life. We love the thrill of the hunt, the sweet first kiss and when it is the right woman, the hunt is over."

This old fart was using the words "love and lust" in the same conversation with my grandma, MaMariah, the sweetest woman on earth. She lives with us, or we live with her. She smoked Pall Mall cigarettes, wore White Shoulder's perfume and read her Bible every day. MaMariah worked to teach us what she calls survival skills: laundry, hemming pants, sewing on buttons, cooking, washing dishes. She said the three of us were so homely we may not get wives. Gene and Roy said they didn't want wives. I at least wanted a girlfriend and a car to ride one around in.

"Mariah was my fourth wife. I just never got around to divorcing the other three. And the fifth one, we didn't have any children. I think I married her because I was just lonely. A lonely heart has a tendency to stray. Big Jack shooting me kind of broke up that marriage. I just hated to divorce and have my children coming from broken homes."

"You should have been a Mormon. So Big Jack really did shoot you?"

"Yes, the circus was in Richmond and Big Jack found me with another woman that wasn't his daughter. I guess I deserved it. I suppose I would have done the same thing."

"It's hard for me to believe Big Jack doing something like that. He is so calm and easy going."

"You have never seen that old man stirred up. I never held it against him for shooting me, and he didn't call the law on me for polygamy."

"Didn't somebody ask questions at the hospital? It was a gunshot wound."

"No. One of the roadies with the circus was an AWOL medic in the army. He got the bullet out and patched me up. I always kept plenty of veterinary supplies on hand.

"Iver, I have made some bad choices concerning my wives. But with all my heart, I have always loved Mariah. If I had met her first, I would not have ever married another woman. I am glad that it was a .22 short that Big Jack had. He could have killed me if he had meant to. He had good aim and got me in the shoulder."

I knew exactly which pistol it was. I remembered seeing Momma take it out of the dresser and giggle. She couldn't have really hated him, or she would not have agreed for me to work there.

"Iver, I've always loved Lauralee and Mariah. Always have and always will. I deserve to be hated for what I did. I just want to try to make up for it, get to know my grandchildren, and make it up to your momma and grandma. Do you still want to work for me? No, let me rephrase that, will you work for me, give me a chance? Stay here?"

I was taken aback. I don't know what I thought this old man would say, but it sure wasn't what he said. I kind of liked him.

"Well, I don't want to haul all those books back home, and I don't want to carry my new clothes back. I want to have a granddaddy, but Doc … I am just having a problem knowing you did something so illegal…and hurtful."

"Iver, I'm working on being a better man. I want Mariah to marry me. Legally."

Well, Iver, was he using you to make points with MaMariah or does he really want an assistant? What if I hadn't come in and asked for the job. What if Momma had said no. Didn't matter, Iver, I thought, seventy-five dollars a week was seventy-five dollars a week.

"Iver, times are changing. I see things in a little different light. I want to help those around me to make up for the pain I have caused in the past. Life wouldn't seem right to me to keep up the old formalities. I treat whoever comes to the door, whether they can pay or not. We are the same under the skin."

I was leaning on the door frame. Doc leaned back in his chair, folded his paper and looked at me. "And Iver, Girlie is a doll, isn't she? She is Henrietta's daughter, grew up in Columbia, finished school at Elizabeth City State College. She's got a teaching degree. Used to be a Normal School for Negros. She won't be here long. With the schools integrating, some principal is going to need her. I know there are some of those Old White Heads that aren't going to teach the colored children and some of them Old Colored Heads aren't going to want to teach the white children. There is a teaching job out there waiting for her. She's smart as a whip and pretty as an angel"

"She is pretty, Doc." In fact, she was as pretty as Sissy Reynolds. I was comparing Girlie to the most beautiful girl I knew. I shouldn't have even been thinking about another girl. I had my heart set on dating Sissy when I got to rolling with some spending money.

Chapter 3

Education and the Federal Agents

It was going to be a long day. School started the first Tuesday after Labor Day. Everybody had their tobacco put in by then, maybe not all of it sold, but in the packhouse. That was the first day of total integration. No more freedom of choice. The colored elementary school in the neighborhood closed. The building was good but there just weren't enough students to keep it open, integrated or not. The students in the area were supposed to go to the newer formerly all black school that was now the elementary school for this end of the county. The boys and I were sent to school the second week of school. I don't know why Momma and Daddy always waited till the next week. I don't remember particularly missing anything.

I was trying to get to Doc's office before eight o'clock and these men came stomping, or walking, in an authoritarian manner into the store. Well, these suit-wearing Yankees came to the store wanting to know why we hadn't been in school. They said that Gene, Roy and I had got to go to school. It was the law.

The three of us were at the store to get some breakfast: Pepsi, sweet cake and a piece of cheese like always, maybe a Red-hot once in a while. I was dropping the boys off at the store and then I was going on to work for Doc. This was the second day of 'official integration.' Momma and Daddy weren't keeping the boys from going to school. They were going next week, really. I wished and I bet those men wished they hadn't tangled with Daddy that particular morning.

I stuck my head into the office up front, "Daddy, they're back." The agents had canvassed all of the county for school children and by God, they were going to school. Damn integration. The agents came around last week explaining about compulsory education and saying that all the children have to go to school, no matter their parent's opinion on integration. Daddy and Momma were fine with integration and so were us three boys. Gene, Roy and I were the ones with problems with education. We tolerated it but that was about it. And Daddy took the opinion that if we didn't want to go to school, apparently, we had something else to do. We went to school as little as possible and passed the tests.

Mine and the twins' education was peculiar. For that matter, our whole family was peculiar. But I could not believe there were federal agents here telling Momma and Daddy that the twins and me have to go to school. I was naive about the power of the federal government. Momma and Daddy said our education was their business and not the federal government's. I am not saying I have not been to school. I started first grade.

I was the only one that could read in the whole first grade. I concluded the teacher could not read. The teacher had these letters on pieces of paper and would rearrange them to make words. It took me a while to realize the other children didn't have a clue. I went home and declared them all to be ignorant. I was wasting my time at school. I finally agreed with Mama and Daddy to try school for a second day.

I was polite to the slow children that sat around me. I raised my hand to be called on, but the teacher skipped over me. I thought that maybe she couldn't read because she couldn't see. She sure couldn't see me. She called on the slow children. I guess she was still trying to cover up the fact that she didn't know how to read.

Time got long so I looked around and saw some story books on the bookshelf. I went over to the shelf, and quietly got a book. Well! You would have thought I was bringing the world to an end. I was told by the teacher that I could not read a book. It was not story time. I was told that we were doing our reading lesson. I informed the teacher I could read.

I said, "I'll just be quiet while you teach these slow children how to read." Several of the prissy little girls started crying. They didn't know they were slow. A couple of the guys got themselves a book and started turning pages.

The teacher took me to Mrs. Cain's office and sat me down. I was kind of happy that I was going to get a smarter teacher. I found out Mrs. Cain was the principal and she had reading problems, too. She asked me to read a little book to her. If that woman couldn't read that little book, she didn't need to be principal. And I told her so.

Mrs. Cain called the store and told Daddy that I had a smart mouth. I was kind of proud she said I was smart. I said, "Thank you." Daddy came and got me from school. Daddy and Mama taught me and the twins at home. Mama would borrow a set of books from the school for a year. And we checked out books from the school library and the public library. Mrs. Cain made it look like I was in school. Momma would bring me to school for any state tests. And we were left alone. I overheard Mrs. Cain tell Momma that I was a handful, and I kept the others from learning because I asked too many questions. I guess the teacher didn't know the answers.

Life was good. Then integration happened.

The agents told Mama and Daddy that the twins and I MUST go to school. Then Daddy began the tirade. The recurring theme was "What is school?" and "What is education? The US government does not need to control the education of our children. Isn't that what the Nazi's did?" Daddy would pontificate for hours to those agents. The agents got tired of it and told Daddy he would have to go to jail if he didn't send us to school. So, Daddy stretched the truth and said he would send us to school. I just didn't go. I went to my job and the agents came Doc's office to take me to school personally. I told them I had quit because I was sixteen and did not intend to attend high school any longer. The agents said if every white child over sixteen quit there wouldn't be any white children in the whole high school. They were personally changing the law, they said. I told them I had read a whole set of law books and I didn't think that is how it worked. Dr. Erastus Rembrandt Edwards stepped in and talked legal speak, real official, right there on the front porch of his office. He told the agents he was going to file some sort of suit. I think he started speaking Latin. The agents backed off and drove off. They didn't try to get me in school anymore that week. They tried again the next week and Dr. Edwards took a piece of paper out of his pocket and spoke to the agents about the constitution and again explained the suit he was going to file. I asked Dr. Edwards about the twins and he said he couldn't find anything just yet but he was working on it. Daddy told the twins they would just have to go until noon on Mondays and that would take care of the problem. Roy and Gene just carried a book to read, and everyone left them alone. This went on for two weeks. Apparently, some folks didn't see them go to school and complained to the federal agents. So, the twins went all day on Mondays for a while and remained on the roll. The federal agents were literally scouring the countryside for students to go to school. Not just the white ones.

Our family wasn't alone in dealing with the federal government. The Samson family had a big problem with the newly integrated school. Rochester Samson did not want his children to go to school with us crackers. The granddaddy of the bunch went up North and hooked up with Elijah Mohammed. When he got to be a Black Muslim, he found out just how evil us White folks were. He probably hated White people before he went up North. Rudolph went and checked out their church. He came back and told us that White people were created by an evil

Black scientist. Rudolph said that maybe high yellows just didn't get turned white enough. Apparently, they were throwbacks.

Rochester Samson lowered himself and came to our house after dark to talk to Daddy about school. Rochester did not want to be seen in any association with us evil White people.

Rochester said, "The government agents said my children had to go to school with the Whites or I was going to jail, and the children were going to an orphanage. So, how come they let you by? Is it because you are White? "

Daddy didn't know that Rochester didn't know how things were working: that Gene and Roy were going one day a week to keep the federal agents happy.

Daddy said, "The first boy, Iver, was such a problem for the teachers that they didn't want him in school every day. We just got him to school for the tests. When the twins came along, we did the same thing."

Rochester said, "Let my young'uns show them what a problem is. I don't intend for them to go to school with you White Devils."

Daddy said, "More power to you!" and gave Rochester the Black Power salute.

Rochester kind of growled and stomped out down the steps.

The Samson's became legendary after Rochester and Daddy met.

A Yankee-accented man named Mr. Scotti was the leader of the federal agents. He went for White, but he would not have passed around here. (There is White and Colored. In the Colored shades there is Pecan Tan, Light, Bright, and Damned Near White. He was a little dark to go for White)

The agents had the idea that if they went to the Samson house again, they could convince them to go to school. That was Mr. Scotti's misunderstanding of the situation. Mr. Scotti and his three minions gathered at the mailbox at the end of the road to walk in. Rochester had dragged old pieces of cars across the road to make a barricade. When the federal agents walked up to ask him to send his children to school, he shot over their heads and called them White devils. Then things got ugly. (The sheriff's deputies were watching from the cars while the federal agents went to the house. That's how word got back about the incident.)

Rochester set his oldest four children on the agents. The children ran at the agents growling and showing their teeth and the four agents just stood there. The deputies that were there had seen this before. They got in the cars, locked the doors and rolled up the windows. The Samsons were known for good teeth. The Samson children jumped on the agents, wrapping their arms and legs around them. Then they buried their teeth in the chests of the agents, right through their suit coats. The agents were screaming, and the children were growling. Rochester was calling out, "Keep biting, you little blue gummers. Yaw poison. Yiiiiii! Gnaw worse than a rattlesnake. Bite!"

To say the agents were shocked is not giving the situation its true impact. Apparently, there weren't any biting children up North. The agents were trying to pull the children off and the children were holding on tighter. One of the girls had worked her way around and was biting one agent's neck and feeling for his gun. She is the one that always has her clothes on backwards. Rochester finally called the children off. The agents staggered back toward the cars. The deputies unlocked the doors and let them in. The deputies were thoughtful and had already called ahead to the hospital and ordered shots and stitches for the "gove-met" agents.

After the attack of the biting Samson children, you could say that the gove-met integration agents declared war on the Samsons.

The agents put on the biggest show to happen, after integration, which had been seen around here since Prohibition.

The agents got the army tank from Fort Bragg. They unloaded it at the crossroads and drove it to the Samson farm. The bitten agents were on top of the tank with shotguns as they rode down the highway. Folks were calling the neighbors to come out and see the sight.

The tank ran over the Samson mailbox as it turned down the dirt path, then drove over some junk cars, pushed some to the side of the road, ran through the hog pen, clipped the corner of the chicken coop, mashed the collards down, broke the light pole, and snatched the electricity out of the house, light bulbs included. Mr. Scotti pulled out a bull horn and told Rochester that the children would go to school. It was pretty impressive.

The Famous Biting Samson children eventually went to school with us crackers.

The Murphy boys still went on Mondays for a while. The Samson children terrified the little White children with their poisonous blue gums. I felt sorry for the little light-skinned Negro children. They were afraid of the blue gummers, too.

The agents didn't come back again to carry us to school. The world settled down. The White children and the Negro children apparently got along pretty good. The grown people had a little problem with integration especially looking at the news from Boston and Alabama. The news on TV was so sad. Doc said that people just don't particularly like to change the way things have always been. He said that after the Civil War change was really hard. Doc said that his father talked about being hungry a lot of times when he was a child before the turn of the century. His daddy said that everybody was hungry, eating possums and poke salad. Didn't mind what color the skin, hunger was with everybody.

I guess integration was our Civil War. We weren't hungry and there wasn't violence everywhere, but things were different. We started going to the same restaurants, using the same bathrooms, and having the same waiting rooms at the hospital. I wondered if Whites and Negroes would get married now that we were going to school together. That Girlie was a pretty girl. She had curly dark brown hair and she had some freckles across her nose. And she had a pretty figure. What was I talking about? She was four years older than me. I was talking about a colored girl. But she was a girl and she told me she didn't have a boyfriend. But she was four years older than I was.

I really liked her. I wondered if she would go out with me. What was I talking about? I was sixteen and she was twenty. She didn't have the time of day for me. She called me Cracker Boy. I called her Zulu. I couldn't ask her for a date. She was colored. And she was an older woman.

I needed to talk to somebody about this. There wasn't anybody to ask.

Chapter 4

The Revival

Mama, Daddy, the twins and I attended Mt. Horeb Presbyterian Church every Sunday. Integration hadn't come to the churches yet, unless you count funerals and the Easter Program. The colored choir sang at the Passion Play. The White people in our church choir were not in the same league as the choir from the AME Zion Church. The twins and I were Christened at Mt. Horeb or sprinkled. If you know Presbyterians, you will understand that I saw my parents sip whiskey and drink wine; I never saw either when they were tipsy. And in my heart, I am still a Presbyterian. Being Presbyterian means everything in moderation and predestination. Things will be as they will be. It is a calm calling. We sing poorly, pass the collection plate, hear about missionaries and believe our preachers can read Greek and Hebrew. We have communion occasionally. We seldom had revival, but the Pentecostals filled the local needs.

We always attended the Pentecostal's revival. It never failed to be a spiritually enlightening experience.

There were stages to revival. First there was finding an evangelist from a fair distance. The event needed to be published in newspapers and on posters with the evangelist's name and home church, the farther away the better and the longer the name the better with capital letters after the name. Most years the baptizing (fully submerged baptizing) was conducted every night, depending on the number that came forward and if the preacher brought his chest waders. The souls were dunked and resurfaced cleansed white as snow. The favorite topics of revival were The Rapture, The Book of Revelation, and The Presentation of the Signs of the End Times and, of course, Are You Ready?

When you went to a Rocking Revival several nights you would observe people who were specialists in worship methods. There were the shouting worshipers: "Amen", "Yes", "Praise the Lord", "Tell it Preacher". There were the dancers: in the aisle, in the pew, at the front, and all the way around. The most fascinating were the ones that spoke in tongues. One person would start, and it would spread like an infection. I was always mesmerized trying to understand what they were saying.

Momma and Daddy seemed to enjoy the services, but they never got baptized. Daddy said you didn't have to be submerged to have your sins washed away. Momma said she was saved enough, and she was not getting her clothes wet around strangers. I knew what she meant. I saw the teenage girls walking in wet clothes with their nipples hard. Their sins were washed away and mine were swelling. I prayed for Jesus to save me from pretty girls in wet clothes.

I generally spent Saturday night and Sunday night in my bed at home. I would stay at Doc's office during the week. Daddy drove me over to the office that Monday morning in the truck, my bicycle in the back. I appreciated it. I could pedal to the office in a little while, but I would end up sweating before I even got started on that day. Daddy said, "Iver, do you want to ride your bike home to go with us to revival or you want me to pick you up here? "

I said, "Daddy, I believe I'll ride my bike home this evening. Mondays are slow and I can leave a little early."

Daddy said, "Why don't you just plan on spending the night here this week. I can run you to the office in the mornings or not. Whatever you want."

"OK, Daddy, but let me stay at the office Friday night. Saturday mornings are pretty early for Doc's customers. That way I can eat Bet's cooking for a couple of nights. I know if I ask her, she'll make some chicken salad and greasy rice one night." Chicken salad and greasy rice were and still are favorites. All these years and mine never tastes just like hers.

Customers had been kind of steady all morning for a Monday. Doc and I stopped for a glass of tea about ten o'clock. Girlie would have dinner at twelve and we would open the office back up at one-thirty. Doc liked to take a little nap after dinner and the patients knew that.

Doc said, "Does Lauralee ever ask about me, Iver?"

I said, "Yes, she asks about you every time I stay at the house."

I didn't tell Doc that her exact words were "The old bastard is still alive? Are you going back to his house?" This woman was certainly a different woman than my mother. I had seen her upset, but this was like war. I had thought of mentioning having him for Saturday-night supper, but I thought better of it. I knew MaMariah wouldn't ask and have Momma have a fit. I would ask Bet how to ask Momma. I was just a young'un, but I thought it would be nice to have him over. MaMariah had said she still loves him. He didn't know Roy and Gene like he knew me. They were his, too. Gene and Roy had sky blue eyes like him. Thinking back, those were some grownup thoughts for a shirt-tail boy.

When I was four, Momma and Daddy had twins. They decided to carry on the firearms theme with their names and added singing cowboys: Gene Remington Murphy and Roy Winchester Murphy. Snap shirts, BB guns, cowboy hats and boots were the wardrobes. Louis L 'Amour adventures were their primers. (At the time I didn't know that all those Louis L'Amour books were Doc's. They were just with the rest of the library.) Nice guys, even for brothers.

I had worked for Doc for four weeks and we had settled into a routine. I swept the front steps, got the fingerprints off the glass in the front door, got the newspaper out of the box and checked the wanted ads. We sat down at the kitchen table and had a good breakfast while swapping sections of the paper. Girlie had on the radio, singing along. She didn't eat breakfast, just a cup of coffee. She said that it was not civilized to eat early in the morning.

"Hand me the want ads, Iver. Never know what I might find."

"Yes, sir. It's right here. I glanced at the cars in the wanted ads. There still isn't one in my price range."

"Keep looking, boy."

"Doc, I saw in the paper that the Fire Baptized Free Will Pentecostal Holiness Church is having a revival. We always go, all six of us, all five nights. Why don't you go? That would be somewhere out in the open to talk to Momma. You talk to Daddy at the barber shop, don't you? And you could talk to the twins after service. Ask them to come by your office. And MaMariah always goes."

I had no idea where that came from. Momma said she hated him, and the twins had heard what Momma said about him. I had worked for Doc for four weeks and I liked him, not loved him like I loved MaMariah but I liked him. He has paid me three hundred dollars and I put two hundred of it in the bank. The other hundred I put as down payment on a used john boat and a Mercury outboard motor. I thought I could get a boat quicker than I could a car. I could borrow Daddy's truck to go fishing. I wondered if I gave Mama the money in the bank would it help her stop hating him? I thought, Don't be stupid, Iver. That doesn't even make sense. Doc says he loves all of us and he has been nice to me ALL of the time. Of course, I have worked for that money.

Then Doc's head kind of tilted back. "That's an idea. It has been a longtime since I've been to a soul-saving revival. I'll think about it."

I couldn't take the words back. I might as well go with the flow. Maybe it was divine inspiration to give him an invite to the revival. Sell it, boy.

"The paper says that the evangelist is from Monroe. That is the furthest, I think, that I have heard, a real coup for The Fire Baptized Free Will Pentecostal Holiness Church. The First Baptist evangelist was from Fayetteville."

I got to the house in time to get a shower and eat some supper. We loaded up in Momma's station wagon and got to the Fire Baptized Free Will Pentecostal Holiness Church by six-thirty-five. Services started at seven. Daddy and Momma always made it a point to get to any church service early, whether it was a funeral or a wedding or just Sunday sermon. They wanted to be in the back of the church or in the balcony so they could slip out if need be. I guess it was a holdover from having little children in services.

Around here revivals were a point of pride for local churches, a major fundraising and social event. The evangelists that led these events were paid for their services with what was termed "a love offering". I have always wondered if they got a percentage of the offerings. They were men of faith, but they were also expected to present a theatrical performance—religious, of course. Revivals started on Sunday or Monday nights and have been known to last until Sunday. Most only lasted five nights; the last night had the biggest "show": visiting choirs, deacons from other churches, and a covered dish supper.

We got a seat in the balcony this particular year. Usually the balcony was pretty hot, but the FBFWPHC put in an air conditioning system in May with the hope that it would improve summer attendance and possibly bring in some new members, worshipping in comfort. It was October when this revival took place, and it was cooling down but when the church got full, so they still turned the air conditioner on. Worshiping in comfort-- on padded pews no less.

The show started.

The lights were dimmed, and the organ began playing softly, not a particular song but kind of like church jazz. This was the signal the service was about to start. Everybody stopped the quiet church chit-chat as this slick, shiny man of the cloth started up the aisle.

The evangelist from Monroe was by far the best one I have ever seen. He walked in then slowly down the aisle to the pulpit. His hair is dyed coal black, so dark it looks like the hot tar the man puts in the cracks on the blacktop, picking up a little sparkle from the low lights. In fact, he was glistening from his greased hair to his blue satin robe to his white patent leather slippers, kind of like I have seen the pope wearing. He was softly reading from the first chapter of John as he walked down the aisle, getting louder as he got closer to the pulpit. He stepped up to the microphone and said, 'Devil beware. I'm going to drive you out of these sinners. Watch out, Satan!'

The preacher says, "All y'all say 'Watch out, Satan!'" And we all did. The tone was set.

I looked over the edge and I spotted Doc. I saw that shock of white hair.

The Evangelist, Fredrick Alan Register, III (Fart, as Roy brought to our attention) delivered a stirring message, Repentance is the Pathway to Glory. Tears flowed as people streamed to the altar. The choir sang What a Friend We Have in Jesus, all the verses, maybe five times with the congregation joining in on the chorus. The deacons from Fire Baptized Free Will Pentecostal Holiness Church prayed with the folks at the altar and asked if they wanted their sins washed away. When they said "Yes" the deacons walked them around the side and up the steps to the baptistery. Without his blue silk robe, The Evangelist and his

Right-Hand Deacon, who came with the evangelist, had on chest waders. It was well-organized. Sinners walked down the steps, got dipped, walked up the steps, and walked out with a clean soul through the side door so as not to drip on the floor.

After the first few baptisms, we slipped out the back of the church. Doc was over to the side near the cemetery. Momma and Daddy started to talk to some folks, and I took the opportunity to steer Gene and Roy over to Doc. It was dark over where Doc was standing around the corner of the church on the path to the cemetery. Even better.

As any doting grandfather would do, he had been to the dime store and had the boys a little gift. Doc pulled a yo-yo out of his coat pocket and "walked the dog". This was a trick that made the yo-yo look like it was spinning as you walked a couple of steps behind it. Then he did a "'round the world". This was a trick that you sling the yo-yo in a vertically oriented arc and then it comes back to your hand. Roy and Gene were under his spell. They weren't old enough to understand the heartache Doc had caused. Maybe I was wanting to forgive Doc because he has been good to me. Doc reached in his pocket and handed each boy a yo-yo just like his. I had looked at the yo-yo's before and they were the really good ones.

Doc said, "I am challenging you boys to a contest tomorrow night. Which one of you is Roy and which one of you is Gene?"

It was on then. Doc was "just right". And what more could a granddaddy want in the entire world but two new best friends.

Tuesday the message was Be Prepared: He's Coming Back, Soon. Gene, Roy and Doc had the yo-yo challenge and Roy won. Doc did a paddle ball demonstration and threw down the gauntlet again.

Wednesday's message was Signs of the Times: What are you looking at? Doc won the paddle ball challenge. Doc brought each of the guys a bag of marbles and told them he had made a place to play at the office. Play date planned.

Thursday's message was He's at the Door: Answer It, Quick. Doc brought the boys Mad Magazines, sketch pads and pencils. He said, "Draw me a cartoon, and we will mail it to the publisher, see if they want you to work for them." I thought it was kind of crazy, but the guys worked with all their might drawing cartoons.

Friday's message was The Rapture: Up from the Graves They Arise. Doc had envelopes addressed and stamped for the boys. He really made a lot over the drawings. They were pretty good. He put the envelopes in his inside pocket.

A wonderful soul-saving revival had come to an end. A record number of folks were baptized, some of them twice. Guess they didn't get all the sin washed away the first time. I told Momma and Daddy we would catch a ride home with somebody. Daddy was fine with it. I think Daddy knew I wanted Doc to carry us home. I guess in my naïve mind I thought Momma did not know Doc had been talking to the twins. And she would never have admitted that she knew the boys were playing with Doc. I think Momma was trying, truly, to do the right thing. Maybe five nights in the Holiness Church was working.

The excitement happened after Momma and Daddy had left.

The dunking was finished, and folks were still shouting as they filed out of the church. I asked the prettiest girl I knew, Sissy Reynolds, if she wanted to check out the messages on the bulletin board in the Sunday school room, and she said "Yes". We slipped in a dark room and kissed standing up. I thought she might have kissed somebody before. We didn't bump noses or miss lips a single time. I had wondered about kissing but she took the guesswork out of it for me. In fact, she knew how to French Kiss, which was amazing. I wondered if it would be in poor taste to thank God for letting me kiss Sissy when I said my prayers that night.

Apparently, while I was exploring Sissy Reynolds' lips, Doc, Gene and Roy were raising the dead.

Doc, Gene and Roy had met at their spot beside the cemetery to confer. After the envelopes were safely placed in Doc's jacket the world kind of rocked on its axis. Doc had his pockets full of firecrackers and a Zippo lighter in his hand. The combination was not good. I heard "Once a man and twice a boy," and I saw it in the flesh that night.

Doc waved the boys over into the cemetery a little way and showed them how to light and throw a firecracker. Doc said, "Watch out, Satan". Doc held the lighter and the boys lit and threw the firecrackers shouting, "Watch out, Satan!"

That was when the earth rocked. The revival attendees were under the impression that The Rapture was beginning. The dead were rising up out of the graves. The end wasn't just near; it was happening in that very cemetery. This wasn't just a soul saving revival; it was a Rapture Activation revival.

There were men and women screaming. A few fainted rights there on the ground, old and young. I slipped out of the Sunday school room when I heard the screaming start.

A few brave souls including the preacher still in his chest waders, ran into the cemetery to see The Rapture. The believers in the church yard and in the cemetery were shouting and crying until they saw Doc and the boys being dragged out of the shadows of the cemetery. Mayhem, chaos, and rage combined in a form seldom seen outside of Hades. I was just guessing; I was young.

The Evangelist and his Right-Hand Deacon were using words I had only heard when Daddy's sugar was out of whack. They grabbed up Roy and Gene and pretty much carried them in the church. Doc was shouting for the Men of God to let his boys go. The boys put up a good fight right up to when the Evangelist and the Right-Hand Deacon held them under the holy water and pretended to pray.

Gene said the preacher said, "Got you now, you little bastard."

Roy said the Right-Hand Deacon held him under until he couldn't hold his breath any longer and breathed out.

When Doc got Roy and Gene away from the Holy Men, we went to the parking lot and let the air out of their tires on all the cars in the designated "Preacher Area". Doc showed us how to wedge a little twig in the valve stem.

Doc brought us home in his Packard. The boys were wet; Doc was red faced and I had on lipstick. Momma grinned and shook her head. She graciously thanked Doc for bringing us home. She walked out on the porch behind Doc and me.

She said, "Daddy, why don't you come for Saturday night supper?"

Doc said, "Thank you, Lauralee. I wasn't expecting an invitation after everything that has happened tonight. Thank you."

"Daddy, a member of the Pentecostal Church called and told us what happened. I can't blame you for playing with the boys. I just wish we could have had a movie of what happened. That was the most excitement Donahoe Creek has had in many years. And MaMariah wants you to come to supper. "

I found out a lot of things that week. Momma could bend. Doc was still a boy at heart. And God answers prayers. I kissed the prettiest girl I knew (not counting my Momma). I was in love with Sissy Reynolds. She was all I could think about.

Chapter 5

Women are Wonderful

"Thank you, Lord, this Friday night is over". That's what I said.

"Iver, are you glad this day is over? I'm sure as hell glad."

"Doc, I don't think I could stand another hour of all the religious activity."

"I hope your parents forgive me for getting the boys baptized by the Pentecostals. Maybe it didn't take with the language those holy men were using."

"No, sir, I don't think that kind of baptism is official."

Doc sighed.

"I am going to bed, Doc. I can't take any more."

I was standing at the sink to brush my teeth when I saw it. Doc didn't say anything about lipstick on my lips. Oh my God! Momma knows I've kissed a girl. Doc knows I've kissed a girl. The whole world knows I've kissed a girl.

"Doc! Why didn't you tell me to wipe my face?"

"All you got was a little sugar, Boy. I was the cause of my grandsons becoming Pentecostal. I hope Walter and Lauralee won't hold it against me. Those supposed holy men were quick."

"A little sugar? Is that all you can say? I'm going to die of embarrassment.!"

"Why? I was kind of wondering when you were going to discover girls."

"What are you talking about?"

"Look, boy. Loving women is what men do. Nations have been lost and battles won for the mere touch of a woman."

"Is that why you cheated on MaMariah or all of your wives?" Thinking back on it, I suppose I shouldn't have said it like that.

"Yes, I suppose so. I love women, the pursuit, the first kiss, the submission to nature."

"Hold on, Doc. I don't want to hear this from my grandpa." I knew then that I had said entirely too much.

"I am sorry son, but has your daddy talked to you about women, about sex?"

"He didn't have to. I've seen hogs do it, cows do it, and dogs do it. I know where babies come from. I've looked at the pictures in the medical books, remember?"

"I'm glad you do, but I'm not talking about intercourse, coitus."

I couldn't believe he said those words out loud!

"Iver, it's time you looked at women as a man, not a little boy, afraid to say penis and vagina."

I thought I was going to pass out or maybe just die. I had never heard Daddy use those words and they are coming out of my granddaddy's mouth. Reading about them in a medical book is one thing, but Doc had said the words out loud, casually. I knew I was surely going to die of embarrassment.

"Iver, sit down. You are as white as a Klan robe."

"Don't talk about the Klu Klux Klan either."

"Look here, boy. Sit down and listen to me. Sex is the most wonderful thing in the world. If it wasn't for sex, none of us would be here."

I was dying right then, dead as a hammer.

"Your parents have had sex. That's how you got here, and they have probably had sex when you were in the house."

Kill me now, Lord. This old man, my grandpa is telling me that his daughter had sex with Walter Scott Murphy. And he isn't upset about it.

"Iver, women are wonderful. God made them to keep us company, for us to take care of them. That's why we like to look at them, to sniff them, to feel their skin. That is just how God made men."

Sissy Reynolds did smell good, and her titties were soft when she leaned on me. And her lips were so soft.

"Iver, listen to me. Your eyes have glazed over."

I couldn't say anything for a minute. I was thinking about when Rudolph carried me to the piccolo joint and those colored girls took me by the hand and danced with me. How easy it seemed when they pressed against me. I could have stayed all night pressed up to the girls. Women were God's gift to man. I didn't need to know this or maybe it was exactly the right time.

"Iver!"

Doc was shaking me. "I think you are having a seizure."

"No. No. I'm not having a seizure. A lot of things suddenly made sense. I guess I can see why you cheated on your wives when you were away from them."

"Well, my loving of women has been…Me cheating on my wives… Having several wives…Oh, hell, Iver. I don't even understand it.

"Did I ever tell you about meeting my first wife? She was beautiful. Not as beautiful as your grandma. I was twenty-six and she was nineteen. I courted her with flowers I picked in the woods. We would sit on her front porch and swing, drinking Coke-a-Colas and eating Hershey Kisses. Her mama and daddy would go off to bed and we would be alone. There would be electricity in the air that would light up my soul. We got married and she caught right away. Lord, there is nothing more beautiful than a pregnant woman. I knew she was having a baby before she did. She just glowed. Her lips were full; her hips rounded.

"She had a little black-haired girl we named Rose. She is grown now, of course. She is the oldest. I had finished my residency and wasn't getting enough patients to pay our bills. I got a chance to be a doctor for a circus. I did other things for the circus, kept books, that sort of thing. People change; circumstances change. I was travelling. My wife was lonely: I was lonely. It wasn't either of us at fault. It was both of us. We came to an understanding. I supported Rosie and she found a nice man that didn't travel. I liked the man. I just never got around to getting a divorce. I visited them a couple of times a year until Rose was grown. Rosie has two sons now. Nice family.

"The pattern was kind of set then. Be in a place for a while, get married, have a child or two. I did that twice more and then I met Mariah. I love all my wives, but Mariah is the true love of my life. I got married after I left Mariah but, Mariah… It's hard to put in words. I kept coming back to Mariah longer than any of the others. When Big Jack shot me, I quit coming to visit. I was ashamed of myself. Mariah was… Mariah is…I just made a poor choice when I didn't divorce my first wife. I just want to make this right. You can understand that."

"Mama said you always sent money to her and Ma Mariah. Did you send money to all of them?"

"Of course, I did, boy. What kind of man do you think I am? I never heard of Mariah getting married. Did she, Iver? You know, my first wife is the only one I was legally married to. All the other children are bastards and their mothers' fornicators. I felt I was married to all of them. I never wanted to divorce. I hated for the children to be from broken homes. It's kind of like I'm thinking in a circle. But I did something illegal."

I was amazed, like I didn't know polygamy was illegal.

"All of the children's birth certificates said their parents are married. At least the world thinks they are legitimate. I hope nobody has any reason to check."

"No, sir. But how did you make enough money for all the women and children? How big a medical practice did you have? Are you some kind of specialist?"

"Oh, no. I've practiced medicine off and on over the years. I've kept my license. I made more money working for the circus. I thought I had told you I owned a circus."

"There is MD on your sign. I wondered where that fit in."

"Sometimes being a doctor can be a heartbreaking occupation. I thought I was prepared when I finished my residency, but I wasn't. I decided to stop practicing for a while not long after I started. I was young and… I saw things I couldn't do anything about. The circus seemed like something completely different, but it wasn't. Fixing problems, fixing bodies. Not a lot of difference. Eventually I was able to buy the circus. I had to work the investment, but it was lucrative, very interesting people, beautiful women. In fact, two of my daughters are contortionists, and trained a couple of the grandchildren, too."

"You don't own the circus anymore?"

"No. I found ways of making money without travelling. As old as I am, I needed to settle down. Making tonics and breaking the joints loose is a good easy life. I make people feel better. I make money. When I get tired of this, I'll practice law. I want to try to have a relationship with Mariah, again. Of all the women I have loved, Mariah was always the one."

"Doc, are you a real lawyer?"

"Yes, I went to law school by correspondence course when I was travelling on the road. Passed the bar exam. I can practice in a few states. Being a lawyer came in handy many times when I was with the circus. I handled all of my own contracts, just about anything.

This is interesting. Doctor, lawyer. Wonder if he will turn out to be an Indian Chief?

"Now, Iver, has Mariah ever dated anybody? She never got married? Does she talk about any other old men? "

Sweet Jesus. My granddaddy made me see that women and sex are the main things that men care about. And he was checking out my grandmother, old people and sex. I had a terrible time getting over Doc saying penis and now I knew he wanted to use one on my grandma. I wanted to slide through the cracks in the floor and bury myself. The closest I came to burial was in the dark and with my head under the covers. I never knew why things hadn't dawned on me before.

Chapter 6

Back in the Family, Again

Bet was the best cook in the world as far as I knew. She didn't like to work on Sunday, so she cooked a big meal on Saturday night. She cooked enough for all of us to have Saturday-night super, Sunday-dinner and Sunday-night supper if necessary. Her Saturday night meal was always the same: chicken and pastry, chicken salad, greasy rice, collards, butter beans, green beans, cornbread, biscuits, a pound cake, a pecan pie and a coconut pie. Everybody could find something they liked. I personally liked to eat the chicken and pastry cold. Mama and Daddy liked the chicken salad after church. Gene and Roy ate all and any of it, hot or cold. Bet said they needed a worm treatment. Rudolph said Mama saw a corpse when she was carrying the twins. Apparently, this caused the boys to be bottomless pits. They ate everything in sight, but they were skinny as clothesline. Their feet were the biggest thing about them.

Momma had invited Doc to Saturday supper when he brought us home yesterday from revival. That was an absolute miracle. After all the trash Momma had talked about Doc, he was coming to eat with us. I didn't dare mention supper all day at the office. Saturday is always a big day for Rooster Juice and the Queen of Hearts Elixir. I guess old people planned to get frisky on Saturday night. I couldn't believe I even said that in my head. I was still traumatized by what Doc, and I talked about last night, talking about sex one moment and Ma Mariah the next.

Grandma Mariah will be at Saturday supper, and Big Jack and Big Judy.

Big Jack (John) and Big Judy (Judith) McLean are MaMariah's parents, so they were my great-grandparents. Big Jack had been a farmer. That was where Momma got her farming experience, on Big Jack's farm. When Big Jack and Big Judy retired, they moved into the house behind ours. Bet cooked for them, too. Ma Mariah and Big Judy visited every day and Big Jack went to the store and sat on the liar's bench drinking little Coke-a-Colas and eating four-corner Nabs every day except Sunday. The store was within shooting distance of the house.

I hoped Momma wasn't going to get everybody together for Big Jack to finish off Doc. Big Jack shot him once. I didn't know if he might keep a grudge.

"Iver, what time is supper tonight?" Doc said in a cheerful voice. A great sense of something dreadful came over me.

"We usually eat at six-thirty." I couldn't stand it. "You are really coming to supper?"

"Well, yes. Lauralee invited me." As Doc said that he stopped and looked at me and asked. "Why?"

"The whole bunch will there tonight: Big Jack, Big Judy, MaMariah, Gene and Roy. I'm afraid for you, Doc. Big Jack has already shot you once and MaMariah has that 410 gauge she loves to play with. I am just scared for you, Doc. "

"Scared? I'm not going to get shot on a Saturday night at my daughter's house. We are not white trash. We are adults that have just had a bumpy relationship. There isn't going to be a gunfight. In fact, I talked to Jack a couple of weeks ago at the barber shop. And I see Walter there, too. If you want to know what's going on, go sit in the barbershop every week or so."

Doc closed the office at five p.m. We got shined up and were walking in the kitchen door at six-twenty-five. Bet looked up at us. She put everything in Pyrex so Roy and Gene could put the lids on and stick them in the Fridge after supper.

Bet was carrying the food into the dining room to the buffet. Rudolph was sitting at the kitchen table looking at the paper, grinning. He always drove Bet and him home at night. She has their supper packed in her bag. Privilege of Tote was tradition. Daddy said if she cooked it, she had to eat it.

I was being my most polite person. "Doc", I said, "This is Rudolph Hatcher and this is Betsy Hatcher. Rudolph, Bet, this is Doctor Edwards."

"Nice to see you Betsy, Rudolph.

Bet said, "Iver, why did you bring Dr. Edwards through the kitchen? Go outside and back around. Use the front door. You have better manners."

"OK, OK, why do you give me such a hard time?"

"Because I'm not through raising you."

"Oh, Lord." I couldn't help but be annoyed by her, especially when she was right.

"So, we walk around to the front door, Doc."

Gene and Roy were lying in wait at the front door. I thought they were going to knock Doc off his feet. Roy was grinning so big you could see a missing molar.

Doc had just as big a grin. He gave them a wink and pointed a finger gun at them.

Big Jack and Daddy were standing by the mantle with their Saturday night drink, bourbon and one piece of ice. Big Judy has one, too. Big Jack said, "Glad you could come to supper, Erastus. Would you like a Saturday night sip with us?"

"Yes. I would, John."

It is strange to hear someone besides Big Judy call Big Jack, John.

Big Jack said, "Erastus, we need to plan a fishing trip, somewhere we haven't been. Have you been to Alaska in your travels?"

Daddy handed him a tea glass with one piece of ice and filled it with bourbon.

Doc said, "Thank you, Walter. No, John, I've never made it to Alaska, but there is no reason we can't go."

Doc turned to Big Judy and said, "You are as beautiful as ever Judith."

"Thank you, Erastus. You always have had a silver tongue. Lauralee will be down in a minute. She put in new automatic waterers in the chicken house today so she worked a little late. Bet has taken care of supper."

Doc said," Still loves her animals." He turned to Big Judy and said, "Judith, where is Mariah?"

Big Judy said, "She had a late appointment at the beauty parlor." Then she winked at him.

Doc was right. This is not a setup to kill Doc. MaMariah wants to spark Doc. And everybody was good with it. Nobody told me! All the family was plotting to get Dr. Erastus Rembrandt Edwards and Miss Mariah McLean together. No. This wasn't going to work. Doc hadn't said anything about being divorced from the first woman. Grandma Mariah and Doc going together. The back of my neck was prickling. My ears were sweating inside. There were black dots in front of my face.

I announced to everybody, "I need to get some fresh air," and stepped out on the front porch and walked around to the kitchen door. Bet and Rudolph were still here.

"Do y'all know what is going on in there? Doc and MaMariah are going to get together. I thought Momma hated Doc so bad that…. I don't know what I thought."

Rudolph shook the newspaper so the next page would turn neatly, "Iver, Miss Lauralee and Miss Mariah have had a change of heart. Miss Mariah is so happy. She still loves the old man. "

Bet was hanging the dish cloths on the rack behind the back door, "Some women love their men no matter what they have done or what they do."

Rudolph looked over the paper, "You like Doc, don't you?"

I said, "Well, yes, he has been very nice to me. I'm learning a lot."

Bet was shaking her apron out and hanging it on the nail beside pantry door, "Some men can do about anything, and women still love them. But after Mr. Jack shot Mr. Erastus he held back from seeing any of us for a long time."

"What do you mean 'us?' You know Doc?"

Rudolph was folding the paper, "All the family knows him. He came by once in a while to check on everybody, Miss Mariah, Lauralee, you boys before he came back to set up practice. He knew you when you were born. Lauralee has raised so much hell over the years; he just kept low. He was just waiting for Miss Mariah to remember how much she loves him. Miss Mariah is the only one that could change your Momma. And she must have got Lauralee to back down. Mr. Erastus doesn't want to die alone. He wants to finish his life with Miss Mariah and Miss Mariah wants to finish her life with Mr. Erastus. They are lonely for each other, like any man and woman would be. Do you understand, IV?

Bet picked the folded newspaper and started fanning me, "Shut up, Rudy. Iver, don't faint. You really are white, even for you."

"Why? He's old enough to know how things work. IV told me he was a man."

I said, "I know men and women have sex."

Rudolph gave a kind of low hum, "No. Men and women love each other, and things get in the way."

"I guess I am confused about how to think about Doc and MaMariah. I suppose I haven't looked at this in the right light."

Bet starts in on me and says, "Let me tell you something Iver Johnson Murphy. Your grandma is a good woman, a good Christian woman and lonely. She married Dr. Erastus in good faith. She didn't know he wasn't divorced. And Mr. John shot him for family honor. And your momma, Lauralee is about to get over it. We need to help Miss Mariah have some happiness."

Rudolph stood up and got his cap off the back of the chair, "Do you understand, IV? Men and women just want to keep each other company. It really hurts when there are a lot of strings on relationships. People ought not to judge people. You don't need to judge Miss Mariah for wanting to spend her time with Dr. Erastus. Look at them. They are both old people."

"I have learned more about my family…no, about people today than I ever wanted to know."

Rudolph said, "You told me you are a man. It's not easy to be a good man. Remember that, IV."

Momma walked in the kitchen and said, "There you are. I thought you would be in here talking to Bet and Rudolph."

I said, "Momma, how are you right with Doc coming to supper? And MaMariah getting fixed up for him? After all the shit you talked about him and what he did to MaMariah?"

Momma said," Don't use that word, Iver. My momma had a long talk to me about my daddy. Momma still loves the old bastard. She told me so. Momma is not young. She's fifty-five and Daddy is seventy. I don't know, Iver. I'm trying to put the hatred away. The Bible says not to let the sun go down on your anger and the sun has been setting on my anger for 20 years. If I am a Christian, I've got to change my thinking. Momma humbled me. I am a grown woman and I still have respect for my mother. And she is right. If she can forgive him, I have to forgive him. Big Jack said he forgave Daddy when he shot him. Close your mouth, Iver."

"I'm sorry, Momma. This is all too much for me. This has been a hell of a week for me."

Momma said, "Quit thinking so much. Sometimes life changes, sometimes good, sometimes bad."

"But Momma…."

"But Iver… my Momma has let it go and I'm working on it. She still loves him. Come on and let's eat. Let's have a big family dinner."

"Momma, can we talk later?"

Momma and I walked into the dining room. Momma said, "Big Jack, will you return thanks? A short Methodist prayer, please, before the pastry gets cold."

Big Jack grinned and said, "Bless the bread; damn the meat. Good God, let's eat".

Big Judy jumped out of the chair, pointing a finger with a long red painted fingernail, "John, you ought to be ashamed of yourself, in front of Iver and the twins."

Gene and Roy busted out laughing and snorting. I was grinning.

Big Jack said, "Alright boys. Do as I say, not as I do. I'm sorry Miss Judith."

Big Jack could yank Big Judy's chain and she loved it.

Doc said, "Jack, you haven't changed since I first met you. You've just got a bigger audience with the boys.

Well, you ought to have seen Roy and Gene with their new best friend.

Big Judy was the first through the buffet line. Big Jack waved Doc to go next and completely oblivious to what they had been taught, Gene and Roy were right behind him. Big Jack just shook his head and picked up his plate. I know MaMariah wanted to sit beside him but there is Gene on one side and Roy on the other. Doc was loving it.

Roy was squeezing lemon in his sweet tea and looked at Doc, "MaMariah said you had a circus. Is that right?"

Doc said, "Well, yes, Roy. I had a small circus."

Gene was doing the same lemon squeeze routine, "How did you get started working for a circus? We might want to do that."

Momma rolled her eyes and MaMariah just grinned.

"When I started working for the circus, I was the front man. I put up posters, bought newspaper ads, lined up feed for the animals. I got goats for the big cats, lions and tigers, coastal hay or alfalfa hay for the elephants and horses, whatever was in the area, corn, oats, groceries for the whole circus."

In perfect timing, the boys say together, "You had lions?"

"I had several over the years, always tried to keep them like pets. They are wild animals, but you get to know them."

Roy said, "Did you get to pet and scratch them?"

"Oh, yes, some of them. The last trainer I had brought one lion with him. She was such a tame cat all she would do was roll on her back to get her belly scratched. The only trick she could do was to eat a hotdog out of her trainer's mouth. I guess that was a pretty good trick. That cat must have been a dog in a previous life."

The twin's eyes were about the size of silver dollars.

And Gene said, "And you had elephants?"

"Yes, three beautiful girls. I named them Sarah, Eloise, and May..."

Big Jack slapped the table and said, "You didn't name one of them Mariah, did you?"

"No, no, no. I had a tiger named Mariah," he said with a little grin.

I think the bourbon kicked in at this point in the story.

Big Judy said a mumbled "Oh, Lord," and emitted a groan. "You are still a rascal 'Rastus."

Gene said, "Tell us about the elephants."

The boys were about to jump out of their seats.

"Sarah was the first one I bought. She was smarter than any animal except a human. I would think of something I wanted her to do, and she just understood. She helped train the others as I got them. All of them are smart. I believe they can read minds. You know they have huge brains. They might have telepathy. Don't know for sure. Sarah could look at the other two, and they would do just what we wanted. I couldn't prove they could read my mind, but it sure seemed like it."

Big Judy said, "Erastus, you haven't changed a bit, filling these boys up with mind reading elephants."

Roy said, "Where are the elephants now? I want to see them!"

"Sarah died of old age. From what I knew of her history, she was sixty-three when she died. She lay down one evening and the other two kept touching her with their trunks. It was a day before Eloise and May would walk away from her. If an elephant doesn't want to do something, you are not going to make them."

Gene said, "Where did you bury her? Or did you have her stuffed?"

"We were in Kentucky when she died. A farmer we bought hay from let me bury her on his land. She was so big I had to hire a track hoe to bury her. I hired two wreckers and we winched her up on a flatbed truck. It was a real production."

All of us were spell bound.

Roy said, "Where are the other two?"

"Well, just couldn't split them up so I sold them to a petting zoo in Georgia. I know the people. They are doing fine. I know they will die of old age there."

Gene said, "What about the circus lions? Where are they?"

"The lion trainer quit the circus and opened an auto shop, took his pet lion with him. I went by to see him, and the old lion was still alive. He let her loose in the junk yard at night. I am sure she is dead by now."

Roy said, "What about the other lions?"

"I sold them to a zoo in South Carolina. They were trying to start breeding lions. It is a nice place."

I could see what MaMariah saw in him. He was charming all of us.

MaMariah said, "Erastus, tell us about the unusual trapeze artist you had."

Doc chuckled, took a swallow of tea, wiped his mouth and smiled real big. "Mariah, are these boys old enough to hear this story?"

"I think so, Erastus. Just be careful of the words you use to describe things." I actually saw MaMariah wink at Doc.

Big Jack made a kind of stabbing motion toward Doc with his fork, "Go ahead, Erastus. I haven't heard that story in years."

Big Judy mumbled in her napkin, "Save me, Lord."

A huge grin was on Doc's face. He was back in the family, right where he wanted to be.

"Well boys, I had this trapeze artist that was afraid of heights when he was sober. He needed to get a little tight before he could fly. If he got a little too tipsy, he wanted to make water when he got to the top of the ladder. Oh, my, excuse me ladies for using such language. "

Big Judy, Mama and MaMariah, all three took their left hands and kind of waved, muttering words like, "No, No, go ahead"', holding their heads down and trying not to laugh.

"Most of the time we caught him if he was too inebriated before he climbed. His wife could do an act without him. He once watered the elephants from his platform. The lights weren't on him, but Sarah knew exactly who had done it. She watered him a while after that. He was walking behind her in the closing parade. Those elephants could hold a grudge."

In unison, the twins said, "Wow" in awe.

"The circus was set up near some power lines in Alabama. Boys, you know the kind I'm talking about, like the Eiffel Tower that carries transmission lines. That is where the tragedy occurred."

Mine and the twin's eyes were fixed on him, like dogs on point.

"Santos the Magnificent, my flyer, got three sheets to the wind and climbed one of those towers naked, with only his gloves and a rope. Apparently, he wanted to swing off of the tower. He had attached the rope but then nature called: he answered it.

"Yes, the stream of water hit one of the transmission lines and the voltage knocked him off the tower. Witnesses said he looked like a naked burning angel when he flew for the last time. When I got there, he was still smoking. I measured three hundred and ten feet from the base of the tower to where he landed his last performance."

Roy said admiringly, "What a way to go."

In my head, I said, "Doc must be the biggest and best liar on Earth. If he's telling the truth he needs to write a book."

Now we are going to have something new to worry about. Gene and Roy are going to want to run away and join the circus.

Momma was pleasant to Doc all evening but she didn't say much of anything to anybody. I could see her looking at Doc and then looking at MaMariah like she was thinking seriously about things. I wondered if she was thinking about how Doc had done MaMariah so wrong. I wondered if she was thinking she might forgive Doc. I know she wasn't thinking about forgetting what Doc had done.

Doc went to church with MaMariah the next morning. Momma wasn't at church that Sunday. She was tending the new chicks. I don't know how she would have felt about Doc sitting on our pew next to

MaMariah. They even held hands, shared the pew bible, the hymn book like two old teenagers. Everybody in town knew the story, no use in hiding it. Still felt kind of embarrassed, Doc being an old rascal, old people making out, old people having sex, MaMariah and Doc having sex. I had all of these thoughts during the sermon. Then I thought, 'Yes, I am on my way to Hades.' Then the back of my neck started getting a prickly feeling. There were black spots in front of my eyes. This was just too much. Oh, Sweet Jesus, I was going to pass on over. This was when I slid under the pew. Apparently, my slide was quiet. MaMariah said the new carpet in the sanctuary kept my head from making a thump. Gene and Roy were on the other side of Doc, oblivious as usual. Daddy was in the choir. He said nobody made a fuss, so he just kept singing. MaMariah said Doc reached down and checked my pulse to make sure I wasn't dead. She said she didn't want to cause a stir during the sermon. The preacher hadn't been with us very long. I woke up sometime and remembered where I was. I laid there under the pew until the sermon was over and the congregation sang the Hymn of Dedication. I crawled out from under the pew as casually as possible and stood up beside MaMariah. I didn't know whether to be hurt that nobody 'tended' to me or grateful that nobody saw me faint.

Doc came to the house after church and had leftovers with us. Momma wasn't at the house when we got home. She left a note for Daddy asking him to come to the layer house after we ate dinner. We ate, straightened up and then MaMariah got in Doc's Cadillac and rode off. I don't know if MaMariah would have left with him if Mama had been home. I am seeing that MaMariah, and Momma's relationship is kind of backwards sometimes. I wonder if MaMariah has forgiven Doc or if Momma was really the one holding the grudge.

Chapter 7

Rooster Juice and Dancing

Doc and I were standing in the kitchen bottling Rooster Juice which was not made from roosters. He made Rooster Juice with some quality white lightning, some sugar, some peppermint candy, some anise, some red food coloring, and one long cayenne pepper in each bottle. It was not deadly to the taste, but the cayenne gave it a little after bite.

I looked at Doc, "Why do you sell so much of this stuff to old men?"

Doc was screwing caps on bottles, "Because they can't dance anymore."

In my naivety, "So your Rooster Juice is going to make old men dance."

"Good God, boy. You are seventeen years old, and you haven't figured anything out. When a man can't dance, he needs something to make him think he can dance."

In my brilliance, "He is going to think he can dance when he drinks the Rooster Juice?"

"That's right. He will think he can and that is all that matters. Doesn't matter how old a man is; he still wants to be in the game. A man wants to feel like he can get the attention of a woman. A man wants a woman to look at him and see the perfect peacock strutting his stuff. You know about the birds and bees, right boy?"

I prayed, "Please, Lord, don't let the words come out his old man's mouth that I think are going to come out."

"Let me tell you about Peacocks", he continued.

Lord, you are not helping me. Save me just this one time. Again. I thought.

"You've seen them strutting and shaking their tail feathers, right? Those cocks are trying to get a hen's attention. The hen chooses who she mates with. The better they look, better they shake, do their dance, the better chance a hen will choose them, the better chance of mating."

In my naivety, again, "So Rooster Juice is going to make old men dance? Shake their tail feathers?"

"No. It just brings back the memories of when they were in the dance. The hope they can get chosen again. Get back in the mating game."

"Doc, so the Rooster Juice is going to make them think they can dance, dream they can dance."

"Good God in Heaven! The boy understands! Females love males that dance. You take a man that can dance, and I'll show you a man with all the women he wants. We're no different from the beasts, Iver. We just understand what is going on."

"So, you're telling me that if I can dance, I can get a woman?"

"Women, your pick."

"I know how to dance, Doc. Mama showed me how to waltz, how to box step.

"No, like a dance, a party. Hot sweating dancing. Men strutting, women rubbing.

"Rudolph carried me to a piccolo joint and I danced with a few colored girls. They laughed at my dancing. He said I was hopeless, so he carried me back again a couple of times. I didn't see any men struttin', in fact there weren't any men there when I was at the piccolo joint, just girls."

"So, you didn't see any of the colored men dancing?"

"No there weren't any there. I think that was why Rudolph took me when he did, up in the day. He said the crowd didn't come in until after dark. I tried to dance but the girls just kept rubbing on me." I don't know where that came from. I can't believe I said that to my granddaddy.

"You see, a man dancing isn't about having sex right there. The dancing is showing the females that you are quality breeding stock. That you are available."

No, Lord, I prayed, Save me. I should not have said "rubbing" in front of Doc. "Doc, I did not say anything about sex." Then after a pause, "Are you saying that is the only reason men dance, to get to have sex?"

"Iver, women pick who is the father of their children. We don't pick the woman. That's all it's about. It's pleasurable and it leads to other things. I had a preacher tell me that dancing was like having sex standing up."

"So, Doc, is it a sin to dance or to have sex? If it is linked together you can't win."

This was another time Doc was telling me entirely too much information. But for some reason I can't stop wanting him to tell me more. When he said things………well, I just had to think about it.

"Doc, where did you learn this from? I need to read this book."

"I didn't learn this from a book. I have just listened and watched people."

"Doc, I need to learn to really dance. I want a wife and children…. eventually."

"Iver, have you been to Carolina Beach?"

"Sure."

"Have you been to Sea Breeze?"

"Sure, Daddy and I went there to buy shrimp when we rented a house at Carolina Beach. What has Sea Breeze got to do with dancing?"

"That's where a white man can go to learn to dance like a black man. You know black men can always have a woman."

"Doc! I can't believe you said that. I don't need to learn to dance like a colored man!"

"Why not?"

"I don't know why not."

"Trust me boy. When you see those men dance at Sea Breeze, you'll understand."

"So, you and I are going to Sea Breeze?"

"No, not directly. We're going to Carolina Beach and staying at a hotel. We are going to eat good food, look at the ocean and then we're going to Sea Breeze."

"Just you and me, Doc?"

Doc said, "Next weekend."

I said, "But Friday and Saturday are your best days."

"We are going to put up a sign this week that we will be closed next Friday and Saturday. Word will get around. Yep, you and me at Carolina Beach."

"Doc, aren't you a little old for the beach and for dancing?"

Doc stopped and looked at me. Dear God. Why in the world did I say that? He was frisking up my grandmother and I had to say that.

"Iver, I know you have heard the old saying, 'There may be snow on the roof but there is still a fire in the stove.' I'm seventy but I'm not dead."

The Great Road Trip began.

We left home early Friday morning with the new rods and reels broken down in the trunk. Doc said that was a great time of year to go surf fishing; the spots were running. I had never been surf fishing before. We always fished off the pier. I think Daddy just liked to sit on the pier. I don't remember that we had ever caught many fish. Daddy always took time to look at the pictures of the sharks and other huge fish that are next to the bait box. The pictures just came to mind. Sharks chasing the spots, sharks chasing spots to where we are fishing in the surf, all I could hope for was an angel to protect me from sharks. Daddy said God took care of fools, drunks and children. That was a good thing.

Doc said, "We are going to stay at Mrs. Blue's boarding house while we are down here. I think you are old enough to keep anything you see to yourself. I mean for you not to tell anything if anything interesting happens."

I said, "If we are going to stay at a boarding house, where are we going to keep the fish?"

Doc says, "We're not coming here to catch a cooler of fish. If we catch any, we'll just give them to somebody else that is fishing. I am not interested in cleaning a bunch of fish this weekend. We have come to Carolina Beach because Sea Breeze is right across the waterway."

"So why aren't we staying in Sea Breeze?"

"When you went to Sea Breeze, where did you see any white people?"

"On the boat selling fish."

"Did you see a hotel you wanted to stay in?"

"No."

"That's why we are staying at Mrs. Blue's boarding house."

"So, what's the deal with Sea Breeze?"

"I want you to see how to dance and try out some steps. There won't be anybody there that we know, nobody white that we know."

"If I understand this right, you want me to watch Negro men dance."

"That's right. I want you to see how the women look at them. I want you to see how the men watch each other dance. You might not understand the value of this now but when you want a wife and want to keep her, you'll remember this."

Doc paused and looked away. "I haven't danced with Mariah in a long time."

I don't think I was supposed to hear that.

Checked in, two single beds, bath down the hall. Could have been better but it was OK. It was six o'clock and I was hungry. We had stopped on the way down and got a drink and cake but that had been a while. "Where are we going to eat, Doc?"

"Downstairs. Mrs. Blue will have spots on the supper table."

The food was good. I could see she had a colored woman in the kitchen cooking. Kind of like home: fresh spots, shrimp, fried oysters, collards, rice, sweet potatoes, sweet tea, served family style on the table. The tea tasted a little funny. Water tastes different at the beach. Bet never cooked fish that good. Doc said it wasn't all the cooks; it was how fresh the fish was, caught today preferably. I ate four spots. Mrs. Blue said the salt air brought out the appetite in men. She had a sly smile on her face when she said it.

Doc said, "Come on, Iver. We've got to walk this fish off. We need to check and make sure the water is still in the ocean."

We strolled down to the boardwalk and looked at the boarded-up stores. It reminded me of the midway at the fair. Now it was tired and resting for the winter. Friday night bingo was open with a few wrinkled, blue-haired old women and leathery-looking old men.

It was about eight-thirty when Doc said, "Let's get some fresh clothes on and ride to Sea Breeze."

"This late?"

"Yes. They haven't gotten rolling good yet. They will be there till dawn."

We rode over Snow's Cut Bridge and turned right and parked on the side of the road. When you turned off Carolina Beach Road, the woods were full of cars and people were milling around. We could hear the juke boxes playing music I had never heard on the radio. I don't know why but I felt relaxed, like I wanted to dance. Maybe it was the soft dark night, the smell of the beach, fireflies blinking and bare light bulbs strung around the clubs. We walked by one and stopped at the second, a concrete block building with a naked light over the door.

Doc walked up to the doorkeeper and handed him a $5 bill. He was a tall pecan-tan man with a black, shiny suit, a red shirt and a bolo tie.

The man said, "Captain, been a long time."

Doc said, "Sure has, Wilson. This is my grandson, Iver."

I nodded my head and smiled standing a step behind Doc.

Wilson said, "You stepping out, Doc?"

"Sort of, Wilson. I wanted the boy to dance with some of these pretty girls and catch some of the steps from these young bucks."

"Y'all enjoy yourselves. The bar is on the left. Card games are on the right."

That night was transforming. I had never seen people dance like that. There was sweat running down their faces. The men's white shirts were wet and stuck to their backs. But there was something in their eyes when they danced. The rest of the world didn't exist. It looked like the men were mesmerized by the women and the women were absorbing their thoughts. Then I saw some of the women sit down and watch the men dance. The men then seemed to try to out dance one another. Doc was right about peacocks and peahens.

Slow music started playing and the couples started swaying together. They began to slip away into the night. I knew what was going on, but I didn't want to think about it. Doc was still in the bar nursing a beer. I walked over to the bar and Doc said, "Get this boy a Pepsi." I had never stood at a real bar.

I was standing next to Doc with our backs to the bar and propped with our elbows. I felt like I was in the game, I was grown, I had gotten the ticket to adulthood, whatever that was. The music picked up again and a colored girl with a tight red skirt and a polka dotted- blouse walked up to me and held out her hand. She didn't say a thing. I looked at Doc and he just nodded and smiled. I caught her hand. She pulled me out on the dance floor and started swaying to the music. I didn't know what to do so I started doing what she was doing, swaying. I was getting pretty good at it, and she got up close to me and took my hands and put on her hips and she put her hands on my shoulders. She whispered in my ear, "Just do what I do." We danced. I looked at her and she was smiling at me. She was beautiful. I watched some of the men dancing and started doing some moves like them. I kept looking at her and she kept smiling at me. One of the men danced over to me and showed me a step and then another and then another. The pretty colored girl sat at a table and watched me dance or try to dance like the men on the floor without her. I was dancing for her, for her to notice me. I danced till I was winded. I sat at the table with the pretty colored girl and put my arm over the back of her chair. She laughed and scratched at my stomach and laughed some more. Then she kissed me, hard and long, like you see in the movies.

She got up, took another man by the hand and started swaying to the music. Doc walked over to my table and sat down. He had a slow smile and said, "Understand now, boy?"

I woke up around noon on Saturday. The windows were open, and the curtains were moving a little bit. Doc wasn't in the room and the fishing gear was gone. I pulled my clothes on and felt my stomach growl. I was hoping there was some dinner downstairs. When I got to the bottom of the stairs Mrs. Blue stepped out of what I think was her room. She smiled and pointed to the dining room. There was a plate of sandwiches on the table. Each sandwich was carefully wrapped in wax paper. There was a note beside the sandwiches that said, "Drinks in the kitchen". I walked in the kitchen and the colored woman was sitting at a little table shelling butter beans. She looked away from the television, smiled at me and pointed at a rusty refrigerator. I smiled back, nodded and got an

RC soft drink. I went back to the dining room, got three sandwiches off the plate and walked out on the front porch. I sat down in a big rocking chair, ate and watched the waves. I don't know how long I sat there. Time seemed to stop. The waves kept crashing. The seagulls kept flying. I relived the previous night in my mind. I could feel that pretty colored girl kissing me again. My body relaxed just thinking about dancing and some kind of feeling was there that I couldn't figure out.

Doc walked up the steps with his rod and reel and mine, too. He leaned the poles on the porch railing and said, "I wondered if you were going to wake up or not. The salt air and the sound of the waves can put a man in a deep, deep sleep. And you are still growing; you need a lot of sleep. Did you have a good time last night?"

"Doc, that was the best night of my life. I don't know what it is, but I can't stop thinking about the music, that pretty girl, the lightning bugs in the trees where we parked the car. I need to write this down. I don't want to forget last night."

"Do you want to go back tonight?"

"Hell, yes!"

"Let me eat some dinner and we'll go back and fish for a while. There was an old man fishing out there that I was talking to. When we go back, I'll carry him a couple of sandwiches. I gave him the fish I caught. He gave me some bait. Nice fellow. He was fishing for something to eat, going to salt the mullets."

We walked back on the beach and the tide was turning, coming in. Doc waded out about knee deep in the surf and cast long. I walked down a little way and started to do the same thing, but I stopped. There was a whelk shell rolling almost on my feet. I had never found one before. I stopped and picked it up. I don't know why I thought of this but maybe this whelk found me so I could remember this trip. That was some kind of sentimental stuff. I knew I was going soft. I carried my shell back to where the tackle box was sitting on the sand, held it to my ear for a moment and then sat it down. Yep, I was going sentimental, a shell to remember the best weekend of my life.

Doc said, "Get to fishing, Iver. We want to get our new friend a cooler of fish before supper."

We fished standing in the rolling waves. I looked for sharks and was positive I felt a few brushes against my legs. I kept seeing those huge fish in the pictures at the pier. I knew God takes care of fools and children and drunks. I wasn't scared.

Supper was the same menu as last night and it was just as good. Mrs. Blue was right. Salt air whets an appetite.

Doc and I walked on the boardwalk again that night. It was still sad and tired. About nine o'clock Doc said, "You ready to go dancing again? I might dance some tonight."

"Really, Doc? I thought you were sweet on MaMariah."

"I am sweet on that beautiful woman, but there is nothing wrong with dancing with another woman."

I got to thinking what Doc said about dancing being the same thing as sex except dancing was standing up. I wondered what MaMariah would think about Doc dancing with another woman.

We parked in a different place that night. There were a lot more cars; it was Saturday night. The club we went to previous night was so full people were spilling out the door. We walked to another one a little farther down. This one was wooden instead of concrete. It was painted a bright blue color, or that was what it looked like in the light of the bare bulbs. There was an old woman at the door. She had bright red lipstick and a tall wig. Her earlobes were sort of ruffled where the pierced earrings had been snatched out. She said, "You crackers can come in but don't start any shit. This is a peaceful place. We serve everybody, even white people. We already integrated," and laughed. Doc handed her a five-dollar bill like he did at the other club. She looked at the money and said, "You keep your money. I make enough money off the bar, you ain't got to pay to get in."

Doc smiled really big at her and said, "You are still beautiful, Alberta. How are your girls?"

"In college, graduated college, teaching school, all of them are good. Thank you for asking, 'Rastus. Is that your boy?"

My God, this old man knew everybody.

"No, this is my grandson, Iver Murphy. I want him to learn how to dance like he ought to."

The red lipped, big wigged Alberta smiled a golden smile. All the upper teeth you could see were gold capped, like Doc's. "There are a lot of pretty girls in here, some of my girls' college friends. Go find one to dance with. Good to see you 'Rastus."

We walked in and I said, "Doc, she called you by your first name."

"Her daddy sharecropped for my grandparents. I met her when we moved to the farm my mama's people left us. We were both teenagers. I'll tell you about it sometime."

I wanted to hear about his grandparents, but I really wanted to dance again. I wondered if I could get my nerve up to ask a girl to dance. A girl asking me to dance might never happen again.

I walked behind Doc to the bar. He got a beer, and I got a grape drink. Doc didn't order; that was just what the barkeep put on the bar. Doc put down two dollars and nodded at the barkeeper. I had drunk about half of mine and Doc had sat down his beer bottle with another dollar under it. In just a second, there was another cold beer. That was how it worked or that was how Doc did it. Doc sucked down four while I was drinking the same grape drink. I couldn't believe what I saw happen next. Doc walked out on the dance floor and cut in on a couple shagging. Doc could really dance; I mean really dance. People moved out of the way to watch them dance. I was still standing at the bar when I heard my name. I turned around and there was Girlie and two more pretty colored girls.

Girlie said, "I heard Doctor Erastus could dance. It's true."

I said, "What are you doing here?"

"I came down here with some friends from school. Kind of a last fling before I start a new job."

"Are you going to leave us?"

"After you left, I got a call Friday for a teaching position. Doc knew I was looking for another job. Doc said you were coming to fish. This isn't fishing," she laughed.

"I'm kind of embarrassed to tell you, but Doc wants me to dance like a colored man."

Girlie and her friends burst out laughing. I was kind of ashamed of myself after I said it, but I don't think there was another way to say it.

Girlie said through her giggles, "That makes sense. We'll even help you learn to dance."

One of the girls that was standing with Girlie took me by the hand, (same story) and pulled me on the dance floor. Doc wasn't there for approval, so I followed her like a puppy on a leash. I didn't start with the swaying method that time; I had her hand in mine from following her and I didn't let go. She pressed against me like a dancer I saw on the Ed Sullivan show. I don't know how I did it, but my feet seemed to know what to do. When the next song started, Girlie came over to me and said, "Let's dance."

It was a slow dance, and it was like a dream. She had her arms around my neck and nuzzled my cheeks. She whispered, "I've wanted to dance with you for a long time." I pulled my head back and looked her in the eyes. "Really?" She nodded. I said, "Me, too." We danced a while, sat a while, watched Doc get drunk and danced some more.

Girlie said, "Let go to the car. Doc will be here a while longer. Alberta will take care of him."

I got the keys for the car from Doc. He was three sheets to the wind and didn't have a care in the world. All he was interested in was dancing with or without a partner. Girlie and I walked out to the car, and she said, "Iver, we have to keep this to ourselves. You understand? My reputation would be ruined if anybody knew about you."

"Because I'm white?"

"No, because you are seventeen and white."

We kissed for a long time, listened to the radio, held hands, and talked. I think the world changed for me right then. My granddaddy got drunk when I was with him. It dawned on me what he meant when he said I was old enough to keep quiet about what I saw. He danced like the colored men and looked pretty good doing it. I thought about a lot of things that night. Thought about Doc and MaMariah, him getting drunk and dancing with the colored women. Thought about Sissy Reynolds, how I wanted her to be my girlfriend and ride around with me in my car that I didn't have. Thought about Girlie, again. Girlie was so beautiful and she was colored. I realized that Rudolph was right; things get in the way of people loving each other. And Doc still had his ways about him. Not all were good, but I couldn't help but like the old man.

Chapter 8

Little Lost Boys

Girlie had left for her new teaching job, right here in the county. The teacher she is was replacing didn't make it to Columbus Day. I guess some teachers get enough of teaching pretty quick.

When Girlie was gone, Doc came up with the idea that I could be the cook now. I have never figured out how he got the idea I could cook. I knew enough not to starve but that was all. Henrietta was going to keep up with the washing and ironing. I was also going to keep the floors. We had a housekeeper before; I didn't know why we didn't have one then.

The first night I cooked we had grits and eggs and I didn't salt the grits. And I forgot to sweeten the tea while it was hot. Doc didn't complain.

After supper we were in the parlor/waiting room, Doc was reading the Fayetteville Observer and I was pushing the carpet sweeper. He had his magnifying glass out reading the stocks. I don't know why the question came to mind, but I said, "Doc, what about your grandparents? You said you would tell me about them. And you've never said anything about your parents. What was everybody's name and where did they come from?"

"You don't want to hear about those old people. I'll write their names on a piece of paper for you. I wrote it down for Mariah one time; don't know why."

"Come on, Doc. You know more than their names. Where did they live? Your grandparents must have been farmers. You already told me they had sharecroppers. Was your daddy a farmer, too? Must have done good for you to get to be a doctor."

"Me being a doctor didn't have anything to do with my daddy."

"Was your daddy a doctor, too?"

"You aren't going to let this go, are you? The past is gone. I'm starting over with Mariah. I've started over before."

I could hear an edge in Doc's voice that I hadn't heard before. He was looking at me like he was thinking what to say to me. Apparently, I have touched a nerve about something.

"I'm sorry, Doc. I just wanted to hear about my family."

"I know, son. I haven't thought much about my daddy in a long time. My old man was a dog, an S.O.B. if there ever was one. I hate him to this day."

"Doc, I…" Maybe I didn't want to know.

"Papa was named Cicero Edwards and my dear mother was named Precious Pauline. Her maiden name was McArthur. It's been a long time since I have thought about either of them."

I asked, "Have you got a picture of them? Or was it too long ago?"

"Not too long ago, just too poor."

"Papa-Cicero married her when she was thirteen. I never knew if my daddy didn't want her to have anything to do with her people or her people disowned her. I don't know which one it was or both. Mother's people sent food sometimes when we were hungry. No, not Mother's people really, but some of her people's sharecroppers that felt sorry for her and us boys. She bore Pa five sons by the time she was twenty-one. I was eleven and she was twenty-five when she left us."

My ears perked up. Doc had four brothers. My family was getting bigger. And his mama ran off?

Doc said, "Little boys without a mama. We were like lost little puppies without a mother."

I said, "She walked out on her little boys? She left five little boys?"

Doc said, "We survived."

Doc was quiet for a long time, just looking at the fireplace.

"Before I tell you this, I want you to remember that we were poor people. Poor like our bones stuck out. Poor like all the meat we had come from the river or out of a trap."

I was quiet, just looking at Doc. I was trying to see him as a poor little boney boy. Now, he had nice suits, drove a Cadillac, had a roll of bills in his pocket, a doctor.

"If you were so poor, how did you get to be a doctor?"

He sighed and looked at the fireplace again. "Mama wasn't always poor. She came from good people. They were farmers and a lot smarter people than my daddy. For some reason, Mama got up with Pa. When her parents found out, they made them get married even though she was only thirteen. They could have had him charged with rape but that would have been a horrible scandal. And Pa had nothing. He had a little shack and an iron pot. But they survived and she had five sons. When she was twenty-five, she was expecting again, showing when she got ready to leave. Papa said she had to get rid of the baby and she was screaming 'No'."

Doc paused and looked hard at me.

"I've never told anyone this. Pa killed Mother."

I sat there stunned. My great-grandpa killed my great-grandma. I couldn't make any sound come out of my mouth.

After a little while I said, "Are you sure, Doc?"

"Yes, I saw him choke her till she quit moving. In my mind I see her apron over her bulging belly."

"You didn't go get the law?"

"Was the law going to bring her back to life? If Papa got hung, what would have happened to us boys? I was eleven and the youngest was four. We would have been sent to an orphanage. He wouldn't have let any of Mother's people have us."

"But you saw him kill her."

"That's right. And I saw my father for what he was, a broken man. He knew I saw him. We looked into each other's eyes as Mama lay on the ground. I saw the baby kick under her apron while she lad there."

"You couldn't have stopped him from killing her?"

"No, there was an animal rage about him that was the devil incarnate. I'm telling you this as a grown man. That was a small boy seeing his father as a flawed man, a devil in a man's skin. I saw an evil that couldn't be controlled."

I could almost see that eleven-year-old boy in Doc. His voice sounded small, like he was ashamed of himself.

"I could not have stopped him. So, I realized that night that I was not perfect but flawed like Pa."

"We grow up in stages and I went through the first stage that night. It was like a veil lifted and I saw the world as a cruel, cold place. I wish I hadn't told you any of this."

"Me, too."

"I've never told anyone any of this, even when the Sheriff came to our shack. I told the sheriff that Mother had left on the train. And I think the sheriff knew the truth. Mother's people must have called the sheriff. Mother would slip to their sharecropper's place when Pa was dead drunk."

"You knew the truth. Why didn't you say something?"

"What good would that have done? Send us to an orphanage? She wasn't coming back and we were five hungry little boys watching Papa boil cornmeal and fatback to feed us. He was cooking for the benefit of the sheriff, just to keep us. Pa was evil. He had about drunk himself to death by then."

"If all were so poor, how did he get the liquor?"

"He made it. He was the sorriest kind of bootlegger; he made it and he drank it. There is an old saying, 'the gentlemen make it, and the fools drink it.'"

I was sitting there with a carpet sweeper in my hand. I had just discovered that my great granddaddy was a drunk and a murderer.

"Doc, how did you go from being so poor to being a doctor?"

"I made liquor as hard as I could when Mother died. I knew how after helping. I kept Pa drunk, which was fine with us. I made enough to keep all of us going-- fed and clothed. I worked as hard as I could, saved money, and kept the money hidden from Papa. The business was lucrative particularly considering I was a child. A hard life makes you grow up early and quickly. I didn't want to be hungry all the time. I did what I had to do."

"But how were you able to keep ahead of the law? You were a child."

"We had help. The sheriff left us alone. I have always thought he knew what was going on and felt sorry for us. Customers looked after us. We didn't do it alone. Neighbors saw to us, fed us, and hid us when Daddy was sober. We had some angels. And I studied and read all I could. Then Mother's parents died, I think of diphtheria, her shame was kind of forgotten. We inherited a piece of land, and I moved the boys away from Papa. I was sixteen then. He didn't follow us, thank the Lord. I expected to see him walk up any day and try to take over, but he never did. It was a nice farm. They already had sharecroppers to run the farm, so we just stepped into a very lucky situation. Things changed for the better for all of us."

I said, "What happened to your daddy?"

There was silence. Doc had the pipe stem in his mouth where his teeth were worn down and the bowl of the pipe in his hand. His eyes narrowed from the smoke, and he sat there for a long time. I sat there watching him, but I didn't think he was seeing me. I was quiet; I didn't want to break the spell he was in. Anything I said would have been wrong. Thank God I was at least that smart that day. I had pried too far into his memories.

Doc said, "He died in that shack. I found him there. He had been dead for a while. He was so thin there wasn't much to rot. He had died sitting at the table; his skull was there with a bottle beside it. If anyone had ever come to see about him, they had left him like he was."

There was a long pause, and Doc looked right through me.

"I set the shack on fire with his body in it. He buried Mother in the woods without a marker. I cremated his bones and left him without a marker."

I said, "I promise I'll never tell anyone. This is too painful."

We didn't say anything else to each other that night. I put the sweeper away and went to my room and read a book. I think Doc must have slept in his chair that night. I never heard him go to bed. I tried to think of myself without Mama and tears started rolling down my cheeks. I felt so sorry for Doc. Nothing I could say or do could change the past. I felt like the past was printed in a book that I wished I had never opened.

I missed Girlie. We missed Girlie. I continued to try to cook. Really, I did.

Tuesday, I made smoked sausage and rice. The rice was crunchy.

Wednesday, I cooked steak and potatoes. The steak was like shoe leather, a little dry. The potatoes were pretty good.

Thursday, we had canned corned beef and grits.

Doc said, "Didn't Betsy teach you how to cook? Your cooking is rough."

I said, "Yes, sir. I helped her cook sometimes."

"Tomorrow night we are going to the café. I don't need to be tormented by your cooking."

My plan worked. I never told Doc I could really cook. I never thought it would have taken a week to starve him out. He was a tough old man.

Saturday morning, we had a housekeeper/cook again. Her name was Theola Burney. She had red hair, freckles and wore red lipstick. She was kind of pretty. Big Judy says if you kiss a red-headed Negro you can get rid of a fever blister. Don't know if anybody has ever tried.

Theola took over the cooking and everything else. My life greatly improved.

Theola said," Doc, what do you want me to cook?"

Doc said, "Anything but chitterlings. And you can cook them in the yard, just not in the house."

Theola was like a woman possessed-- on a mission-- cleaning. She started in with the parlor and finished with the yard.

She told Doc she needed a television in the kitchen. She was missing her stories.

Doc said, "If that woman wants a television, she will have it."

Chapter 9

Hooked

It was a normal Monday morning. Maybe not really normal, whatever that was. Daddy opened the store up. Big Jack was on the liar's bench. Doc told me at church the day before to go by the store before I came to the office. I hung around the store for a while. I rang up some nabs and a Pepsi for me. I didn't put any money in the cash register. I just put a note in the register. Daddy liked to keep track of his inventory. Big Jack said to watch your dimes and the dollars will take care of themselves. I don't know how that worked but Daddy stuck with it.

Daddy walked out of the office and said, "Go onto work, son. Rudolph and I have the store. "

"All right, Daddy. But I am sure it would be alright with Doc if I took a day off."

"Iver, have you heard Doc mention fishing since y'all went to Carolina Beach? Since Lauralee isn't out for him to die anymore, I thought I might see if he wants for all of us men to ride to Holden Beach and fish off the pier. I thought I might ask T.R. if he wants to ride with us. I can call and see if the spots are biting." (T.R. was Daddy's brother)

"Close the store for a Monday?" Maybe a space alien had invaded Daddy's body.

"Rudolph can keep the store. Any of us could drop dead and he could handle it. We need to do some things that are fun, make some memories. Ask Doc if he wants to go."

I couldn't believe this was my daddy talking. He never took off except Sunday and Thursday afternoon. Everything in town was closed on Thursday afternoon. He was going to take off on a Monday leaving Rudolph and Henry to keep the store. I thought better of pushing the subject. Daddy might change his mind.

"When I get to the office, I will ask Doc and call you. I know Gene and Roy will want to go. Skipping school is always on the list."

"You and Doc had a good time fishing at Carolina Beach?"

"Yes, sir. We went surf fishing. The water was warm. All I could think about were those pictures of sharks we look at when we go to Holden's Beach."

Daddy was nodding as he listened to me. "That's the reason I fish off the pier."

"Did Doc take you to Sea Breeze?"

I was shocked he would know anything about what we did.

"Didn't you bring us a mess of shrimp? I figured you picked them up at Sea Breeze."

My heart had nearly jumped time. "Yes, sir, Sea Breeze shrimp."

Doc didn't open that Monday. We all met at the house at nine o'clock. Roy and Gene had all the tackle together and two coolers. Doc brought his own tackle and cooler. Uncle T.R. showed up with two poles and a tackle box. Big Jack had a rod. We got in the store truck with the camper shell: Daddy and Uncle T.R in the front, Gene, Roy and me in the back. Doc and Big Jack were in Doc's Cadillac. I slipped the cushions off the front porch and put them in the back of the truck. I would have hell to pay if the cushions got dirty so I ran in the house and got a couple of sheets to throw over the cushions. Bet made a box of sandwiches. Daddy swung by the store and got drinks, nabs, cakes and Vienna's, two bags of ice and some cups. We boys played cards, ate and drank on the way down. I don't know what they talked about in the cab.

We got to the pier about eleven o'clock. Apparently, the spots were really biting. We saw two men carrying a big cooler of fish to their truck. Daddy walked over to the men's truck and said, "Spots biting good?"

One man had cut-off pants, a ball cap and old muddy tattoos and he said, "Yep, that's all I want to clean."

Daddy was nodding, "I know what you mean."

The man in short pants said, "I hope you fellows can find some rail to fish from. It's shoulder to shoulder right now."

We gathered our stuff up and went into the building at the end of the pier. We walked up to the counter and an old woman with a cigarette hanging off her bottom lip counted our rods and gave us a little ticket and a safety pin. Daddy paid the woman, and we dutifully pinned the tickets to our shirts.

Daddy said to the cigarette woman, "What kind of bait are they biting?"

She didn't even look up, counting money into the drawer, "Blood worms and shrimp."

Daddy was pulling his wallet back out, "We'll take some of both."

We got all of our stuff on the pier, and it was chaos. There wasn't a foot of rail that wasn't taken. We walked from one end of the pier to the other.

Doc said, "Walter, do you have a rod you wouldn't mind losing?"

Daddy said with a grin, "Yes, I do Mr. Erastus." Daddy knew what Doc was going to do. We didn't.

Doc wandered over to a trash can and fished out a beer can. He took his pocket knife out and made a hole in the can and tied the fishing line to it.

Then the show began.

Doc rooted around in his tackle box and brought out what I believe to be two of his favorite things: a string of firecrackers and a Zippo lighter. Daddy didn't say a thing; he just handed Doc a filtered Pall Mall cigarette. Doc stuck the end of the string of firecrackers in the cigarette next to the filter. This was a delay fuse. He unbuttoned a couple of the buttons on his shirt, stuck the string of firecrackers with the cigarette fuse in his shirt to hide them and walked toward the end of the pier. He came back with the Zippo, no firecrackers. Then Doc pulled his shirt off, and made a little handkerchief hat for his head, the kind with a knot in each corner. We just stood there as Doc started staggering around on the pier and shouting, "Fish! Fish! I said come here fish!"

He shouldered his way to the rail and hollered, "Come and get it!"

About this time there was a commotion three light poles down the pier. A man was dancing and hollering around a string of firecrackers popping off. And at the end of the rope of firecrackers was a mysteriously positioned cigarette filter. Everywhere the poor man stepped the string of firecrackers followed him. Everyone was watching the dance show while the real show was happening. Doc cast the beer can parallel to the pier toward the far end. And then he started reeling the can in. He caught about fifty lines. He put the rod down and walked away. There were some hot-- and I mean smoking hot-- mad people trying to get their lines loose. Doc put his shirt on and took the handkerchief off his head. Magically there was plenty of space for us to fish.

Then this ashen faced old drunk man staggered by and said, "Bo, I don't know what it is, but something down there will scare the hell out of you."

Doc said, "Really, brother? I'm sorry to hear that."

The old drunk man said, "Tell your boys here to watch out." He was pointing at the three of us. We just nodded.

I was in absolute awe of my granddaddy. He executed a perfect plan with two diversions to get us a spot to fish. I wanted to be just like him when I got old.

We were pulling spots in two at a time. In about an hour the six of us had caught two coolers of fish. It was fun while it lasted.

Daddy said, "Well, boys, we're going to have a fish fry tomorrow. We need to get the ice on them quick. Let's head home."

"Roy, Gene, think you are strong enough to carry the cooler? T.R. and I will get the other. Iver, get the rods and tackle boxes."

The twins grabbed the handles of one cooler and strode down the pier like they were grown. They were pretty good size for twelve years old. Things were going good until Roy got hooked in the nose. This pretty woman was learning to cast and wasn't very good at all. She caught Roy by the nose. Roy dropped his end of the cooler and fish slid across the pier deck. When Roy got his nose pierced, apparently the initial piercing wasn't bad. It was the snatching that got his attention. The barb of the hook went all the way through and out his nostril. The woman kept pulling on the rod trying to cast over her head. Roy kept hollering, trying to hold his nose and the line.

Daddy yelled, "Whoa, you're killing my boy."

Roy was crying, "Stop, woman!"

Gene was picking up fish oblivious to Roy's problem. Daddy pulled his knife and cut the line. I couldn't do a thing but stand there with the tackle boxes. Roy was standing silently with tears rolling down his cheeks. The blood worm was still on the hook and there was about two feet of line hanging off the leader. It was a pitiful sight.

Daddy and Doc were looking at Roy's nose. The woman couldn't stop apologizing to Roy. She pulled out a ten-dollar bill, stuffed it in Roy's shirt pocket, gathered up her stuff and ran off the pier. The man that was beside her gathered up his stuff and left, too, without the rod that the woman got Roy with. The man said, "Young man, after what has happened, you just keep the rod and reel."

Roy said in a noble voice, "Thank you, sir," with tears dripping off his chin.

Doc was maneuvering Roy to get some good sunlight on Roy's face, "Don't worry. Let's prop you up on the rail. I'll get that hook out."

Roy screamed, "Noooooo! Don't pull it out!"

Doc said, "Calm down, Gene."

"Doc, I'm not Gene, I'm Roy."

"Sorry, Roy. The barb is already through. All we have to do is cut the barb off and pull the hook out."

Roy gasped, 'Don't touch it, Doc!"

"But I've got to cut the end off to get it out. It's going to hurt a little extra right now, but I'll be quick."

"Doc, I'm sorry to ask you, are you really a doctor?"

Doc stopped and looked at Roy, "You had better hope I am," and laughed.

"But are you?"

"Yes, Roy. I am a doctor."

Doc rooted around in that magic tackle box, pulled out a flask and handed it to Roy.

"Roy, take you a big swallow of this."

"But Doc, this is whiskey. I am too young for whiskey."

"Son, this is for medical use, Lauralee won't mind."

Roy took the flask and pulled off a big drag. Then after a second, he gasped. Just when Roy sucked in a bunch of air, Doc cut the barb off the hook with some pliers, pulled the hook out and dabbed a little firewater in the hole on Roy's nose. Doc started packing up his tackle box and Roy was holding onto the rail. Daddy was patting Roy on the back. Gene was sitting on the cooler, oblivious to anything but a seagull walking around on the pier. As I observed this chaos, I realized that Doc was an official member of the family.

It was at this time that I realized human blood, or Roy's blood, was something that I could go without seeing for the rest of my life. I guess I had dreamed about being Doc Adams on Gunsmoke too much. Television was one thing but a real-life operation on the fishing pier kind of put things in perspective. There was no way I was going to be a doctor. Doc could have it.

As we walked off the pier, Daddy was looking around, "Where is Big Jack? I saw him helping pick the fish up."

We found Big Jack dead, leaned up beside the men's restroom on Holden's Beach Fishing Pier, knees locked, elbows on the rail. He was still standing up like he was posing, resting, chin on his chest, hat still on his head, the brim pressed against the wall.

The lady with the cigarette stuck to her lip was unphased. She called the coroner. The number was written on the wall. She said they generally had one every year when the spots were running. We laid Big Jack down in the bait shop waiting for the coroner. Daddy called Momma and told her. Momma called the funeral home to come get Big Jack. I wish we could have carried him home in the truck but apparently that was against the law. We kind of rolled him in the sheets and put him in the back of the truck with a cushion under his head until the hearse got there. Daddy said we just couldn't let him lay out in public on the floor of the bait shop with people looking at him, even with the sheet on him. Roy, Gene and I rode back home with Doc. I was in a state of wonder that Daddy, Uncle T.R and Doc acted like it was an everyday thing. Gene and Roy were crying their eyes out most of the way home.

When we pulled up in the yard Doc said to the three of us, "Dry the tears up, boys. Big Jack had a great life, had a great family and died doing something he loved-- being with his family. Now get in there and love on Big Judy, Lauralee and Mariah. They need our help now. Boys, it is time for you to be the men I know you can be." Doc called us men.

The first time anyone had called us men. We stood up straight, tucked our shirttails in, got the water hose to wash our faces and followed Doc in the house. We waited for Daddy and T.R. to come back from the funeral home.

Rudolph took the coolers with the Spots and gave them away. No fish fry for us but somebody had one.

Chapter 10

Big Jack Is Dead

Doc said, "That's just like him, even died with that golden horseshoe up his ass."

Daddy looked at him for a moment and laughed. "Big Jack has always been lucky."

I said, "What does luck have to do with dying? Big Jack is dead and y'all are laughing."

Daddy said, "Look how he died, son. He died propped on a fishing pier, standing up, posed like a movie star. Lucky or blessed, it doesn't matter. He went out in style."

Doc said, "We all should be so lucky."

Big Jack and Big Judy only had one child, Mariah. And Mariah and Doc only had one child, Lauralee. And Lauralee and Walter had three children. I'm glad Momma, Lauralee, had more than just me. I bet MaMariah was lonesome when she was a child and I bet Momma was lonesome when she was a child. I had a good time with Roy and Gene.

Big Jack was a regular kind of farmer around here, I guess. He quit farming row crops and tobacco not long after my Momma and Daddy got married. He leased the cleared land to a neighbor and my momma took over the livestock and poultry. He sharecropped the tobacco with a neighbor. Momma was the farmer and Daddy was the storekeeper. Big Jack and Big Judy did whatever they wanted. I learned later that Doc made sure MaMariah had whatever she wanted. I hoped I could get old and do whatever I wanted. Big Jack always had a hunting story to tell.

I thought he was making up stories about all the places he went fishing and hunting but after hearing Big Jack and Doc talk, he might have been telling the truth. He did carry us fishing in the creeks around here, and dove hunting, quail hunting, and deer hunting with Rudolph. He wore a white shirt; necktie and a suit coat every day. He said that he didn't intend to get dirty farming anymore so he was dressed up the rest of his life. He would be sitting on a bucket on the creek bank, fishing with a suit on. And he died wearing a starched shirt and double Windsor tied necktie. When he retired, they moved into the house next to ours. It was a nice house, but it didn't have a good view of the highway so Big Jack bought a new recliner and put it in the living room of our house.

He would sit in the recliner and smoke his pipe when it was too cold for him to sit on our front porch or the porch at the store. When you asked what he was doing, he would say, "I'm watching the world go by and wondering."

Once I asked, "Wondering about what, Big Jack?'

"Wondering if all those people know where they are going."

Daddy came in the living room, "Son, Iver, come with me to the funeral home. We need to make arrangements, pick out a casket."

Doc had his arm around MaMariah's waist and MaMariah's head was on his shoulder, "I'm going to the office and put on a suit. I need to talk to Theola, get her to come over and help Betsy with the house. There is going to be a crowd." He kissed MaMariah in front of all of us, I guess for the first time.

Daddy was standing at the door and said, "Iver, come on."

I looked at Daddy and tears were coming down his cheeks. That was it. Then I started crying. Big Jack was dead. I wasn't going to talk to him again. I wasn't going to sit beside him at Saturday night supper. And Big Judy, she was going to be alone and lonesome. He was MaMariah's daddy. Her daddy was dead. This would be even more awful if it was my daddy that was dead. I was going to miss Big Jack so much. I was going to miss Daddy when he was dead so much. My chest was hurting, and my nose was running. I could be in MaMariah's place, losing my daddy. Or Momma's place losing her granddaddy. I lost my great granddaddy. He had left a hole in the family. I knew that everybody dies but I never thought of how I would feel when one of our family died. I was crying for myself.

In my mind I was thinking, "Big Jack, was there anything I should have told you that I didn't? Was there anything that I did wrong to you? I can't tell you now. I can't change anything. I wonder if you can hear my thoughts. Have you already left or are you hanging around like a haint?" This was crazy. Was I praying to Big Jack or just thinking about him? He wasn't going to be here anymore. I felt…I don't know how I felt about it. My soul had shrunk.

Daddy said, "Come on, Iver. We'll get through this. Death is part of life, just like birth. Big Jack is starting something new. We know where he is, resting in the arms of Jesus. I need your help."

I sucked in a deep breath. Daddy handed me a clean handkerchief from his pocket and peppermint from the jar in the kitchen

Daddy needed my help. He was the one always helping us. I stood up straight and nodded at Doc, looked at Daddy and nodded. I was going to help Daddy. If my Daddy needed my help, I was a grown enough man to help him.

I had been to the funeral home many times for wakes but never to 'do business.' Mrs. Jackson met us at the door. She said, "So sorry for your family's loss. Big Jack was a pillar of the community."

Daddy said, "Thank you, Mrs. Jackson. This is really a shock."

"Death is always a stranger, Walter."

"We saw Mr. Maultsby and Mr. LaGrange when they got Big Jack." Daddy's voice cracked. "I never thought his end would be like this."

For some reason, at the very wrong time, I blurted out, "Who is at the house taking care of everybody?" Panic just overcame me.

Daddy nodded and said, "You know Bet is there with them. Doc is over there by now, and Theola. Rudolph is closing the store. Things are going to be OK."

When Daddy said that I felt a wave of relief in my chest. Something about Daddy saying things would be OK. It was good to hear that.

Mrs. Jackson said, "Do you want Mr. Jack embalmed? If we don't, we will need to bury him tomorrow. Embalming will give you a few days."

Daddy paused before he spoke, "Big Jack said he wanted to go naturally. And he did. He didn't say anything about being buried naturally. Sure, go ahead."

Mrs. Jackson asked, "Does he have a burial plot picked out?"

"Oh yes. They even have a stone up. They had a picture taken of themselves in front of the stone and used it for their Christmas card. They thought it was a great joke."

Mrs. Jackson said in a soft voice, "I remember."

We climbed the stairs to the second floor. The hand railings weren't but knee high and the treads short. We were all kind of hunched over walking up the stairs.

Daddy said, "This banister must have been made for a dwarf. And these little steps."

Mrs. Jackson was puffing a little bit, "As a matter of fact it was. The lady that built this old house was four feet tall and this was a boarding house. All the windows are low, too."

I wondered what a dwarf woman would think about her boarding house being a funeral parlor. We straightened our backs at the top of the stairs.

I had never been anywhere but the visitation room in the funeral home, never the casket room. The room had a bunch of caskets open and on the inside of each one was a little tent of paper with the price. There was gray carpet and kind of dusty pink curtains, soft music played from the ceiling. Maybe grey and pink was to get you in the mood. We were sending Big Jack to a soft, soothing place: heaven.

Mrs. Jackson was doing a salesman's sweeping hand gesture pointing to the interior of the caskets, "The cards that are in the caskets are the package price: family car, visitation here at the funeral home, the complete services."

And Daddy replied, "Hold it right there. We're not doing a package price."

I must have gasped. Daddy and Mrs. Jackson looked at me.

"We're not going to have the wake here. Take that off the price. In fact, let me tell you what we are going to pay for."

I prayed for the Lord to please save me from whatever this was. Daddy was negotiating at the funeral home. Big Jack was dead, and Daddy was trying to make a deal. Sacrilege. This was just too much.

"Daddy," I pulled on his sleeve, "Step over here and look at this wood casket. It looks like a piece of furniture."

"Iver, we are not going to bury Big Jack in a pine box."

"No, Daddy, over here."

"What, Iver?" Daddy was annoyed.

Daddy walked over to the wood casket, and I said, "Daddy, please don't negotiate with Mrs. Jackson. She is such a nice lady."

"Son, it's nothing to do with her being a nice lady. This is business to business. You don't leave any money on the table."

"But Daddy, Big Jack is dead."

"Who do you think taught me how to negotiate? This is what he would do for me and enjoy the whole thing."

I don't know if I was embarrassed or in awe. Big Jack was a corpse downstairs, and Daddy was working a deal to bury him.

Daddy walked back over to Mrs. Jackson and said, "Let me tell you what we want. Embalm him, wash him, I'll bring a suit over and put him in a modestly priced metal casket with a metal vault. Bring him to my house tomorrow or late tonight when you get him ready. We will have the wake Wednesday night. Come and get him Thursday morning and carry him to Mount Horeb Presbyterian Church for an eleven o'clock funeral. Y'all dig the grave, cover it back up and do the paperwork."

Mrs. Jackson was starting to hem and haw, "Well, Walter, I believe you have put me in a position I'm not used to being in. My business is a service, a service program, a package deal."

"That's not what we want. And we can drive ourselves to the church. Put a price beside each thing we want."

"This is not the way we do business."

"I know that, but this is the way I do business."

I was mentally digging a hole through the floor. There was a good chance that I would die from embarrassment. Daddy was negotiating and Big Jack was a corpse. I walked over to the wall to have something besides a casket to hold on to. Near where I was standing was a door open to a closet and the closet had a hole in the floor. For some reason I couldn't stop myself from walking to the closet and looking in. So that's how they get the caskets up here. I looked down through the hole in the floor and jerked my head back. Big Jack was down there. I walked back over to Daddy and kept my mouth shut. The negotiations took about an hour. Mrs. Jackson was going to bring Big Jack to the house as soon as she got him ready.

Daddy said, "Big Jack didn't die at home, but he is going to be at our house until he is buried."

Word spreads quickly in a small town. The fried chicken, casseroles and sweets were coming to the house before supper. The hearse backed up to the front door about midnight. I took the spring off the screen door and propped open the front door. Mr. LaGrange worked at the funeral home and part time as a butcher at the grocery store until too many people complained, pulled a shiny accordion looking folding stand into the den to put the casket on. Being helpful, I took upon myself to get the stand exactly in front of the windows looking out on the porch where he always liked to sit in his recliner and look out the window watching the world go by. He could see the highway from the front window at our house. Mr. LaGrange, Mr. Maultsby (who wore a straw textured and colored hair piece), Rudolph, Henry, Gene, Roy, Doc and I got the casket in the front door. It was a task. Big Jack was a big man. I wondered if there weren't a few cinder blocks in there, too.

We got the casket in the house then we had to get it centered on the window and on that little buggy. I supervised this and things were going well until I backed up and stepped on Big Jack's little black feist squirrel dog, Flash Gordon. Flash Gordon yelped like I was killing him. Mr. Maultsby tried to snatch his head out from under his little hair hat. Mr. LaGrange sounded like he was swallowing his liver and blanched white, like light bread. All of us were panting. It was a miracle we didn't all pass out for lack of oxygen. Flash Gordon rocketed out the front door like his name's sake. I made the executive discussion that Big Jack was in the right place. No one but me knows the little shiny buggy was a little to the right. I stood beside Mr. LaGrange when he opened the casket. There he was.

Daddy walked up and said, "He doesn't look right without a pipe in his hand."

I asked, "Can we put the pipe in his hand?"

Mr. LaGrange said, "Sure, Iver. Go get one."

So, I stepped over to Big Jack's chair and picked up a Meerschaum pipe that Momma gave him when she was a child. He always said it was too pretty to smoke. Daddy and I bent his fingers around the pipe.

Mr. Maultsby pulled this little crank out of his pocket and put it in a little hole in the casket. I wouldn't have ever noticed the hole if I hadn't seen the little crank in it. He proceeded to crank Big Jack's head up and then put the little crank in another hole and tilted toward the open side a little. It was a very slight adjustment, but it made a big difference. He looked a little more relaxed. I guess you are totally relaxed when you are dead.

I said, "He looks a lot more like himself now."

Daddy told me, "Go get Lauralee and see if Big Jack looks alright to her."

So, I got Momma. She looked really close at Big Jack for a long time. "He looks like Big Jack to me."

Momma walked back to the kitchen and Daddy stepped back to the casket. He said, "Iver, let's work on his fingers a little bit. Let's see if we can bend his fingers a little more."

So, Daddy and I bent Big Jack's stiff fingers around the pipe some more and pointed the stem toward his face.

I asked, "Mr. Maultsby, can I adjust Big Jack a little?"

"I don't know why not", he answered.

I cranked and Big Jack was looking out the side door. I was thinking, this would be a fine greeting for the visitors coming to see us.

Mr. Maultsby said, "Iver, you are going to flip Big Jack out of that casket if you don't stop. If you do it will take all of us to get him back in the box."

Big Jack in the box, Big Jack out of the box. I prayed, "Lord, please forgive me for snorting. But I am sure you thought it was funny, too."

The next day, Tuesday, neighbors, friends, and business contacts showed up at the house with more fried chicken and more tea. The van from the florist brought wreaths and potted plants; our living room was the visitation room. People filed in and out. Momma, Big Judy,

MaMariah, all came into the living room together holding hands. Big Judy and MaMariah hadn't been in the living room before Daddy and I fixed the pipe. Momma gasped and MaMariah put her arm around her back like she was going to hold her up.

Big Judy scolded, "What is wrong with you? You know he is in a better place."

Momma was leaning over Big Jack, "I know but I think that pipe is different than it was a while ago. He couldn't have moved it. You know, he is dead."

MaMariah said, "Lauralee, I know you are not drunk at Big Jack's wake."

"I am not drunk. That pipe stem was pointing to the right when I was in here a while ago. Now it has moved, pointing at his face. You tell me how that has happened."

I didn't say anything. It was too good, Momma thinking that Big Jack had moved the pipe. I hope I don't spend time in purgatory for that.

About ten o'clock the preacher said, "Let's have a prayer and leave so these folks can get some rest."

He said to Big Judy, "I'll be here in the morning, and we can get the service planned if that is alright with you?"

For some unknown reason I blurted out, "We are going to be sleeping in the house with a corpse."

Big Judy said, "Yes, he is dead and gone. You slept in the house with him last night."

I was so tired last night I just hadn't thought about Big Jack being downstairs. I think Momma stayed with Big Judy last night. They weren't here when we brought Big Jack in the house. That was a good thing.

I started talking teenage stupid. "He might be dead but he's not gone. He is right there in the den." I sat down in one of the folding chairs that the funeral home brought to the house. Big Judy was standing next to Big Jack, talking quietly, and holding his hand. We left the den so they could be alone. We went to bed. I think Big Judy slept in Big Jack's recliner.

Funerals draw old cousins. You don't hear from them for years but somehow word gets around through the family like lightning when one of them is dead. Funerals are like family reunions. I like the reunion part, two or three days of extra company, lots of old stories. I have always felt guilty that I see a funeral as an enjoyable experience. Our religion teaches us that the death of a Christian is a joyous occasion. It took me a while to figure out why there was crying at death. People cry for themselves. It is their own shortcomings that bring the tears. Tears are for missed opportunities to tell the dead that they are loved. It's very simple. We cry for ourselves.

It was going to be a long day. The wake was that night. People were drifting in, signing the guest book at the door. Bet had on her white dress that she wears when she ushers at church and a lace circle on her head. She and Momma have gotten out the good tablecloths and all of the silver. Momma said we were going to do it up right for all the cousins coming. "Putting on the Dog" as Bet called it. Bet said there were a bunch of nosey white people coming. She liked to say, "If you can't come when I am alive, don't come when I'm dead." She had a point.

Bet caught me on the way through the kitchen and gave me a quick lesson on polishing the silver candlesticks. I was sitting and laboring at the kitchen table when we heard a "Hellllloooooo" coming up the back steps. It was kind of high pitched, melodic and kind of male. We both turned and looked through the screen door and saw this old man with an artificial leg pulling himself up the steps by the handrail.

Bet said, "My God, I thought that one was dead."

I asked, "Who is it, Bet?'

"Your cousin Braddy, from D.C."

I stepped to the door and pushed it open. The old man looked at me and smiled a perfect false-teeth smile. I still had the polishing cloth in my right hand as he put out his hand to shake. I switched hands and shook his hand.

I said, "Hello, I am Iver Johnson Murphy, and you must be Cousin Braddy."

"Nice to meet you, Cousin Iver. I see you are a man like me that loves to polish silver."

"Well, no, not really. I got snagged to help finish up."

Cousin Braddy said, "Bet, good to see you, again. Let me speak to everybody and I will come help you get everything organized."

"Thank you, Mr. Braddy. I appreciate that," she responded,

After Cousin Braddy went hobbling to the front of the house, I said to Bet, "I can't believe that old man wants to help you in the kitchen with all this crowd. Is he trying to make time with you?"

Bet said, "My Jesus, that man is sweet. Can't you tell that? Your momma said you were slow about some things."

"You never say I'm sweet when I have to help you."

"Iver, you are not sweet like that old man. That old man likes men. He should have been a woman. Close your mouth, Iver. Sometimes you are slow on the uptake."

Lord, Lord. A funny as Miss Judith calls them. I didn't know we had any in the family. He walked—limped-- back into the kitchen in a few minutes and asked me to bring his bag in from the car. He drove a new Beetle. When I brought the bag in, out came a chef's coat and a chef's hat. He was serious about the kitchen. In a few words--he took over. Bet went back to polishing silver, which she apparently likes, and started smiling at Cousin Braddy. He organized the sweets on the buffet, asked Bet where some meat platters were and started in. He wiped the tea glasses, so they sparkled.

"Iver? Your name is Iver?"

"Yes, sir."

"Could you give me a hand moving the platters? It's hard to put two hands on a platter while holding a cane."

I looked at him and all I could see was Chef-Boy-R-Dee. I couldn't help but smile. "I will be more than happy to help, Cousin Braddy."

I was getting to play with Chef-Boy-R-Dee. And Bet was smiling at Chef-Boy-R-Dee. And Cousin Braddy really was a chef, the high-class kind.

There is no doubt that the Chef Cousin Braddy could talk. He started talking and kept talking. Didn't matter who was in the kitchen. It was like a LP playing all the time or talk radio late at night. He talked. We found out where he worked, who he served wine to, who ordered what meals, who liked fish or steak, what movie stars had given him jewelry, who did his dead mother's hair, awards he had won. We found out entirely more than we needed to know. But I'll give it to him; he had some very good points. He made chicken salad from some of the fried chicken, made something with cake, pie and whipped cream in a punch bowl, and made little animals with pickles and toothpicks.

As good as funeral food is, Cousin Braddy made it better. And we learned a lot. I said, "Cousin Braddy, what happened to your leg?"

Cousin Braddy said, "I was traveling with Princess Grace as her wine steward when I stepped on a land mine. I lost two toes on my other foot, too. She wanted to give me a medal for saving her life, but I refused it. I am a humble man."

All I could or needed to say was, "Wow."

He went on. "I did accept a gold chain with a tiny bust of Prince Rainier, part of the Crown Jewels, you know. Would you like to see it?"

All that came out of my mouth was, "Sure." Few words were needed around Braddy.

He reached into the neck of his chef's coat and sure enough pulled out a gold chain, about as big around as a cigarette, with a little bust of Prince Rainier on it. The chain was so long it went to his belt. Maybe some of what he was telling was true. Cousin Braddy was what Big Jack referred to as an "Expert": a hundred miles from home and you were not sure if he was lying. I hadn't thought of Big Jack for a little while. I wondered what Big Jack thought of Cousin Braddy. I wouldn't get a chance to ask him now that he had died. I wondered what else I didn't think to ask him: about his hunting trips with Doc, about how he farmed, about…about a lot of things. And then I felt the tears coming again. Cousin Braddy was looking at me and he stopped talking.

Cousin Braddy was still looking at me when he said, "There is nothing wrong with a man crying, Iver. Tears for Cousin Jack won't make you less of a man."

All I could do was let the tears roll down my face. Cousin Braddy put his arm around me and patted my shoulder. His words were kind, not patronizing. I saw him as a man, not Chef-Boy-R-Dee, just a truly kind man.

Momma came in the kitchen and said, "Cousin Braddy, can we talk on the back porch for a minute?"

"Of course, Cousin Lauralee."

"Cousin Braddy, we have a little problem."

"Well, of course, but have I caused a problem? I can stay at a hotel."

"Oh, no, Braddy. We are so happy you came. We are thankful you came. It's just that Helen is here."

"OH, God! Iver! What are your twin's names? Twins! Come quick! Where are you going to put me and the boys? I will personally protect your sons."

I pretty much jumped out of the back door when I heard Cousin Braddy scream my name.

"What's wrong, Momma?" I asked.

Momma said, "Let's just settle down. We can handle this."

Braddy was almost panting, "No one told me my sister was out. I thought she was going to live there the rest of her life." Braddy was had blanched white. He pressed his back to the side of the house. I had never seen pure fear in a human before. It was awful. I couldn't do a thing to help him.

Momma said, "She just came in on the bus. She must have gotten a pass or just slipped out to come to the funeral. She hasn't been here in years. I would love to know who told her, unless the funeral home already has it in the paper."

"Momma, what is going on? Who is Helen?"

Momma said, "Iver, there are a few of our cousins that we don't talk about and one of them is Braddy's sister, Helen. She has been locked up a while."

I said, "Locked up where? In jail?"

Cousin Braddy said, "No Iver. At Dorothea Dix in the insane asylum."

"What?!" came out of my mouth in a very high-pitched voice.

Braddy pointed at my crotch, "That's what you will sound like permanently if she gets ahold of your testicles."

Again, I said, "What!" I could feel my testicles drawing up. Sweet cousins, crazy cousins, Big Jack a corpse.

Momma said in a quiet voice, "Iver, just calm down. We have had to handle this before. We are just going to have all of the men stay at Daddy's office until she gets picked up. I hope we can get her picked up before bedtime. There are extra rooms upstairs at Daddy's from when it was a home." Apparently, the separation of the sexes was a necessary precaution when Helen was out and about. I didn't go with Cousin Braddy and the twins to Doc's office. I saw them just grinning getting into Cousin Braddy's VW Beetle. I wonder if the twins would be punching each other going over to Doc's.

After I calmed down, and my testicles began to descend again, I knew I just had to talk to Cousin Helen or, at least, get a good look at her. This was entirely too good a story to miss. For some reason when I got to the door of the dining room, I just couldn't go in. I stood behind the door and peeped in between the upper and middle hinges.

Cousin Braddy had done a wonderful job arranging the dining room. It looked like something out of Momma's Ladies Home Journal or Good Housekeeping. Some of the church ladies and Cousin Helen were sitting around the dining room table drinking coffee and eating pie. Helen had taken her saucer and put it on top of her cup. She was swatting things on the table that the church ladies couldn't see. Cousin Helen stopped hitting the things that we couldn't see and picked up the coffee cup. She took the saucer that was on top of her cup and put it to her forehead, slurped a sip of coffee, put the saucer back on and put the cup down, quick as lightning.

The church ladies, being the ladies, they were, of course, were attempting to make small talk over the invisible critter swatting and unique style of coffee consumption.

One of the ladies, Mrs. Maultsby, Mr. Maultsby from the funeral home's wife, asked, "Where are you from Miss Helen?"

"I am from Winston, but I live in Raleigh now. The police made me move. All the men in Winston were getting castrated and they said it had started on my street. They said I had to stop, so I moved."

Mrs. Maultsby didn't bat an eye and said, "Raleigh is a nice place to live, isn't it?"

"I told the police in Raleigh to tell those men I sleep with my drawers on." Cousin Helen was mashing the bugs with her fingertips by then.

Mrs. Maultsby said, "I will be happy to relate this to the local police."

Cousin Helen stopped mashing the invisible bugs and started thumping them off the table. "Thank you, I will sleep better knowing the police know I sleep with my drawers on."

Mrs. Maultsby said, "Ladies, let me take these dishes to the kitchen and save Bet a few steps."

She stepped in the kitchen with the dishes and said, "Did you hear that, Bet, what Miss Helen said?"

"Yes, ma'am. I think you and the ladies need to leave. Missy is calling Raleigh to tell them to come and pick her up. She gets away once in a while. This is the first time she has shown up when the boys are home. We sent the boys over at Doc Edward's office. Iver, this one, just had to stay and watch."

Mrs. Maultsby said, "You don't think she will mess with Mr. Jack, do you?"

Bet actually lost a little bit of her color. She was kind of light already. She tore out of the kitchen, straight into the living room. I was right behind her. There was Cousin Helen beside the casket with a pair of scissors, standing there like she was thinking. About that time a deputy walked in the front door and said, "Hello, Miss Helen."

She turned to the deputy and said, "Hello, Dwight. Have you still got your testicles?"

The deputy said, "Yes, Miss Helen, and I am planning on using them in the near future. We need to get you home. Your friends from Dix are going to come pick you up. You haven't done anything to Big Jack have you?"

"No, Dwight. Nothing you can see."

Deputy Dwight looked around and saw Momma, smiled at her and handcuffed Cousin Helen, just to make sure. Momma motioned to Dwight to bring Cousin Helen to the den where they could watch TV while they waited for the ambulance. Bet set up folding TV trays for Dwight and Cousin Helen to have some refreshments while they watched the television.

I don't know if she did anything to Big Jack. I don't think so. I just wanted to know how she got word that Big Jack was dead. And did they let her go or did she slip out? She did come to pay her respects. I had to give it to Cousin Helen for family loyalty.

Momma and Bet insisted I stay at Doc's with the men until the ambulance from Dix Hill picked up Cousin Helen. I wasn't leaving, so I said gallantly," Dwight is the only man here and he might need some help." She said Cousin Helen could slip away from about anywhere.

I had never gotten a good look at a real live schizophrenic, that I knew of. I was kind of disappointed that she looked "regular." As Daddy would say, "There must be just a scratch between smart and crazy." After World War II she worked at the State Department with displaced refugees during the day and spent her nights at Saint Elizabeths Hospital. Saint Elizabeths is a big mental hospital in Washington, D.C. She had a driver that picked her up and carried her back to the hospital. She must have been good at whatever she did for the government. Things went well for a couple of years until she ran across some photos of wild animals being housed on the grounds of Saint Elizabeths until the National Zoo was finished. She demanded a long arm weapon, shotgun or rifle to protect herself. Apparently, she was denied her request and she just left Washington. Her brother, Cousin Joseph, finally hired a private investigator and he found her in Yellowstone. The private investigator got her back to Washington without any problems. The Big Shooting Incident happened when Cousin Helen was using a telescope to look in the neighbor's houses, nice homes, in Arlington. Across the street was a Canadian ambassador, attaché, something important, that was a Robert

C. Ruark type, a big game hunter. Cousin Helen spied a water buffalo head mounted on the front wall of his foyer and she proceeded to stalk it and kill it. Somehow, she had gotten a weapon from her stay at Yellowstone in her suitcase. (Cousin Joseph said he didn't have a .308 rifle in the house. He just used the weapons that were provided on a safari.) She shot the wall beside the water buffalo hoping to get a shoulder shot. While she was reloading to kill the full-sized walking, saddled, stuffed tiger the ambassador had make for his grandchildren, the ambassador's chauffeur took the rifle away from Cousin Helen and put handcuffs on her. Cousin Joseph came out of the house with Bermuda shorts, smoking jacket, and those funny genie shoes with the turned-up toes. His wife, Cousin Wanda, came out the house with red silk pajamas with little snorting dragons on them and matching genie shoes. Momma and Daddy knew what they had on because that was how they showed up at our house. I guess they went to Spiro's, too. I would love to have seen those shoes. The chauffeur had suggested they put Cousin Helen in the trunk of Cousin Joseph's Continental so as not to draw attention. The ambassador, owner of the magnificent tiger, handed Cousin Joseph a wad of money and some official looking diplomatic papers out of his car and suggested they head to Raleigh and deposit Cousin Helen at Dorothea Dix Hospital. The chauffeur offered to drive, he said he had diplomatic immunity, also, but Cousin Joseph and Cousin Wanda said it was a family matter and thanked the chauffeur for not killing Cousin Helen. Cousin Joseph said they were waiting for them when they drove up at Dix. I have always wondered if the chauffeur had thought to give them the keys to the handcuffs.

The ambulance came; it looked like a white hearse. Big Judy told Cousin Helen she was glad that she came. She said that Big Jack would have appreciated the effort she made, riding the bus and controlling herself long enough not to get arrested on the way down here. Big Judy was always gracious. She walked Cousin Helen to the ambulance from Dix, kissed her on the cheek, tucked a twenty-dollar bill in her brassier and made sure she didn't bump her head getting in the back seat. Cousin Helen said she wished she could have seen Big Jack one more time, alive. Big Judy started tearing, I started crying, and Cousin Helen said we would all be together again soon. With all her problems, she still knew the Lord.

The Funeral

The hearse came and got Big Jack at nine o'clock in the morning. I heard Momma tell the men from the funeral home to leave the casket open before and during the service. I guess she wanted Big Jack to hear his own funeral. I know I shouldn't make any jokes about Big Jack's funeral, but I just couldn't help it. The men from the funeral home got the guest book and podium and put it at the church. They said they would be back the next day for the folding chairs.

The service was at eleven o'clock on Thursday morning. I know folks understood the office being closed and the store being closed. Big Jack was liable to be fussing that we weren't making any money today. Some of us got in Big Jack's new red Cadillac: Daddy driving, Momma, MaMariah, Gene, Roy and Big Judy. Three in the front, three in the back. Rudolph, Bet and I were riding in Big Judy's red Cadillac, last year's model. Rudolph was driving. Theola was staying at the house while we were at the funeral. Henry was staying at the store taking care of things just like he always did. We got to the church and the hearse was parked at the side. There were people milling around in the church yard; some folks were already at the tent. The church was full. Big Jack was already on display.

Most people understand how the family lines up to go into the church at a funeral, oldest to the youngest. We lined up on the front steps of the church, Big Judy, Mariah and Doc, Mama and Daddy, me, Gene and Roy. Bet and Rudolph sat with the family. The pall-bearers were eight old men from the Masonic Lodge, old men like Big Jack.

I suppose it was a regular funeral. The minister led the family in. Same scriptures as the last funeral I went to, Twenty-third Psalm and for the message, Ecclesiastes Chapter Three. The preacher related meeting Big Jack the first time at the store. Apparently, Preacher Jenkins got stung by a wasp while he was standing on the store porch. Big Jack pulled a pinch of pipe tobacco out of his pouch and doctored the sting on the back of his neck. One of the elders read the obituary that was printed in the Bladen Journal.

Bet's sister, Louise, from the AME Zion sang "Sweet Low, Sweet Chariot". Then Bet and Louise sang a duet, "If You See My Savior". The congregation sang "Beautiful Garden of Memories" and "Blessed Assurance", just a nice quiet funeral. I cried; all of us cried. We must have used up five or six of those little pocket-size packs of Kleenex. The preacher covered everything in the bulletin. I was making sure I had stuffed all of the wet Kleenex in my pockets getting ready for the dismissal to the cemetery when the preacher said, "Does anyone have anything they would like to say about Mr. John?"

Oh, oh. This wasn't in the program. I opened my bulletin and checked. The preacher was freewheeling. This was not good. I've heard about these things going wrong, very wrong. I was hoping nobody would bring up Big Jack shooting Doc. What happened next was beyond the pale.

A woman at the back of the church stood up and began to speak. None of us recognized the Yankee voice. The whole family turned to the left to see where the voice was coming from. She was a tall white woman with a black hat, black dress, black lace gloves and the biggest set of boobs I have ever seen. The cleavage between the boobs must have been twelve inches deep.

The big boobed woman said, "Big Jack was the sweetest man I have ever met. He was always so nice to me and the other girls."

At that moment, three other women stood up, two that were white and one looked Indian, like from Robeson County. Two had big boobs, one just kind of regular. I might not be mentioning the boobs but the black dresses they had on were about to let the appendages fall out the front. Tight black dresses, long black gloves, big hair and movie star makeup. 'Memorable' did not touch the looks.

There was a collective and audible gasp from the congregation.

Big boobed continued, "Big Jack was the only customer we had that remembered our birthdays and sent us Christmas presents. We just wanted his family and friends to know that we have never had a customer as nice as him, always generous and thoughtful.

Another gasp, and a couple of giggles. These were hookers.

"Big Jack came every Friday at noon and ordered the same thing. We rotated serving him. He was so generous with his tips."

I looked at Big Judy and she was nodding. All the rest of us had a look of horror. Why was Big Judy sweet when these women were telling that an eighty-six-year-old man went to a whore house every Friday and ordered the same thing. Those had to be hookers; who else would have boobs like that and that hair and that purple and blue and green eyeshadow? These had to be hookers; who else would wear dresses that tight to a funeral?

"We all work at the truck stop."

Nooooooooo. Road whores.

The second woman to speak had bleached blond hair and earrings so long they touched her shoulders. She said, "Big Jack was always so patient with the new girls. He was always good natured when they were first getting started."

Big Jack trained hookers.

The Indian woman said, "He made sure I got paid the same as the other girls. We Indian girls usually don't get the same pay."

Civil rights for Indian hookers.

The last girl in the line had the tallest hair-do I have ever seen but she didn't have as big a set of boobs as the others. I have always thought she was compensating for not having giant boobs. The small boobed, big haired one said, "Big Jack bought me a car so I could get to work on time. The manager will fire you if you're late to start your shift. If all waitresses had customers as wonderful as Big Jack, being a waitress would be the best job on Earth. Thank you, Miss Judy, for calling and asking us to come."

There was a flutter of laughs and giggles. I wasn't the only one that thought they were hookers. Big Judy had tears running down her face. Surely, Big Judy wouldn't pull a fast one on us, making us think Big Jack went to a whorehouse every week. She did that on purpose, a cunning old woman. I couldn't believe she did that. Waitresses at a truck stop. Big Judy gave them a little wave and laughed. She couldn't hold it any longer. I didn't know she had a mean streak like that.

We walked out of the church to the cemetery for the graveside service. The pallbearers were little, old and feeble Masons, so Daddy, Roy and Gene, and I stepped in and helped carry Big Jack. When we got the casket on the frame over the grave all of us were blowing. Roy and Gene had their hands on their knees trying to get their wind back. Big Jack was a good-sized fellow and apparently that was a quality casket.

From where he was hassling, Roy could see under the casket into the grave. He straightened up and said, "That doesn't look six feet deep. We can't let them bury him too shallow."

Gene stepped over, put his hand on the casket and looked in the grave. "It does look shallow, Roy. We need to get tape and measure it. Let me find Daddy."

Gene walked over to Daddy and said, "Daddy, do you have your measuring tape? We don't think the grave is six feet deep."

Daddy walked over to the grave again as everybody was gathering, squatted down and looked under the casket.

"Boys, I think it's deep enough. Big Jack will be alright."

Gene and Roy nodded exactly the same and said in unison, "OK, Daddy." The twins did that a lot. It still bothers me, them speaking in stereo.

After the committal, we all stood and watched them lower Big Jack down. White people at funerals leave and come back: colored people stay. I guess we were like colored people. We had to see it through. We stayed until the end. Momma and Bet arranged the flowers around the grave. It was sad knowing all the flowers would fade away, just like we do. Alive and then gone.

After the funeral, I think the whole church came to the house to eat dinner, including the waitresses from the truck stop. There was Braddy in the kitchen. It was evident that he was in his element. Ham salad on little rolls. I mean it was high class. Olives and cheese on toothpicks. Bet filling tea glasses and the twins collecting plates. Theola was in the kitchen washing the dishes. She had on a pretty white dress. I sat on the stairs eating a roll and surveying the crowd. Big Jack would have loved this. Not a tear to be seen, laughing and tale swapping, his two favorite things.

The party broke up at about 5 o'clock. The folks just kind of slipped off. Big Judy walked back to her house. Theola walked with her. Big Judy announced she was tired and needed to be left alone, but Theola didn't come right back. I knew Theola was making a little fuss over Big

Judy which was what she needed, "Extra loving" was what MaMariah called it.

Momma and Daddy were at the kitchen table. Daddy said, "Laura-lee, let's go and get a steak. It has been a good day. I want to ride around."

Momma said, "Walter, we just buried my granddaddy."

"And it was a fine affair. Let's go celebrate. Iver and the boys can go to the Dairy Queen in Whiteville."

"What about MaMariah?" said Momma.

"Her and Doc can do whatever they want," said Daddy.

"I can't think of a reason not to go."

Daddy handed me two twenty-dollar bills and gave me a wink.

Roy, Gene and I needed to have a party, too. Rudolph gave me the keys to Big Judy's red Cadillac. I have never taken the boys out by myself. Shoot, I haven't taken myself out many times.

I hollered up the stairs, "Don't change clothes boys. Daddy gave us money to go to Whiteville. Let's go ride around."

Roy said, "Where are we going? What's for supper? Where are Momma and Daddy?"

That boy had a turbo charged tongue. No wonder Gene didn't have to say anything. He didn't need to.

"Daddy gave us money to go to the Dairy Queen?"

Gene said, "Come on y'all. There might be girls there."

Apparently, Gene could talk, we just didn't know what about. Now we knew.

Gene said again, "Come on y'all" impatiently. He was in the front seat before we got to the car. One seventeen-year-old, twelve-year-old twins, dressed in their Sunday best riding in a red Cadillac on a Thursday night. We had to be the coolest guys in the whole county.

God blessed us that night. Sissy Reynolds was at Dairy Queen on a school night, with her two little sisters, twelve and thirteen. Just right for Gene and Roy. Gene ate and looked at the girls. Roy talked. Sissy's parents had a barbeque restaurant. I never thought of it before, but I guess they get tired of barbeque and fried chicken all the time. Sissy sat beside me in the front seat, let me hold her hand and I got a close look at her. She really was beautiful. I don't know what we talked about. When she and her sisters had to leave, I walked them to Sissy's car, opened her door and kissed her before she got in the car. That was the second time I kissed her. I hoped she hadn't forgotten the kiss at revival. The third time would be the charm. Wait a minute, Iver. Charm for what? I was planning to kiss her again; that was all. I just wanted to sit close to her, to hold her hand. I wondered if we could date for years and then get married. I was thinking that this might have been something I would talk to Big Jack about. Big Jack and Big Judy were married forever--over sixty years. Big Jack was gone; I couldn't ask him. Doc was next on the list. He had definitely kissed several women. Doc had told me.

Chapter 11

Theodore Roosevelt Murphy and the Nurse

It was Sunday afternoon, and I was sitting in the Emergency Room waiting area looking at Daddy and Aunt Naomi. Uncle T.R. was in the back. I could have been motoring around in my new john boat with a pretty girl from Sunday School. I was not sure which girl, but I know I could have gotten at least one to spend the afternoon with me. I already had the boat loaded in the truck.

Daddy said, "Naomi, what happened to T.R.?"

T.R. is Daddy's brother, Theodor Roosevelt Murphy. Naomi is Uncle T.R.'s wife.

Naomi rocked side to side and grunted kind of low, "I caught T.R. with a woman at the hog pen this morning. I took a tobacco stick and started yelling 'skeeters' as I was beatin' him. When I finished with T.R., I started checking that little strumpet's hair for lice, one clump at a time."

Daddy said, "Good God, Naomi! You could have killed him with a tobacco stick."

Naomi said, "I wasn't trying to kill him. If I wanted to kill him, I would have shot him and fed him to the hogs."

"Naomi, you pulled the woman's hair out? It's bad enough to beat T.R. but you jumped on the woman, too? That was crazy. That woman can file charges on you."

I couldn't move. This woman was talking so calmly about killing Uncle T.R. Daddy said T.R. and Naomi are both idiots. He said that T.R.

has a stiff pecker and a weak mind and Naomi has a weak mind and wants a pecker. She wasn't an idiot; she was just crazy and on the loose.

Naomi continued her rant. "T.R. 's latest girlfriend is the veterinarian's nurse where he carries his coon dogs. He has always run around and I've always knowed it. I had a woman call to tell me T.R. was running around and I told the woman calling to be patient; T.R. would get around to her eventually. This has been going on the whole time we've been married. I have just had enough. T.R. met his girlfriend at his hog pen this morning. And when they were doing the deed, I stepped out of the woods and proceeded to beat him with a tobacco stick. He was in such a position that he couldn't run. I was yelling that I was going to whomp those 'skeeters off his back. When I finished with T.R, I proceeded to choke the nurse and pull her hair out in little clumps. I told her I was checking her head for lice. I made it back to the house before T.R. He drove up in the yard naked. I had flung their clothes in the hog pen. I just walked to the truck with my purse and him a set of clothes, pushed T.R. over and drove him here to the emergency room."

I was sitting there looking at Aunt Naomi picturing the scene in my head when the doctor walked out and said to Daddy, "Mr. Murphy, we'll have your brother ready to go in a while. I've gotten the paperwork started."

Aunt Naomi said, "Doctor, I am his wife. I'm here to carry him home."

The doctor said, "Yes, Ma'am, but Mr. Murphy wrote us a note to call his brother."

Aunt Naomi said, "What do you mean he wrote a note? Y'all got to have everything in writing to cover your asses?"

The doctor said, "No, ma'am. The end of his tongue has been bitten off and we were having a problem understanding him. He wrote that a nurse left with the end of his tongue. It has been too long to try to sew the end back on, but I want to write a complaint to go into her work history."

Naomi said, "It was a veterinary nurse that took the end of his tongue."

The doctor said, "A veterinary nurse was giving Mr. Murphy first aid?"

Naomi answered, "Not exactly. I bet T.R. bit the end of his tongue off when I whomped him up with that tobacco stick."

The doctor said, "On that note…I called the police in to take pictures of Mr. Murphy's injuries. We usually have cases like this with a wife being the injured party. We wanted to get pictures in case he decided to press charges to whomever injured him. He has several broken ribs and some bad bruises."

Aunt Naomi said, "Forget about all that. I caught him messin' with his girlfriend and I whipped them both. I'm here to carry him home."

The doctor didn't change his expression.

The doctor said, "Ma'am, Mr. Murphy wrote that he wanted his brother to carry him home."

Aunt Naomi was getting mad. I could see the blood rising on her neck. I had seen it before. When her forehead got that vein popped out, it would be on then. She was on her feet so fast I am sure her butt cheeks just snapped together and popped her out of the chair. The doctor stood up and backed up. Aunt Naomi started cussing. She said some cuss words that I didn't know women knew. She told the doctor and everyone who was listening, whether they wanted to hear or not, from what kind of canine Uncle T.R. was descended. She also elaborated on the lineage of the women that he had engaged in coitus. As she continued educating us, I noticed a man with a tool belt holding a wet sheet and a male nurse with a syringe. The needle on the syringe looked like a matchstick.

The doctor took the syringe and said, "Ma'am, you can calm down or I will help you calm down."

Aunt Naomi took a step toward the doctor. She slapped the doctor on the ear with her open hand. The wet sheet was around her before she could squeak.

The doctor was patting his pants pockets and he turned to Daddy and said, "Mr. Murphy, have you got a blade on you?"

Daddy reached in his pocket and pulled out his Old Timer. He flipped the blade out and handed it to the doctor, handle first. I could see blood starting to trickle out of the doctor's ear. I know she hurt him. The doctor took the pocketknife and sliced a hole in the sheet over her arm. He said, "You've got a good edge on that blade," he observed. To which Daddy replied, "Thank you, Doctor."

Aunt Naomi was screaming, and the doctor said, "Mrs. Murphy, you can either calm down or I will help you calm down while you wait for the deputies."

Aunt Naomi had her cheeks puffed out and she was snorting through her nose like a little pig. It was sad to see a grown woman contained like that. She looked kind of like a peeled banana with a curly metal pot scrubber on top. The deputies came in and Aunt Naomi acted surprised. I don't think it crossed her mind that she had gone too far when she slapped the doctor. She cranked up the cussing again and the doctor turned the volume down with the syringe of magic sleeping medicine. Two deputies came in and picked her up like a piece of pulp wood. We walked out behind the deputies, I guess to see if she was going to do anything else. The deputies kind of chunked her in the back seat, headfirst.

The doctor spoke to the deputies, "I'll be down to the magistrate's when I get off my shift. I'm pressing charges."

Daddy looked at me and said, "Let's go find a drink machine."

"Daddy, are you doing to bail out Aunt Naomi?"

Daddy said, "T.R. has been a sorry excuse for a husband but he didn't deserve to be beaten like she did. And she slapped that doctor. I think she needs to stay in jail at least one night to cool off. "

"Daddy, if Aunt Naomi is this crazy all the time, maybe Uncle T.R. had a reason to run around."

"You might be right, Iver."

Daddy called Mama from the pay telephone in the lobby to give her a heads up that he was bringing Uncle T.R. home. I think I heard her scream a cuss word over the phone.

We drove T.R. to the house and parked him in the den so he could watch a ball game on the television. Daddy and I rode back to the hospital to get Uncle T.R.'s truck. Aunt Naomi wasn't going to be driving it tonight.

"Daddy, what about Uncle T.R.'s coon dogs and hogs?"

"Well, T.R. is going to be up and around in a day or two. You run over here before you go to Doc's in the morning, maybe Tuesday morning, too. Give Doc a call and tell him you are going to be late in the morning. I'm going to call the magistrate when we get back to the house. I wonder how much bail Naomi is going to have to put up."

I went first thing Monday morning to feed up for Uncle T.R. I didn't think it would be any problem. I drove around the back of Uncle T.R.'s house and the dogs weren't barking. I looked across the yard and saw the dog pens were open. Blue and Joe were gone. Then I noticed the trash barrel was burning. I walked over to the barrel. There was the leg of a green leisure suit kind of melted to the side of the barrel. Then it dawned on me that these were Uncle T.R.'s Sunday clothes. And there was a kerosene can beside the barrel. A pair of Hush Puppies were stuck up under the barrel and kind of curled up. Kerosene and polyester must give off a lot of heat.

Aunt Naomi and Uncle T.R. went to the Methodist church together every Sunday. Uncle T.R. would go to the prayer rail every Sunday wearing a green leisure suit and his Hush Puppies. Uncle T. R. went to the prayer rail so much he has his own permanent knee tracks in the cushion.

Aunt Naomi had been devilish to Uncle T.R. in the past. She once taped a black snake to the steering wheel of his tractor with black electrical tape. And she hung a rattlesnake under the hood of a car he was working on one time. One time she took all the money out of the bank and burned all the checks. Uncle T.R. had to buy gas on credit to get to work. He was the millwright at the local sawmill, Tall Pine Lumber Company, or as we called it, Have You Seen My Finger Lumber Company. I knew she had done more, but Uncle T. R. was probably just ashamed to tell. I was wondering who set the barrel afire. Then it dawned on me! Somebody had stolen T.R.'s coon dogs! I looked at the back door and it was open. Thieves! This was a perfect time; T.R. was at our house and Naomi was in jail. The hogs! I jumped in the truck, drove around the field to the hog pens and there were the Samson boys loading up the hogs. I needed to call the law. I didn't need to go back in the house; the thieves might still be there.

I got to the highway and started to turn toward home but I thought better of it and decided to go to the local store, Albert Sommersett's. Albert's was the local coffee- drinking, lie-swapping, gas station that was essential to the whole area and the nearest phone I could think of. I drove to the store and there were so many trucks I had to park on the road shoulder. I walked in and said, "Morning, Mr. Albert. Could I use your phone to call the sheriff's department? I don't even know the number." Everybody in the store stopped talking and looked at me.

Mr. Albert said, "Here's the number," pointing to a piece of cardboard nailed to the wall. "What happened, Iver?

"Uncle T.R. has been robbed. His coon dogs are gone, and the Samson's are stealing his hogs. They are loading them up right now."

"Wait a minute, Iver. I know where the dogs are and who is getting the hogs. T.R.'s hunting buddy, Earl, lined up a sale for the dogs after Naomi called him and said T.R. needed ten thousand dollars to pay some gambling debts off. She said he was in the hospital after a New York mobster beat him up. She called me and I got the Samsons loading the hogs to go to the sale this morning in Chadbourn. We were going to take up a collection for the rest."

I leaned on the ice cream box and said, "So, that is what Aunt Naomi said?"

Mr. Albert said, "Yes, she called me to see about getting the hogs sold and called Earl to sell the dogs."

I said, "Mr. Albert, I know Uncle T.R. appreciates all of your concern, but Aunt Naomi has lied to y'all. Aunt Naomi whipped him with a tobacco stick when he was messin' with the veterinarian's nurse at the hog pen Sunday morning."

There was complete silence in the store, everybody was listening to me.

Mr. Albert snorted, "Well. This is an interesting turn."

"She slapped the doctor at the emergency room and got put in jail. I saw it happen."

Mr. Albert said, "She is trying to get the money to pay the bail bondsman. She is slick. I bet Bernard posted her bond on credit. He knew those dogs were worth at least $5,000."

"Daddy called the magistrate last night and he said her bond was a thousand dollars."

Mr. Albert said, "She's cleaning T.R. out. I bet she will be at the bank when it opens. Let's see; it's eight-fifteen now. Iver, go on home so you and your daddy can go with T.R. to the bank. I'm going to call your daddy right now and tell him what is going on. "

I tried to make T.R.'s truck fly. I couldn't believe this was happening in our family. This was ridiculous, absurd, embarrassing, trashy; I don't know what else. I didn't know who to feel sorry for. I felt sorry for Aunt Naomi for a while, but I thought she had evened things up. I thought selling his dogs evened up with his tomcatting around, surely. I don't know why I thought of it right then, but I could see Uncle T.R. coming back to the pew after two verses of a hymn with tears in his eyes. Selling the man's dogs was about the meanest things I had ever heard of. When I drove in the yard Daddy was waiting on me.

Daddy said, "Albert called me to tell me what happened. Don't say anything about the dogs just yet, one crisis at a time. We know Earl has the dogs. Albert said he would send his hired man, Toby to T.R,'s to watch the house till we get there."

Uncle T.R. had on a set of Daddy's clothes when he stepped out of the house. I wondered if Aunt Naomi had burned all of his clothes.

Daddy said, "We'll take the Cadillac. You drive, Iver."

We got in the car, and nobody said a word as we drove to the Pioneer Bank. I hoped T.R. and Naomi would just go their separate ways. Maybe they won't be like some people that break up and get back together on and on. That would be torturing each other over and over again.

We got to the bank before it opened but not before Naomi got there. Daddy said, "Iver, run down to the Excalibur Pool Room and ask them to call a deputy to come over here."

I sprinted around the corner and there was a deputy sitting in a booth finishing up a hamburger. I said, "Could you step down to Pioneer with me? I think there is going to be trouble when the bank opens." The deputy cleaned up the wrappers, dropped the trash in the can and put the bottle in the rack.

"No problem, son." He got up and walked out to his car and called on the radio, "Assistance at Pioneer. You are Walter's son, T.R.'s nephew, right? Come on and get in the car with me. I heard Naomi cut a shine at the magistrate's office."

I said," She made bail and figured she would come down here to the bank and clean out the accounts. Did you know she got Earl to sell his coon dogs?"

He just about screamed, "WHAT!? That little she-devil. Now that was uncalled for. She sold Blue and Joe? That was low."

"Uh-huh. She told Mr. Albert Somerset that T.R. had gotten beat up by New York mobsters for a ten-thousand-dollar bet. She must have told the same thing to Earl. He's got the dogs and gone to sell them. Naomi is the one that beat him up."

When we drove in the parking lot, Aunt Naomi was standing with her back to the front door of the bank hollering at Uncle T.R.

The deputy said, "Iver, I didn't tell you my name. I'm Benji Purcell and T.R. and I are coon-huntin' buddies. We've won some trophies together."

Benji Purcell stepped out of the patrol car, put on his campaign hat, patted his gun, sucked on his teeth, spit on the sidewalk and strode up to the door where Aunt Naomi was standing. He calmly said, "Miss Naomi, can I help you? Let me see if I can help you work things out. I'm just here to make sure everybody gets what they are supposed to have."

"You're just one of T.R.'s asshole, coon-hunting buddies. You're here to cheat me out of my part. I know you bastards."

Officer Purcell said, "I'm here for you to get what is yours and for things to be quiet in the bank."

She looked at T.R. and said, "I deserve all of it and I'm going to get all of it."

Mr. Jim Parks, the bank manager, was standing at the front door with keys in hand looking out the door at us. Aunt Naomi stepped up and slapped the glass. "I want my money now!"

Officer Purcell kind of nodded to Mr. Parks and he unlocked the door. Aunt Naomi had a checkbook and savings account book in her hand. She ran to the first window, slapped the books down on the marble shelf and said, "I want all the money out of these accounts."

Uncle T.R. walked over to the teller and pulled the little spiral notebook out of his pocket, wrote a little bit, ripped the paper out and passed a note to the teller. I'm not sure what it said but it dawned on me that Uncle T.R. might be having problems talking, the end of his tongue being gone. I hadn't heard him say anything since we brought him home. The teller said, "Benji could you read this and verify what it says?"

Deputy Purcell said, "It says, 'Leave my half where it is and take her name off the accounts.'"

Aunt Naomi said, "No, I was here first; I want it all." It went round and round, but Aunt Naomi finally agreed to getting her half, took it in cash in two envelopes, stuffed it in her brassiere, said a few choice words and stomped out of the bank. She tried to slam the door, but the hydraulic door closer slowed it down.

Deputy Purcell, Uncle T.R., Daddy, and Mr. Parks all shook hands. Daddy said, "Let's go get a hamburger. We haven't had any breakfast." Officer Purcell and Mr. Parks begged off so Daddy, Uncle T.R. and I drove around to the Excalibur Pool Room. Uncle T.R. just shook his head and sat in the car while we went in. We brought the burgers and Mountain Dews back to the car. Uncle T.R. tried to eat his burger but we could tell he was having a hard time. I kind of felt sorry for him. Uncle T.R. handed Daddy his little notebook and Daddy handed it to me. "I want to go by my house", it read.

Daddy said, "I've got to tell you something, T.R. Naomi has gotten Earl to sell your coon dogs and she got the Samsons to carry your hogs to Chadbourn this morning."

Uncle T.R. just nodded slowly. Daddy told Uncle T.R. the whole story of what Naomi had done, and he didn't show any feelings. He tapped the notebook again and pointed toward his farm, so I pointed the Cadillac to Uncle T.R.'s.

Toby, Mr. Albert's right-hand man, was sitting in his truck on the side yard of Uncle T.R. 's house. He got out of his truck and said nobody had showed up. Uncle T.R. was trying to get out of the car and moaned. I had forgotten he had his ribs taped and his pain killers may be wearing off. Uncle T. R. pointed to the house and gave a little grunt. I walked along beside him on the steps to the back door. When he stepped in the door, he straightened up and took a deep breath and made a little moan. He walked over and got two shot guns out of the closet and a pistol out of a bureau. Then he walked over and got a hunting trophy off the mantelpiece when I realized what he was doing. I stepped back in the kitchen and got a clothes basket. He started putting the trophies and the photos of his dogs in the basket. He went to his recliner and got his Bible and handed it to me. As we were starting out the back door, Naomi bumped and scraped her car down the passenger side of Daddy's Cadillac. Daddy said, "It's just a car. Let it go T.R." Uncle T.R. shook his head.

Daddy and I walked to the trunk of the Cadillac and put the shot guns and the clothes basket inside. Aunt Naomi was jumping up and down and screaming things I could not understand. Then Uncle T.R. acted like he wasn't in any pain at all. He walked over to his charcoal grill, poured some kerosene on it, pushed it to the side of the house and lit it. The house caught pretty quick. Aunt Naomi started doing laps around the house hollering "Help!" Daddy, Uncle T.R., Toby and I stood there watching the house burn. When the roof was burning, Uncle T.R. walked over to the Cadillac, opened the back door and sat down. Daddy slid across the front seat and I got behind the wheel. I had to scrape down the side of Aunt Naomi's car to get out. She stopped lapping the house and started running around in little circles, screaming.

As we drove out of the driveway, a fire truck was pulling in. Uncle T.R. pointed toward Mr. Albert's store. When we got there, most everybody was at the fire.

I pulled the car between the gas pumps and the front door so Uncle T. R. wouldn't have to take many steps to get in the store. Mr. Albert held the door open as Uncle T.R. walked in. Uncle T.R. walked a few steps and sat down on a wooden keg, took out his little notebook, handed the book to me and pointed at Mr. Albert.

"You're welcome, T.R. I am sorry about your dogs." T.R. bobbed his head up and down. Daddy and I got a Mountain Dew out of the box and Uncle T.R pointed at the Coke box.

We didn't say anything. I was afraid to say anything. I looked at Uncle T.R. and thought, "I bet his balls wouldn't fit in a baseball cap." He was making a break in his life for sure."

Mr. Albert kept a wheel of cheese next to the counter along with produce scales, a topless cigar box for pens, pencils and another topless cigar box for the cheese knife and a cash register. He sold about a wheel a week. Daddy had the same type of cheese at his store, but he kept it in a cooler. Daddy cut a turn of cheese first thing in the morning, one-pound wedges and snack pieces. He said it was more sanitary as Mr. Albert's cheese tended to ripen during the week, especially in the summer. I never saw any mold on Mr. Albert's cheese or on the knife he used. The technique he used was tried and true. When you wanted a piece of cheese, he would pull a piece of wax paper and slap it on the scales. Then he would take the wooden top off of the cheese, take the knife out of cigar box cut the amount of cheese you wanted, pierce the cheese with the point of the knife, throw it on the scale, get the weight, fold the wax paper around the cheese, put it in a paper sack, tape the bag closed, write the price with a wax pencil on the sack and ring it up. In the store you would normally see old men sitting around with pocketknives out eating little pieces of cheese. It was awfully good cheese. The reason I have told all of this about Mr. Albert's cheese business is because Aunt Naomi walked in the store, picked the knife out of the cigar box, stabbed Uncle T.R. in the neck, and tossed the knife back in the box. We all just stood there and let her do it. I have no idea why we didn't stop her. I felt like we were watching a movie. Naomi walked back out of the store and drove off. Uncle T. R. was hissing air out of his neck. Daddy grabbed a couple of paper sacks and put them over the hole in his neck. Mr. Albert pulled off a piece of tape and ran it around his neck to hold the bag in place. Daddy kind of drug Uncle T.R. to the Cadillac and put him in the back seat. I jumped in the front seat and jumped over in the back. Daddy got under the wheel and said, "Iver, keep the hole in his neck covered." Uncle T.R. was bleeding pretty bad. I guess it was good the Cadillac had a red, crushed-velvet interior.

Mr. Albert was standing by the car and said, "I'll call the hospital and tell them to be looking for you." He called the sheriff's department and filled them in. Then he called the Farm Bureau and told them T.R. Murphy's house had burned down and they needed to send an agent.

Aunt Naomi got arrested again, no bail this time. We left Uncle T.R. at the hospital. All they did was put a big band aid over the hole in his neck. The doctor said the hole was where he would put in a tracheotomy in any way. Apparently, the doctor thought it was no big deal and Uncle T.R. had already had a tetanus shot on Sunday, after the tobacco stick beating and tongue biting incident. Daddy asked them to keep Uncle T.R. at least overnight. I think Daddy needed a rest.

When we got to the house, Bet met us at the door. "Where is T.R.? I cooked some chicken and rice soup for him."

Daddy said, "I'm going to the store. I need a rest. We left T.R. at the hospital."

I said, "Could I have some soup, Bet? It has been a long day."

Bet said, "It's only two o'clock, Iver. Toby called me and told me what happened, Naomi stabbing him and all."

"Daddy, I hope we never have a day like this again."

"Tell it, boy," and he walked out the door.

I sat down at the table where Bet had put the bowl of soup, "Thank you, Bet. We left Uncle T.R. at the hospital. The doctor said the hole in his throat would heal up. The knife missed the vital stuff, just poked a hole in his windpipe."

"Have they found Naomi?" Betsy asked, putting a glass of iced tea in front of me.

"I haven't heard anything, Bet."

I decided to go back to work. I was already seven hours late. I walked in the office and Doc said, "You look like hell. Go upstairs and go to bed. You're no good to me right now. I'll get you up for supper. Bet called and told us the scoop."

God Bless Alexander Graham Bell.

I walked in the kitchen and Theola pointed at my chair. I sat down and she put a piece of lemon meringue pie in front of me. Lemon meringue pie is sweet and tart. Maybe this is how marriage is; the sweet and the tart just work things out. Well, not with T.R. and Naomi. I needed to ask Doc about this. He has been married so many times, maybe he could counsel with T.R. about the tart factor. What even makes a man want to marry? Aunt Naomi was set on killing Uncle T.R. I couldn't figure him marrying her. He had to have known about that wild streak for a while and she wasn't pretty like Momma or MaMariah or Girlie. Maybe I just couldn't see Naomi in the same light as T.R.

Naomi actually made me a little afraid of women. There could be a lot of meanness in a little package. Girlie was a little package. I thought about the trip to Sea Breeze when I kissed Girlie. Different girls, different kisses.

Chapter 12

Flaming Goat Tacos

Daddy got T.R. home from the hospital on Wednesday evening. Considering everything, Daddy said my uncle was in good spirits. Daddy had called the sawmill and told them T.R. wouldn't be in for at least two weeks. Of course, everybody already knew the whole story except they thought Naomi had set the house on fire. News moves like lightning in little place.

Things settled down around our family. T.R. was staying with Momma and Daddy. He was using my bedroom. I just decided to stay with Doc on the weekends for a while to keep the house from being so full. I drove Doc's old car now like it was my own, so I came over a couple of nights a week to see everybody. It was a Thursday night when I came by that particular time. Everybody was sitting in the den after supper watching television.

Uncle T.R. said, "I had some quiet time at the hospital and the preacher came by to see me. We were talking and he said God must have a plan for me. Naomi didn't kill me so I must have something else to do."

All of us were nodding while he talked. He said, "Earl brought me ten thousand dollars for Blue and Joe last night."

Everybody tried to suck all the air out of the room when he said ten thousand dollars.

"When school starts back in January, I am going to community college and major in English. I always liked to read." There was a pause. "The crowd I ran with in high school didn't care about college, so, I didn't."

Daddy said, "The only books I have ever seen at your house were the Bible and Hot Rod magazine."

Uncle T.R. said, "I kept my library books in the Hot Rod magazines. You know how Naomi fussed about everything. I don't know what she would have thought if she saw me reading real books."

All of us were quiet. I was just figuring how old Daddy and T.R. were. Daddy is forty now and T.R. is six years younger, so he is thirty-four. Going to college at his age isn't a big deal.

T.R. said, "I can get some G.I. bill money for my expenses. And I've made some real money with my dogs: stud fees, bets, contests, all in cash. Naomi didn't know anything about that money. She wouldn't even pet the dogs, so I kept that money. With that money and the money Earl brought for Blue and Joe, I can live without working for a while."

We all sat there in awe. Who would have ever thought he would be interested in English?

Uncle T.R. said, "I know I was a bad husband for Naomi. I have always been weak when it comes to women. And Naomi didn't help things, either. When she had that second miscarriage, well, she just turned bitter toward me. I couldn't make things better for her, so I guess it was my fault. I started chasing women. I just wanted a woman to say a few kind words to me. A nice conversation goes a long way.

"I have prayed for strength to be true to Naomi. I prayed for her to have a baby. She wanted one so bad. I have thought about it a lot the last few weeks and I'm going to ask the district attorney not to press charges against Naomi. I just drove her to it. When we went in the house, I noticed all her things were gone. She was leaving me. It didn't matter that I set the house on fire. It was paid for and in my name and there wasn't any insurance on it."

All of us were just sitting there, listening to T.R. talk so calmly about Naomi. And objectively about himself. I don't know if I could have gotten over her selling my dogs.

"I know Naomi is in Myrtle Beach. She always said that is where she wanted to live. And I know this is crazy, but I want y'all to start calling me Teddy, you boys, too."

Mama said, "O.K., but why?"

Teddy said, "I'm starting new today."

When Saturday night rolled around, we had the fish fry. Daddy cooked them in the yard. There must have been thirty people besides us there. There was enough fish, slaw, cornbread and sweet tea for an army. I don't think anybody asked Teddy about where Aunt Naomi was. After all the wrinkles shake out, I'm sure someone asked him about it. No wife, no dogs, no house.

The Friday of the following week, Teddy drove over to the office at closing time. I saw him walk in and thought, "Surely, he isn't here for a treatment." He had on a new suit of clothes, new shoes, mustache trimmed and his ponytail was gone.

Teddy said, "Come ride with me tonight over to Emerson; I'm feeling a lot better."

As usual, I didn't have any plans. I said, "Sure. Who or what is in Emerson?"

Teddy said, "A very old friend of mine."

It was close to dark when we left Donahoe Creek. I said, "Uncle T.R.—Teddy--, what did you do about Aunt Naomi?"

"I filed for divorce and there aren't any charges against her. We are both starting over."

We didn't talk much. I didn't take but about thirty minutes to get where Teddy was going.

There was a mailbox with two reflectors on the post where we turned in. I couldn't see any light from the road. We went around a curve on a two-lane path and came up on a mobile home with a huge screen porch on the front. There were four picnic tables in the yard and kerosene lamps on them. It was just a nice setting. When I stepped out of Teddy's truck, I was struck with the most wonderful smell I have ever smelled. "What is that smell, Teddy?"

"Supper. Goat tacos."

Teddy led the way. He walked up on the screen porch steps and said, "Daphne," and a string of words I think was Spanish. This man is amazing. "I didn't know you spoke Spanish."

A pretty woman opened the screen door and motioned us both in. She kissed Teddy square on the mouth. You could tell she had done it before. They started talking. The lady walked over to a high-fi on the porch and started playing Mexican music. Teddy laughed and I felt left out.

Teddy said, "Iver, come on out here and let's sit down."

We sat at a picnic table in the yard. It was a warm night, a just right night. In a few minutes, two boys about eleven or twelve years old came to the table with paper plates of tacos and beer.

I said, "I didn't order beer. I didn't order anything."

Teddy said, "The beer comes with it. Just eat and enjoy it."

And I did. And I ate another plate of something and drank another beer. It was good and I was eating the second round, not because I was hungry, but, because it was just good.

My belly got full, music was playing, Teddy was talking to the lady in Spanish, I didn't know what was going on, so I laid down on a table and went to sleep, hard asleep.

Teddy shook my awake by my shoulder and said, "Let's go back home."

I got back in the truck and looked at my watch. It was after midnight and I had to be at work in the morning. "Teddy, how do you know that woman?"

"I was married to her before I married Naomi. She didn't want to move from Texas where I was stationed, so we just got divorced. She wrote to me last summer and said she wanted to move her business up here, so I bought her a piece of land and the trailer. The two boys here are her little brothers. I couldn't tell anybody. My reputation with women is bad enough."

Yes, we had underestimated him.

We got home at about one o'clock. I got awakened at my usual time anyway with no alarm clock. There is no way to say it nicely, but my bowels woke me up every morning at 6:00 and they did that Saturday morning. I got up, picked up the book I was reading, crossed the hallway, flipped on the light switch and just did make it to the toilet. I was holding on to the toilet seat with both hands, like I was going to blast off; my hind part was on fire. I took a deep breath just to make sure I wasn't dead and in hell. I didn't faint but I did see a couple of spots in front of my eyes. This was not good. I looked down; positive I would see smoke coming up from between my knees. I hesitated to wipe my behind in fear of setting the toilet paper on fire. I got in the shower but there was no relief. I ran some cold water in the tub and suspended my behind in the water. I kept my feet hung over the side so they wouldn't be cold. Even though my behind was on fire, the water didn't get any warmer. Then that cramping sensation hit me again. It was about six-thirty by then. I sat on the toilet sideways that time so I could have a better grip on the sink. I didn't faint but it was pretty painful, and the pain didn't stop even after the paperwork was done. The only thing I could think of was to blow cold air on the offending part.

I went into my bedroom and turned on the air conditioner and stood on a chair with my hind parts to the air conditioner and my face to the door, naked as a jaybird. It was about seven o'clock by then and I was still suffering. For some reason, maybe a signal from God, Doc walked in my room and looked me square in the eye. "Goat tacos" was all I could say as the tears were rolling down my cheeks. I was in awful pain.

Doc came back upstairs in a few minutes with an emesis basin with a scoops of vanilla ice cream and a tongue depressor. Doc said, "See if this won't cool you down. Theola has breakfast ready." I started to eat the ice cream and then thought, This if for my flaming ass.

I was sitting straddle the emesis basin with the ice cream cooling my bum down and couldn't do anything but think, those goat tacos were good, but they could kill a man. Big Jack used to eat hot peppers whole. Those peppers couldn't have set his asshole on fire like those goat tacos did mine. That old man must have been made of asbestos.

Teddy and Daphne got married again. We never saw Aunt Naomi again. Teddy went to college for a while and decided to be an electrician. I was not permanently damaged by the goat tacos, but I was always cautious of Aunt Daphne's cooking.

Chapter 13

The Hunter and The Hunted

Big Jack was gone. September was gone. October was half gone, and hunting season had started. Daddy had stocked the store with ammunition like he did every fall. He had gotten in a few long guns that he kept in the back. Daddy didn't deer hunt, but he didn't mind us going with Rudolph and his brother Ike. Hunting was a pastime that most males enjoyed except Daddy. He said he wasn't going to stand in the cold wind waiting for a furry, tick-laden Bambi to run out of the woods. Then you had to dress it to go in the freezer. He said that it was a troublesome piece of meat. But Rudolph made sure we had venison in our freezer, too. Bet cooked Bambi once a week as long as we had some in the freezer. Daddy said that Bet's venison would make a bulldog break his chain.

Hunting was and is a ritual. It is a coming-of-age rite for young boys. When little boys first go, they just ride around, mostly with whoever is working the dogs. When they get a little older, they get to be on a stand with somebody that's grown, some old man with a lot of patience. When the boy gets about ten or eleven and can behave, they get a stand of their own. Standing in the cold for hours for some reason was thought of as fun. It really didn't matter if you killed a deer or not. It was all about getting in the Big Boys Club.

Rudolph had always carried me hunting on the first day of the season since I was six-years old and did the same for the twins. Rudolph kept a pack of deer dogs all year. In August and September, he would let the new dogs run with the old dogs, so they get the idea of what they are supposed to do. He blew the horn on his truck when he fed so he could catch his dogs-- Pavlov's dogs, Rudolph's dogs. All three of us boys had twenty-gauge pump shotguns. All three were exactly alike and Daddy engraved our names on them. Daddy didn't want any questions about whose was whose Most of the time we hunted on Big Jack's farm. It had two creeks with a swamp between them, lots of good stands if you were dog hunting. 'Dog Hunting' means turning a pack of dogs out in a spot with the hope they flush a deer. The hunters wait around the perimeter and wait for the deer to run out, then you catch the dogs, maybe.

We got on stands around the edge of the woods and Rudolph would let his dogs loose at one end with the hopes of the dogs jumping a buck. We didn't always see a deer; sometimes we saw a fox. Most deer dogs would chase about anything. If somebody tells you that their dogs only chase deer, they are lying. The reason I knew this was because Rudolph's cousin, Willie Blanks, killed a bear in front of Rudolph's dogs. It was the best day hunting that I would have in my lifetime.

It was the first Saturday in November and Doc had given me the morning off and the twins were following Rudolph. When we got our stands assigned, Willie said he wanted the stand in the run of the bigger creek. He had on his waders. That stand had about four inches of water around it but that was his favorite stand-- out of the wind. Things were going good for Willie for a while and then the stomach pains hit. There wasn't anything he could do but start peeling his clothes down. He usually had a piece of a roll of toilet paper in the inside pocket of his hunting coat, but it had gotten used the last time we went hunting. His tee shirt would be sacrificed for this event.

The event was progressing calmly until he heard the dogs crashing through the creek, water splashing, twigs breaking. Willie was kind of squatted over with his gun across his knees when the splashing bear appeared. Now, if it had been a deer, he would have let it go. He was in need of privacy for a few more minutes but the bear was coming straight to him. The bear got in front of him and stood up on his back legs. The bear was standing there growling. Willie did the only thing he could do in that situation. Willie raised the gun and shot the bear from a squat. Willie later said he wondered if that was the bear's spot, "We know bears do their business in the woods. I might have been trespassing," he speculated.

Well, when anybody discharged a weapon, everybody'd come to see the deer you had hopefully killed. That time it wasn't a deer. Willie was struggling to pull his clothes back up without dropping his gun. Rudolph was the first to get there. He walked over to the bear that Willie had shot. The bear wasn't but about ten feet from Willie's stand.

Rudolph said, "Why did you let that bear get so close?"

Willie said, "Well, Rudy, it just snuck up on me."

Rudolph said, "No, he didn't. You were squatted down and couldn't move. And there it is, right there", pointing to a pile of fragrant material with a piece of tee shirt beside it.

"Rudy, don't say anything. Let's step over here."

"Oh, hell no. All the picking you have done on me, this is too good not to tell. Willie Blanks, you are crazy to think I'm not going to tell this."

Rudolph brought the three of us back to the store before lunch. We didn't have a hunt that afternoon. It takes a while to skin a bear and Willie wanted to do it while the bear was still warm.

Rudolph told it. I told it. Gene told it. Roy told it. Everybody told it.

I made it back to the office by twelve-thirty. I couldn't wait to tell Doc. He was waiting on customers. The Rooster Juice was a hot item.

"Doc, Willie Blanks shot a bear this morning."

"That's interesting. Not many bears are killed around here."

"Once in a while somebody kills one, but Willie shot this one with his pants down."

"So, how do you know that?"

"We heard the shot and went to see if he got a deer. And there was the bear."

"How did you know he killed it with his pants down?"

"He admitted it and the bear was shot in his paws and chest."

"I would have given a silver dollar to see Willie Blank's bare-assed and shooting a bear. You wait till I see him here in the office. I want to hear him tell the story."

The customers slowed down, and we locked the door.

While we were standing on the porch I said, "Doc, I need a little advice. I want to date Sissy Reynolds and I want to do it properly."

I got ignored on that request.

"I haven't hunted in years. Did I ever tell you about hunting quail in Mexico?"

"Doc, how do you think I should ask Sissy out for a date?"

"All of us boys need to go to Mexico and go hunting like Big Jack and I used to do."

"Doc, did you say that you and Big Jack went to Mexico hunting?"

"Yep, we went right after he shot me in Richmond. Yes, we went on hunting trips together. We got over our disagreement when he shot me. Lauralee held the grudge. Well, you know about that."

"And y'all would go to Mexico together?"

"Yes, and Canada deer hunting and trout fishing here in North Carolina. But that trip to Mexico was something."

Doc was going to tell the hunting story no matter what I asked. So, I just sat down and listened.

"We rode the train to Texas and got up with a farmer that was a friend of mine who sold us goats for the cats when the circus was down there. He had a ranch just over the border in Mexico that only he hunted and had a small lodge there.

"Well, when we rode to his ranch…well it was beautiful. He had an old long car that the top folded back, a Hispano Suiza. I don't think you have ever seen one. It was like a Rolls Royce that was made in Spain and that was what we hunted out of. He had a driver in the front; the dogs were trained to get back in the car, so we just stood up in the back and shot. There were birds everywhere. And we feasted that night. There are a lot more quail down there. The second day, I just gave out. I shot till I was tired. Jack went the third day, but I just walked around the ranch near the lodge. I was carrying a pistol for snakes. I didn't kill any snakes, but I shot the biggest rabbit I have ever seen. When I carried it to the cook, she acted like I was a champion, a star. I got treated like a king that day. She said I was *macho*. She cooked that rabbit; it was something. Never did figure out how she seasoned it."

"You know, boy, hunting is what men do to leave their problems behind. You go and look for an adversary, something to kill or to catch. Sometimes men will hunt in groups, in a pack together. It doesn't matter if anything is killed, just that they went on a mission. They get away from the routine, away from the everyday jobs for a while. Sometimes it is a good excuse to sit quietly in the woods."

"Whoa, Doc, we hunt to get free meat to go in the freezer."

"Iver, that meat isn't free. The way y'all do it, it would be cheaper to buy steak in the grocery store or feed out a pig than to get game. Dogs, guns, trucks-- all those cost money. When I was a boy and we were hunting to survive, a rabbit box or a dove trap would get a lot of meat without much effort. I was told that after The Civil War you couldn't find a possum. Could get a deer with a snare but the deer had about been hunted out. We hunted to eat year-round. I've hunted some with a crowd, but I didn't load my gun. It was an excuse to sit in the woods and contemplate the world. You do some good thinking on a stand, don't you?"

"You are afraid to kill a deer?"

"No, just don't want the responsibility: dress it, put it in the freezer. That's a lot of work."

"I can see what you mean. But what has this got to do with getting a proper date with Sissy Reynolds?"

"The Thrill of the Hunt, planning on what to hunt, what weapon, how to stalk the prey."

"That sounds sinister. I was just wanting to know how to ask a girl on a date, not how to stalk her."

"Son, dating is the same thing. You are finding a girl versus finding a deer. You have to have a plan."

"Hunting a woman? That's not what I'm asking you, Doc. I am asking you how to ask a girl on a date. I appreciate that I know how to dance but now I want a girlfriend. You've been married all those times and now you are sparking MaMariah again. You have got to know the answer."

"Who is it, Iver?"

"Sissy Reynolds."

"Lipstick girl from the revival? You already kissed her."

"Yes, at revival and at the Dairy Queen in Whiteville and I want to kiss her some more. I don't want to wait for the next revival. I want to see if she will go with me, you know, be my girlfriend."

"You've already done the first thing: you have chosen your quarry."

"Sissy is not a quarry."

"She has already proven she is alive and wild, kissing at revival."

"Alright, I may not be the only one she has kissed, but Doc, she is so pretty. I want her to be my girlfriend. Maybe do a little more kissing."

"That better be all you do. You are kind of young to start making babies."

"Doc, she isn't that kind of girl," I said in a soft voice.

"OK, Iver. The best place to start is at church. Does she go to the Presbyterian Church?"

"No, she is Pentecostal."

"Son, you need to go to the Pentecostal Church on Sunday. Go to Sunday school and make some small talk. Ask her parents if you can sit on their pew."

"I can do that. But how do I get her for a girlfriend?"

"Next Sunday, go to church with her, whisper in her ear that you like her and would like to come to Sunday supper. Then you can start the plan."

"What plan?"

"You make friends with her parents. Bring a box of Whitman's to her momma. Bring Sissy a bag of Hershey Kisses. Be a smooth, southern gentleman."

"I'm not sure about a smooth, southern gentleman."

"All of this is easy. Make friends with her parents. Sissy will be impressed. Her parents will be impressed. You will get invited back next Sunday. Then you will ask her daddy if you can ride around with her for a little bit. Daddy says to be home at nine o'clock; you bring her home at eight-thirty."

"This sounds simple. Daddy never told me any of this."

"That's because your mama and daddy met at Myrtle Beach after her senior prom, at a shag club. Your daddy came back from Korea and they got married, none of the proper techniques. That is the reason he doesn't know about it. "This girl is young, fifteen, sixteen?"

"She's seventeen. And yes, I am going to treat her like a lady.

I went to the Pentecostal Free Will Fire Baptized Holiness Church Sunday morning, early for Sunday school and to scope things out. Sissy and her parents were not there at Sunday school or in church.

I asked a boy in the Sunday school class if he knew Sissy Reynolds. He said that the Reynolds family had been turned out of the church because they had put a dance floor in the restaurant and that they played rock and roll, jungle bunny music, devil music.

Two different girls asked me to sit with them and their families. The mother of the girl I sat with asked me to Sunday dinner. I already had some camellias I had picked in the truck. I followed them home, ate dinner and helped with the dishes. Her daddy said, 'Take my truck and y'all ride around.' I guess things go faster than when Doc and MaMariah were courting and sparking. I made a startling discovery. Some girls will kiss on the first date. Lucky me.

So, I changed my plans. I went home and worked on how I was going to ask Mama and Daddy if we could go to Reynolds' Restaurant to eat supper Friday night.

I hemmed and hawed how to bring up the subject of Sissy Reynolds. I hadn't talked to Daddy about Sissy. After work Monday by the store to talk to Daddy.

"Daddy, did you know that there is to be a dance floor at Reynolds' Restaurant, out on Highway 74?"

"Yes, Iver. I took your mama out for her birthday there. I saw they were building on and heard there was going to be a banquet room."

"Well, Daddy, I'm not supposed to tell this but…."

"If you aren't supposed to tell, don't."

"A bunch of people already know."

"All right, if I'm not going to be the only other one that knows."

I sucked in a deep breath and said, "The Pentecostal Church turned the Reynolds out of the church. They are Methodist now."

"Yeah, Bet told us something about that. The cook at the restaurant told Rudolph that there was a big stink about the dance floor and the music. Sam Reynolds had told the cook about getting booted out of the church. Kind of wished they had come over to the Presbyterian Church. We can always use new members."

"Daddy, I went to the Holiness Church Sunday before last and found out the Reynolds had changed churches. I didn't know you had already found out. I wanted to talk to Sissy Reynolds, so I went to the Methodist Youth Fellowship last night. She told me she wouldn't date me until her parents met my parents. Can we go to the restaurant and y'all meet her parents? Can we go Friday night?"

"Of course, son. You sound pretty serious."

"I was visiting with Sissy when the boys got baptized."

I stopped and wondered if Daddy had seen the red lipstick that night when Doc brought us home. Or did Doc tell him about it at the barber shop? Daddy knew I had already kissed her. Then I stopped and thought, "I have seen Daddy kiss Mama a hundred times. Not like I was kissing Sissy…. well, maybe. I had never thought about the different kinds of kisses. The kissing I did with Sissy was the kind that could have led to sex. My parents have kissed like that, and I bet it had led to sex. And I had kissed Girlie. Those kisses from Girlie were sweet and long. They were relaxing. Girlie acted like the world had stopped for us when we kissed. Sissy's kisses were frantic like she was trying to achieve something. No, surely the prettiest girl- no, the prettiest white girl- I had ever seen gave me the kisses that lead to…. Now I was seeing a mental picture. I was going to disappear and hope this conversation never happened with Daddy but it was too late.

Daddy said, "Son, why are you turning red? Something you want to tell me? Is she pregnant?"

"No, Daddy, nothing like that!"

"Because, if you want a girl to have sex with, I don't want you having to get married at seventeen.

Please, Sweet Lord, let this conversation stop.

"Daddy, I just want to date a nice girl, take her out to dance. I'm a good dancer, Doc told me so."

Daddy stopped and looked at me for a long minute. "I heard Mariah say that Doc was a good dancer. Did he teach you how to dance?"

"Not exactly. He just made sure I knew what a good dancer looked like."

"Didn't Rudolph carry you to the joint at the bridge?"

How did Daddy know this? I never said anything.

Daddy continued, "I know what you are thinking. Rudolph told me. He carried me there when I was young. He says that white people have to be taught what comes naturally to Negros. Sounds bad, doesn't it?"

I must not have any secrets from Daddy. Rudolph has told him everything. I held my head down and nodded.

Daddy said, "Between Doc and Rudolph, all the important things have been covered. Not like I would have done any of those things, but I figured they were going to do it anyway. Does this girl work at the restaurant?"

"Yes, sir, she is a waitress on Friday and Saturday nights."

"So, when are you going to see her if you start dating her?"

"Sunday afternoons. The restaurant is closed on Sunday."

"You've got this figured out, boy. We'll go Friday night, you, me and your momma."

I was going to get to have a date with Sissy Reynolds. No, I was going to ask Mr. and Mrs. Reynolds if I could take Sissy on a date. Lord how I hoped this prayer would be answered. I sure did want to kiss Sissy again. And I wanted to feel a titty. I was going to hell. I was going to hell just praying to see a boob. I wondered which side of the furnace my seat was on. I was plotting and scheming to get my parents to help me get a date with a pretty girl. Her parents might say no. Sissy might have changed her mind. But that kiss this summer---the way she leaned on me when I put my arms around her. I wondered if it was love or lust. I think it must have been lust. All I wanted to do was kiss and hug her. Now I had gone from kissing her to hugging her. Maybe we could get married and have intercourse. What was I thinking? You didn't have to be married to have sex. I had figured that out before, but I was pretty sure going to hell was attached. In fact, I had seen people have sex in a magazine and I looked, and the participants did not have on wedding rings. I had dreamed about sex. I had dreamed about sex with Sissy. Maybe love and lust go together. Maybe they were supposed to go together. Why did I think I was in love with Sissy? She was the first girl I kissed. I kissed the other girl from the Pentecostal church. And I had kissed Girlie. I guess it is like Doc says, "That first sweet kiss." That first kiss with Girlie was so sweet. Girlie was older than I am, and she was colored. I just put that away.

I took some of my savings and got a new suit of clothes including shoes to wear that Friday night. I wanted to look my best. I went to the City Barber Shop and got a haircut. I had been shaving for a while. I got some new aftershave and a new toothbrush. I hadn't gone to that much trouble since Easter.

Tonight, was the night. We got to the restaurant at six-thirty and there was a line out on the porch. We could hear rock and roll music, jungle music. Whatever it was, I liked it. I didn't think about it, but Mama and Daddy might want to dance. I had seen them dance at home.

Daddy noted, "Iver, this is a hopping place. We may have to be here a while to meet that girl's parents. Friday night might have been a poor choice."

"Daddy, I didn't know this place had this kind of business."

A lady with a short skirt and big hair turned around in line and said, "Y'all need to put your name on the list the hostess has," pointing to the front door.

And there was Sissy, the hostess! She was standing there with a yellow legal pad and a Bic pen.

Daddy looked at the front door and nodded "Iver, go up there and put our name on the list."

Well, I strolled myself up to the front of the line and said with a big smile, "Hey, Sissy."

Sissy didn't miss a beat. She said, "Are you here to dance or to eat? How many are in your party?"

"We came here to eat supper. And there are three of us. Do you think Mama and Daddy could meet your parents?"

Sissy said, "Mama is managing the dining room and Daddy is the disc jockey in the banquet room. I'm not sure when you will get to talk to both of them. This is the biggest crowd we have had so far. I'm supposed to keep count of the number of people in and out."

Right then Mrs. Reynolds walked up to Sissy and says, "How many are on the list, honey?"

Sissy answered, "Eleven want to go in the dining room and sixteen in the banquet room."

I said, "Hello, Mrs. Reynolds. I am Iver Johnson Murphy."

Mrs. Reynolds said, "Nice to meet you, son."

Sissy said, "This is the boy I told you about."

Mrs. Reynolds said, "Oh, good."

There was a pause and Mrs. Reynolds said, "Have you ever worked in a restaurant?"

I said, "No, ma'am. I work for Dr. Edwards. But I would be happy to help you tonight."

"I need a bus boy. Sissy, seat Mr. and Mrs. Murphy in the banquet room. Give them a menu. Is that alright, Iver?"

"Yes, Ma'am. Mama and Daddy might like to dance."

So, from the back of the line there came Mama and Daddy. If looks were knives, we would all have been dead.

Daddy said kind of under his breath, "Iver, you've got the golden horseshoe up your ass this time. Big Jack must have left it to you. You scored the mother lode: a pretty girl, a restaurant and a dance hall."

I just gave Daddy a big grin. Momma shook her head as she was walking.

Reynolds Restaurant was a paper plate joint. Your food was served in little red and white paper trays or paper plates, paper cups and plastic forks. They had a one-page menu, barbeque, fried chicken, slaw, hush puppies, sweet tea and bottle drinks. You got your plate in about five minutes. The waitresses walked around with tea pitchers in one hand and mop towels in the other. The new banquet hall had tables around the edge of the room. The lights were low, and everyone was smoking. There was a jukebox at the front but there was a stage, too. There were two turntables and speakers set up on the stage. And there was a mir- rored ball hanging in the middle of the ceiling. It looked like Bandstand. Mr. Reynolds was putting records on the turntable and was grinning from ear to ear.

Sissy sat us in the obviously sacred booth in the corner. We knew it was special because there was a telephone on the windowsill with a phone book under it. Mr. Reynolds waved at us from the stage.

Sissy said, "Mama said you need to eat before you start to work. Can I order for you?"

In about four minutes two waitresses came out with our food, family style. I mean they put on the dog and left the tea pitcher. The food was great.

Daddy said, "I hope they take a check. I don't think I brought enough cash for this meal."

We were about finished eating and Mr. Reynolds walked over and said, "Hello, I'm Charles Reynolds. You must be Lauralee and Walter Murphy and you must be Iver."

He shook hands all around.

"Hope you folks like to dance! I want everybody to have a good time. Let me get back on stage." He stepped back to the stage before that record ended and started a record on a second turntable. He timed the visit to the length of the record. It was slick the way he worked the music. And you could tell he was having a good time.

Daddy said, "I think we have met the parents."

Momma said, "Pretty painless."

So began my One Night Stand Friday Night job. Mrs. Reynolds wouldn't give Daddy a ticket that first night. Momma said when they came back, they were going to pay like the other customers. Mrs. Reynolds agreed.

At the start, the work wasn't bad. I wondered why the busboy quit. Take the plates and cups off the table, wipe the table off with bleach water, dry the table off with another towel, and sweep under the table. The kitchen quits serving at nine o'clock.

By eight-thirty I know why the busboy quit. I was bushed and people were still sitting down. I didn't get to see Mama and Daddy again. It was all I could do to keep up. If I was supposed to bus the banquet room, it just didn't get done. I never noticed how fast some people eat. By nine o'clock things were winding down.

The money I cleaned off the tables, I put in a jar at the cash register. It was full when I put my change in there the last time. Mrs. Reynolds split the jar with the help, and I ended up making $6.57. At ten-thirty, I sat down with Sissy.

Sissy said, "Did you have a good time? Mama says you are good looking and can work."

I looked at her with my best smile and thought to myself, they have worked me like a rented mule. We came for a proper introduction, and we got a free meal. I worked from seven o'clock to ten-thirty for six dollars and fifty-seven cents. Doc pays me fifteen dollars a day to help old men get in the door, serve them a cup of coffee, get them on the Knee Cracker Bicycle, sell his tonic, eat his food and drive his everyday car. I didn't know I had such a plum job. This restaurant business was hard work for less money. But I got to see Sissy. She was pretty.

Without any preamble, Mrs. Reynolds said, "Iver, be here at five o'clock tomorrow night."

"Mrs. Reynolds, Dr. Edwards won't be closing his office until 6:00 tomorrow evening. And tomorrow night is a birthday party for my grandmother, Mariah Edwards." I was lying through my teeth about the office times and the birthday party. I had decided I was not going to be a bus boy again.

"What do you mean Dr. Edwards? Are you a nurse or something?"

"No, I'm Dr. Edwards' assistant."

"I didn't know you worked for him. He has a lot of coloreds come in there doesn't he?"

"Yes, ma'am and a lot of white people, too." The way she said 'coloreds' struck me in some kind of way. Colored was one of those words that was just used to describe people. Colored was not a slur, just a description, but the way she said it, well, she meant it differently. And for some reason, I just didn't like that woman.

Right that minute Mr. Reynolds stuck his head out the kitchen door and looked me straight in the eye. Mr. Reynolds was a Rooster Juice regular, and I bet Mrs. Reynolds didn't know it.

Mr. Reynolds walked out the kitchen and said, "It was a real loss for the area when Dr. Edwards left years ago. I'm happy he wanted to come back."

I didn't know if I wanted to work for this woman or not. This woman didn't know Doc was my granddaddy. And the way she said "colored", I decided I was going to let that drop from the conversation.

"Yes, it has been a really good experience working for Granddaddy."

Mrs. Reynolds looked and me, "He's your granddaddy?" I don't know if she said it with condescension or surprise. It didn't matter. I still didn't like her.

There was a long pause in the conversation.

Mrs. Reynold broke the silence, "Your granddaddy helped us adopt our beautiful Sissy. In fact, Doc delivered her. He has come by to check on her a few times over the years. He has acted like she is very special to him."

Doc had never mentioned that he even knew the Reynolds, much less delivered Sissy. I wondered why he had never said anything. Just how many more secrets did that old man have?

By this time Mr. Reynolds had stepped into the dining room and sat down at the table. He said, "Iver, how do you like working in a restaurant?"

"To be honest, sir, I didn't like it and I don't need a second job. I just want to date Sissy, not get a job."

There was a gasp at the table then Mr. Reynolds busted out laughing.

Mr. Reynolds said, "I'll give it to you, boy, for being an honest man." Then he put out his hand for a shake. I felt redeemed.

"You have passed the test. You lasted the night without complaint and told the truth. Do you know of anyone else that would like a job on Friday and Saturday nights? What about those brothers of yours? Do you think they would like a job?"

I said, "They aren't but thirteen, sir."

"I didn't know they were that young. They are kind of tall for thirteen."

"Mr. and Mrs. Reynolds, I want to cut to the chase. May I come to your house Sunday and visit with Sissy? Could we possibly ride around town and get an ice cream?"

Mrs. Reynolds spoke up and said, "Yes, Iver. That will be fine. In fact, you can come at two o'clock for hamburgers."

I said, "Thank you. Is there anyone I can catch a ride home with tonight?"

Mr. Reynolds said, "I'll carry you home."

We got in his truck, and he already knew where Doc's office was. He said in a very calm voice, "Iver, if you get my little girl pregnant, I will cut your pecker off and stuff it down your throat. Do you understand, young man?"

I swallowed instinctively and said, "Yes, sir. I understand."

I didn't say anything on the way to the office. I put my hands in my pockets to make sure my equipment was still intact.

As usual, Saturday morning was kind of busy. When the rush was over Doc asked, "How was the meeting with the parents?"

"It sure didn't go as I envisioned it. I worked busing tables for three hours, mopped the dining room and got my pecker threatened by an old man."

"Interesting."

All I wanted to do was to do things the right way. Now, I knew what he thought of his daughter. Hell, he knew his daughter was fast. And that was what got my attention to start with. Maybe this wasn't going to be worth the effort. In my mind, I just wanted a nice girl.

I think Doc was reading my mind like the elephants did his. He said, "Iver, do you think this is going to be worth all of the trouble?"

"What?" But I knew what he was thinking.

"All of this trouble you are going to, so you can kiss this girl."

"That isn't the point. Doc, you don't know this girl."

"I might not know her, but I know men. What are you going to want to do when you get tired of kissing her? You are going to want to give her a poke and then what are you going to talk about? What are you going to do, look at each other? You catch the dream, and the hunt is over."

I was not going to admit it to him, but he was right. All I knew about her was that she went to school, worked at a restaurant, and French kissed a boy the first time she got a chance—at church. Her daddy knew she was fast, so he knew what we were going to probably end up doing, this was not good. Her people were going to think we were going to get married if I slipped up and said, "I love you". Her picture would be in the paper with the date set. I had heard of this happening. Iver, I thought, what are we going to do about this situation? When I thought about it, I didn't know if I wanted companionship or the chance to get frisky. I guess I wanted both. To be honest, it's the frisky I am really looking forward to. Apparently, that's what's on her mind, too. So, what is wrong with this situation? There is a good chance I am going to hell for even having these thoughts and my penis might become detached. Why am I going through this for the first girl I have kissed?

Doc said, "Are you obsessed about this girl because she is the first girl you kissed?"

I'm getting embarrassed, "Yes, sir."

"Iver, most men fall for the first girl they kissed, but it will most likely wear off with time."

"I think this has gotten out of hand in my own mind before the first date. You are right. What are we going to talk about?"

Doc said, "Don't worry what to talk about. Smile and ask her daddy if you can carry her to the Dairy Queen. When you get there just follow her around as she shows you off to the other girls."

I said, "I'm not a bull at a 4-H show!"

Doc said, "Yes, you are. You are being inspected for breeding stock."

I am horrified, "What? I haven't bred with her. What are you talking about?"

Doc said, "It's simple, son. Females pick the father of their children. They look at how you act around her friends, around her parents and then she will want to see how you especially behave around your mother. All of this is important because if you are an ass, you will sire asinine children. Some women like that kind of man but most don't."

I was absolutely flabbergasted, again, by my granddaddy. But now that I think about it, it does make sense. Dating is checking each other out. All I wanted was to kiss her some more and I have already married her.

"Doc, I am going to her house at two-o'clock Sunday afternoon for hamburgers. I am going to ask her to the Dairy Queen, and I am going to kiss her goodnight. While we are riding around, I am going to ask about movies, books, religion and politics. That will cover it. I am not sure what there is left to talk about."

"Sounds like a plan, Iver. Keep your fly up. Don't let your pecker lead you astray."

At precisely two o'clock I rang the doorbell at the Reynolds' home. It wasn't a simple doorbell; it was the first part of the William Tell Overture. I should have taken that as a sign from God. Sissy opened the door and kissed me. I am not sure how she got her jeans on, but I believe it must have involved Crisco and pliers. I believe if they had been touched with a sharp object, they would have exploded. And she had a turtleneck shirt on that was so tight I could see the little flower on the front of her brassiere. All of these were signs that today was going to turn into an adventure. She grabbed my hand and pulled me into the living room. I wanted to greet Mr. and Mrs. Reynolds and give them a box of candy but she kissed me again. I asked, "Where are your parents? I have a little gift for them."

Sissy said, "They are in the dining room, and I told Daddy we are going to the Dairy Queen after dinner. We just need to be back by dark. I have to have my beauty sleep."

"That's fine but I thought I should ask your parents. It would be more proper."

"I already told them."

Sissy looked at me like I was crazy. She was fast.

Sissy said, "They don't care what I do. They both say, 'This is the '60's,'" I can make my own decisions. I'll just tell them where I'm going-- maybe."

This is not the impression that Mr. Reynolds gave me when he threatened my penis.

Dinner was kind of quiet. Mr. Reynolds asked if Doc was really my granddaddy. "Yes, ma'am", I answered

Mrs. Reynolds asked if my mother ever cooked. "No, ma'am." I said.

They both said that Big Jack would be missed, a pillar of the community.

Sissy finished her dinner first. I was finishing my second hamburger when I felt a foot with the toes wiggling go up my leg, I didn't miss a beat eating. Sissy looked at me with a blank stare. This is what Mama refers to as "a little wild ass heifer." Sissy is not a bovine, but she was acting like one. I'm not saying I didn't believe that was happening. I just didn't expect it to be so quick. I thought her legs must have been pretty long to reach under the table. She finally quit when I finished my glass of tea. I still had a problem, so I just left my napkin tucked in my belt like I had forgotten it.

I said, "Mr. and Mrs. Reynolds, would it be all right for Sissy and me to ride to the Dairy Queen and around the lake?"

I was trying to do my best, do things properly, even though Sissy did not see proper as a priority.

Mr. Reynolds said, "That's fine. Dairy Queen, ride around the lake and home by dark. Sunday night is a school night."

Sissy dragged me out the door. We got to the car, and she gave me a shock if you can believe that after the foot action.

"Iver, did you bring some Rooster Juice and Queen of Hearts?"

"No, woman! How do you know about that stuff?"

"The pit boss at the restaurant, Sterling, buys some and the other cook, Berta, told me about it. She said it will make you want to 'do it'. Does it?"

"No, Sissy. I didn't bring any."

"Have you tried it? Did it make you want to 'do it?'"

"I've tasted it, but it didn't make me want to 'do it.' "

"I want to drink some Queen of Hearts and see if it makes me want to 'do it.'"

"Sissy, I don't think you need any."

"I found a bottle of each in Daddy's underwear drawer with the dirty books."

"You snooped in your parent's bureau?"

"Sure, that's how you learn things. I found a box of rubbers and I took one. You want to see?"

"No, I don't want to know about your parent's sex life. You don't need to know about your parent's sex life!"

"I brought the rubber so we could do it."

"What? This is our first date? What are you thinking?"

"I'm thinking I want to get poked by your pecker with one of these on it."

"This conversation is all wrong."

"Iver, it is 1969. Haven't you seen all the posters about love? Free love? Have you listened to the radio? The Rolling Stones. 'Can't Get No Satisfaction?' I want to give you some satisfaction."

"Sissy, I am not that kind of man. Right now, I'm not sure what kind of man I am, but I am not going to have sex with you today. I do have morals."

"Well, it is your loss."

"I'm taking you back home. I can't be responsible for you."

"I am not going home."

"Yes, you are."

"You can't make me."

"Look, Sissy, you are about the prettiest girl I have ever seen. That's why I asked you out, met your parents, and worked at the restaurant. I just wanted to go out with you, maybe a little kissing to start with. I don't want to marry you."

"Who said anything about getting married? I didn't."

I said, "Well, generally, when people have sex, they are married or going to get married."

Sissy said, "What world do you live in? What about the stuff your granddaddy sells? Does he just sell it to married people?"

She was right. I have to say, she made the separation of love and lust. I didn't think girls made the separation. I always thought they were just into love, hearts and flowers. I didn't know young girls like that existed. I thought that the only ones that were like that were hookers. I thought, she is just a girl. Maybe she is a nymphomaniac, every normal guy's dream. So why isn't she my dream girl anymore? She scared me so bad I thought I was missing some of my equipment.

Sissy said, "I don't know why you are so worried about us having sex. It's not like I'm a virgin."

"What? So why did I have to meet your parents to have a date with you?"

"I've never had a boyfriend before."

"Huh? So, who...so where?"

"At the restaurant, at church camp, band room at school, locker room."

I was standing there with my mouth dropped open. I was turning down sex with a pretty girl who brought her own condom. I thought, "Just carry her home and write this off as an interesting experience".

"Hey, Iver, are you queer? You don't act queer."

"How do you know what queer acts like? No, I like girls. Apparently fast girls just don't turn me on."

"You are the first one to turn me down."

"What? How many have you had sex with?"

"Eight so far."

"Aren't you afraid of getting pregnant or getting some kind of disease?"

"I always have sex standing up. Everybody knows you can't get pregnant when you do it standing up. And I don't have sex with nasty people."

"Sissy, I am sorry to inform you, but you are a nasty fast-behind heifer."

So ended my pursuit of the prettiest girl I had ever seen. I was the dog that caught the car. I caught the car and couldn't do anything with it.

I had an epiphany. Women were the hunters, sly and cunning, and men were just innocent victims, oblivious that they were being stalked.

For some reason I went by Bet and Rudolph's house on the way home. Bet was at church. Rudolph said, "I heard you were going to the Reynolds house today for some courting and sparking."

"I did and I carried her back home. You want to know why? She wanted me to screw her and all we had ever done was kiss twice."

"You turned her down?"

"I think she scared me, to be honest. I have heard of fast women, but I never thought a girl that was seventeen would be that fast."

"Kind of bad to be that way at seventeen."

"She asked me if I was queer."

"Iver, for her to be seventeen and asking you questions like that, she knows a lot."

"I just decided that she isn't the girl I thought she was."

Rudolph looked at me kind of hard and said, "What are you going to do now?"

"I am going to go home and tell Mama and Daddy 'thank you' for going with me to the restaurant."

Rudolph said, "Don't say anything to anybody about the girl. Word will get around on its own."

"She isn't as pretty as she was."

"Next time, you need to grade a woman on more than looks. You'll miss a lot of good ones if you just grade them only on looks"

So ended my quest for Sissy Reynolds.

Chapter 14

Carry Your Problems to Daddy

I came downstairs that Monday morning to the smell of country ham. I was starting a new chapter in my life like I did every Monday morning. Mondays still are the best day, the start of something new. Now, it is years later, and I still like Mondays. I was not sure how that week's chapter would work out, but if it was as good as the smell of that country ham, it was going to be a keeper. And Monday is a good day to start something new.

Theola had us spoiled. Her cooking was wonderful, and her biscuits were good all day. She made a pan of biscuits Monday through Friday mornings. I took a biscuit, a piece of ham and some grape jelly and made a sandwich. I got a Pepsi out of the fridge and sat down. I had an appreciation of my simple life; no, I was living like a king.

Doc was already seated at the table, "Doc, are you finished with the first section of the paper?" I asked.

Doc said, "Yes, Son. Take all of it. I don't want to read any more tragedy. This bad news makes my heart hurt. I want to read a little good news."

Theola said, "I think I hear the bell on the front door. Iver, you finish your breakfast. I'll check."

I said, "Thank you, Theola." Being the doorman was part of my job.

Doc put his coffee cup in the sink and was looking out the kitchen window at the squirrels.

Doc leaned closer to the window, "It's been a long time since I've eaten squirrel. Iver, think you could get us a mess of squirrels after the first of the year?"

I said, "Yes, sir, but I'm not eating any. They look like fuzzy-tailed rats."

"Come on, boy. Flesh is flesh, muscle is muscle."

I said, "I'll get you a mess but I'm going to pass on eating 'em."

Theola walked back into the kitchen, "Doc there is a white woman out here that says she is your daughter."

I belched at that moment and the fizz came out of my nose. Doc straightened his tie and walked in the waiting room.

At the sight of the visitor, he said, "My girl! Mary Margaret! What a wonderful surprise. You have made quite a trip from West Virginia to North Carolina. Would you like some breakfast? Some coffee? A Pepsi?"

"Oh, Daddy, I was worried that you had moved again. I used the return address on my birthday card to find you."

"Yes, yes, girl. Come on in the kitchen and eat a little breakfast. Let's visit. I am so glad to see you."

Theola set another place and scrambled some more eggs. I hadn't eaten all the ham or biscuits.

Doc said, "My darling Mary Margaret, Mary Margaret. You are just as beautiful as your mother."

Mary Margaret said, "Thank you, Daddy."

Doc said, "Where are my manners? Mary Margaret, this is your nephew, Iver Johnson Murphy. Iver, this is your aunt, Mary Margaret Edwards. She is Eloise's daughter."

Aunt Mary Margaret said, "Nice to meet you. Daddy, who does he belong to?"

Doc said, "He belongs to Lauralee, Maraih's daughter. And this is Theola, our housekeeper."

Aunt Mary Margaret said, "I have never met Lauralee, but I have seen her photograph. She has blue eyes, too, doesn't she?"

Doc said, "Yes, all of my children have blue eyes and a few of the grandchildren."

There was a long pause in the conversation.

Doc finally said, "How is Eloise?"

Aunt Mary Margaret said, "She is dead, Daddy. I couldn't decide what to do with her, so I brought her here to you."

There was a very long pause.

Aunt Mary Margaret said, "Mama said that you would take care of things. I've got her in the trunk of my car wrapped up in a pretty bed sheet in a suitcase."

There was a pause that I thought lasted for eternity.

Doc said, "Mary Margaret, how long has your mother been dead?"

Aunt Mary Margaret said, "She died Sunday a week ago. I couldn't get up with John Oliver. He is somewhere in South America. I don't have a husband right now. I just figured the best thing to do was to let you handle things."

Doc said, "How cold is it in West Virginia?"

Aunt Mary Margaret said, "In the twenties and thirties. Some of the ski lodges are open."

"Mary Margaret how did Eloise die?", Doc asked.

Theola and I are looking at each other. There is a dead body in the trunk of Aunt Mary Margaret's car and Doc is asking if it is cold in West Virginia. It has been in the trunk of her car since last Sunday and she has driven her mother, the corpse, from West Virginia.

Aunt Mary Margaret said, "She was getting the leaves out of the gutters and fell off the roof."

Doc said, "She was still doing an aerial act at her age, an amazing woman."

Aunt Mary Margaret said, "There was some ice on the roof, and she just lost her footing. She said the ladder to reach the second story was too heavy for her."

Doc said, "Yes, she was a petite person. I always loved to see her on the high wire."

Theola and I were looking at each other. She was petite. That was why she was in a sheet in a suitcase.

Theola said, "Miss Mary Margaret, would you like some more coffee? Anything else?"

Aunt Mary Margaret said, "No, thank you. This breakfast was delicious. I hope I haven't disturbed your schedule, dropping in for breakfast."

Theola said, "Oh no, Missy, my day isn't on a strict schedule. I am sorry about your mother."

Aunt Mary Margaret, "Thank you. Mama was fearless. I thought it fitting for her to die in an aerial act. She was so feisty; I wondered how she would be if she ever got down and I had to care for her."

Doc said, "Iver, what is the temperature outside?"

I got up and stepped out on the back porch. When I walked back in, I said, "It's thirty-six and the wind is blowing."

Doc took his cup out of the sink and rinsed it out and poured a half a cup of coffee. He reached in the cabinet and pulled out a bottle of Wild Turkey and finished filling the coffee cup. I had never seen him do that before, drink alcohol before noon.

Doc said, "Mary Margaret, does anybody know that Eloise is dead?"

Aunt Mary Margaret said, "Yes, the deputy that took the report. The coroner came and declared her dead. I could have told him that she was dead."

Doc said, "I was just curious why you didn't call the funeral home."

Aunt Mary Margaret said, "I did, Daddy, the funeral home handled the cremation."

There was a collective sigh in that kitchen. I don't think Aunt Mary Margaret heard the sigh, but I sure did.

Aunt Mary Margaret said, "Daddy, I have no idea where to bury her ashes. The minister helped me organize a memorial service. Her bridge club, the ladies circle, the book club and her gymnastic students came to her service. There was a nice crowd. I brought the memory book for you to look at. I thought you might remember some of the folks."

"Thank you, that was very thoughtful."

Aunt Mary Margaret looked at Doc, "I just thought, for some reason, that you needed to decide what to do with her ashes. We don't have a family plot."

Doc said, "I don't have one, but that can be remedied. Iver, who takes care of the cemetery at the Presbyterian Church?"

I said, "Mr. Harris has a map. I think that is who you need to talk to. Isaac Harris."

Doc stood up with his coffee cup in hand, "Y'all visit for a few minutes."

Doc walked into his office and got out the phone book from his desk. He started dialing the phone. Then he put the phone down and walked over and closed the door. He came back in a few minutes and said, "If it is alright with you, Mary Margaret, we can bury your mother in the cemetery where I am going to be buried."

Aunt Mary Margaret just busted out crying. Doc stepped over to her chair at the breakfast table. Aunt Mary Margaret stood up and Doc wrapped his arms around her. She was sobbing. She looked a lot like my mama, especially crying with Doc's arms around her. There was nothing I could do to help. She looked a little older than Mama and her hair was a little grayer than Mama's. Seeing a woman that could be my mama crying, sobbing, gave me a sense of helplessness. She was an adult and adults aren't supposed to be weak and crying. For some reason, I felt I needed to protect this woman, to comfort her. I stepped around the table and patted and rubbed her back. It was all I could think to do that might help.

Aunt Mary Margaret hiccupped a couple of times. Theola handed her one of Doc's handkerchiefs off the end of the ironing board.

Theola said, "Missy, I know you are tired from your trip. I bet you drove straight through, didn't you?"

Aunt Mary Margaret nodded and sniffed.

Theola put her arm around Mary Margaret shoulders, "Come on upstairs with me. Iver, go out to her car and get her things. Miss Mary Margaret, I think you need to lie down for a while."

When I got Aunt Mary Margaret's things out of her car, I looked in the suitcase in the trunk. There was a brass urn shaped like the ginger jar on the mantle at Big Judy's, carefully wrapped up. I looked at it for a few minutes. I decided to bring it in the house. I carried all of Aunt Mary Margaret's stuff up to her room. The door was open and Theola was lighting the heater.

I said, "Aunt Mary Margaret, I think I will put Miss Eloise on the mantle in the parlor, if it is alright with you?" I wasn't sure what to call her and I thought Miss Eloise would be proper enough.

Aunt Mary Margaret nodded, "Yes, Iver. That will be fine."

I put the brass urn on the mantle. She looked kind of lonely there, so I went to the kitchen looking for some flower vases. I couldn't find any.

I said, "Doc, I'm going to the store for a few minutes for some vases."

Doc was holding his coffee cup, "Fine, Iver. I'm going to just sit here for a little while."

Doc looked kind of old and sad. Well, he was old, and I knew he loved all his wives. He reached into his pocket and handed me his car keys.

When I walked in the store, Daddy was putting Pepsi's in the cooler.

Daddy said, "How are you doing, Iver?"

"Well Daddy," and I stopped. Daddy stood up and dried his hands on his apron.

"What is it, Son?"

"A sister of Momma's is at the office, Mary Margaret. She brought her mother from West Virginia for Doc to see about burying her."

Daddy said, "She drove a corpse from West Virginia?"

"No, no, no, Daddy. I'm sorry. She brought Eloise, Doc's second wife, back as ashes. She didn't know what to do with them. She is pretty tired, so Theola has put her in one of the bedrooms upstairs, turned on the heater. I put the urn on the mantelpiece. The mantel looked kind of bare so I came to see if there are some vases or something I can use. The camellias are blooming so I can break some of them."

"Son, you are on the right track, but we are going to call the florist. That is your Momma's …. half-sister's Momma, I think. I am not sure what all the connections would be. Call the florist and tell them the situation. There isn't anything they haven't heard before."

Daddy shook his head, rolled his eyes and shrugged his shoulders at the same time. Daddy said, "We need to call the house and tell Mariah and Judith. I'm not sure what Emily Post would have to say about this. Son, stay here for a few minutes and let me run to the farm to tell Lauralee".

About that time MaMariah and Big Judy walked in. I was old enough to keep the store. I guess I was old enough to relate family news or whatever kind of news this appeared to be.

Big Judy and MaMariah walked over to the cooler, and both pulled out a Mountain Dew and then both walked over to the Lance jar and got a pack of square nabs. MaMariah said, "How are you doing, Iver? I didn't think you would be here keeping the store. Is there anything going on?"

I said, "Well, something came up and Daddy needed to talk to Mama."

Big Judy and MaMariah nodded their heads. Both took a bite of a nab. They liked the Toast Chee flavor.

I said, "I guess I need to tell you. A woman named Mary Margaret has brought her mother Eloise's ashes to Doc for him to bury. Eloise was one of his wives. I put the woman's ashes on the mantelpiece. I came to get something to put some camellias in, but Daddy said we needed flowers from the florist."

Big Judy said, "And Walter is exactly right. Mariah, you call the florist and have two matching arrangements for the mantel and an arrangement for his foyer. Have them make the door badge with black ribbon instead of white. I don't want anyone thinking Erastus is the one dead. It will still be proper but not as noticeable."

MaMariah said, "Erastus loved this woman, and probably still does and always will. I know he loves Mary Margaret, and he sure loves Lauralee."

MaMariah stepped behind the counter and got the phone book. She dialed the florist. All I could hear about the conversation was, "You don't need to worry about who died; you just need to fix the flowers and deliver them." MaMariah had a little Texas Pete in her tone.

Big Judy said, "Mariah, let's ride to Erastus' office and offer Mary Margaret our condolences. And we need to get with Theola about fixing a nice meal tonight and for lunch tomorrow."

MaMariah and Big Judy, both pulled me across the counter and kissed me on the cheek. They were walking away, and I heard Big Judy say, "Erastus and his marrying, not divorcing, polygamous, Mormon-assed self, can't help but love the old bastard."

Daddy got back to the store and called Preacher Jenkins. It took Daddy a few minutes to relate the highlights of the saga. Preacher Jenkins said he would go by Doc's office later this afternoon and talk to Doc and Aunt Mary Margaret. I said, "Daddy, what did Mama say?"

"Lauralee said she had always wanted to meet some of her siblings, and she was going to welcome her with open arms. She said they had a lot in common."

Everything went just fine. I suggested Big Judy write to Emily Post and tell her how we handled things. At least write to Ann Landers.

That evening the folks from the funeral home brought some folding chairs over to the office. Wednesday morning, all of us were at the graveside service including Rudolph, Bet, Henry, Theola, Gene and Roy. Preacher Jenkins did things just right. Theola sang "Asleep in the Arms of Jesus." When Theola was singing, I imagined that was how angels must sound. It was beautiful. We all ceremoniously signed the memory book. We left Momma, Mary Margaret and Doc by themselves to visit. I went and stayed with Daddy after the service. I didn't want to intrude on Momma, Doc and Aunt Mary Margaret's time together. Theola was there to take care of them.

Aunt Mary Margaret left the next morning, Thursday morning, with a promise that we would go to West Virginia to visit. She said she had a poster of Doc's circus that I could have if I came to visit. Talk about bribery!

We waved at her car as she left. Doc said, "I am sorry Eloise is dead, but it was nice to visit with Mary Margaret. I need to make a road trip and visit all my children. I wonder if Mariah would want to ride with me. All of them are on this side of the Rockies. Well, except John Oliver. He has been in South America for a long time."

I said, "Doc, if MaMariah doesn't want to go, I'll go with you. Give me the names and addresses and I will work on a plan for us, get us some maps and figure the mileage. You could write them letters and tell them you want to come for a visit."

Doc looked at me and smiled where I could see his gold teeth.

Chapter 15

An Honorable Man

It had gotten cold quickly in November. I don't think it was really that cold, but that fall had been so pleasant-- no hurricanes, no big storms. That was the first frosty little snap.

Doc said, "About a week after the first frost the Artificial Blood Circulation business will pick up. The cold weather brings out the 'ritis."

I didn't have the nerve to ask him what the cooler weather will do with the Rooster Juice and Queen of Hearts Elixir sales. I am afraid he might tell me something I didn't want to know.

Doc said, "The cooler weather slows up the tonic business. The women wear more clothes and the men put their shirts back on. Clothes cover up a lot of ugly men and women. Paint covers a lot of the extra ugly on women. Ugly men just stay ugly."

But that Monday got a little off center, quick. I went to the front door to unlock it with a broom in hand to sweep the steps and there was an old man with bibbed overalls. I had seen him in town, but I had never seen him in Daddy's store. He was sitting on the steps, barefooted; and there was a little frost that morning. I thought he was a colored man at first or maybe a mulatto, but his features were definitely white. I looked hard at him. Yes, it was a white man. He was so dirty he looked colored. A little waft of aroma came by me which made the inside of my nose burn. It is rough for a man to smell like that on Monday morning and with frost on the ground. His feet were huge, swollen and purple-ish.

On his inside right ankle was an ugly, black wound. I could tell that he had cut off the inside of his pant leg to keep it from touching the scaly mess on his ankle. He was trying to stand up as I was opening the door. It was a pitiful sight. He was really suffering. I jumped down the steps and took the old man by the arm.

"Please, may I help you, Sir?"

"Yes, son. Thank you."

I helped him into the treatment room and sat him down. I stepped in the kitchen where Doc was drinking his coffee and reading the paper and hollered, "Doc, you need to come in here!" I didn't intend to shout like I did. I was a little panicked.

Doc walked in and said to the man, "Hello, friend. I am Dr. Edwards. What seems to be the problem?" This was the first time he hadn't said "Masseuse and Artificial Blood Circulator" as part of his title.

"I'm Nelson Munroe, Doc. I've got a problem I hope you can help me with. I don't have any money to pay."

"I'm not going to turn you out for lack of money. I'm just a plain old country doctor. You can bring me some eggs, OK?"

Doc pulled his glasses out of his pocket and put them on. Then he pulled a little note pad out of the desk. I was suddenly reminded that Doc was a real doctor, not a root doctor, not a quack, not a charlatan. Doc got up and pulled the door closed to the waiting room. I really didn't know what to do. I just stood there and waited to be told. I walked out the front door and around to the kitchen door. I got my morning Pepsi out of the Frigidaire.

I stood there and Theola asked, "Why are you standing in here and not helping Dr. Edwards?"

I said, "Doc is seeing a new patient and he closed the door."

"Well, Iver, he is a doctor."

I said, "Yes, but there is a sick man in there. I have just not thought of him as a real doctor. I just see him with that big crazy machine and tonic. And seeing him make the stuff, his tonics, here in the kitchen. ``

Theola said, "Dr. Edwards set up a practice here about fifteen or twenty years ago. I am not sure exactly when."

"I didn't know that."

'He was a doctor that would come to your home. I think that was about 1955, sometime along there. I don't know why he left."

I figured in my head: I was born in 1952: this was 1969. That would be seventeen years ago, 1954. He was here when I was a baby. He must have come by to see me sometimes. That sneaky old man. He has known me my whole life.

Theola said, "He even delivered babies at home."

I was shocked at the news. Again, I had to put Doc in a different light.

Theola said, "He was the cheapest doctor to deliver a baby. If you didn't have any money, he would take a bushel of sweet potatoes. He was with a lot of mamas and babies when there was no one else."

I was learning more and more about Doc. I wondered what else he that had done I didn't know about.

Doc stepped in the kitchen and said, "Theola, would you get the white enamel foot tub and bring it in here with some hot water? There is one in the cabinet somewhere. And put a capful of Clorox in the water. He reached under the sink and got a box of Epson salts. He walked back in the office, turned around and came back to the kitchen. He got an apron off the back of the door and a hand full of dishtowels.

Doc said to me, "Come here and talk to this patient while I work on his leg."

I walked in behind him, and he said, "Iver, this is Mr. Munroe. Mr. Munroe, this is my grandson, Iver."

Doc had never introduced me like this before. I was a little stunned.

I said, "Hello, Mr. Munroe. Nice to meet you. Do you live here in town?"

"No, son. I live in Beaver Dam. Doc treated me and my wife years ago when we lived here. I knew I needed an old doctor to fix this leg."

Theola brought the big enameled foot tub in the office. She had the tub in one hand and a steaming pitcher in the other. Doc helped Mr. Munroe put his foot in the foot tub and slowly poured the hot water over his leg. I could smell a little Clorox. Doc shook some Epson salt in the foot tub and stirred it around a little with a tongue depressor. Theola was back in a minute with another pitcher of hot water and she slowly poured it into the foot tub.

Doc said, "Mr. Munroe, we need to get some of this dead flesh off this wound so it will drain. This is a pretty big spot."

Mr. Munroe said, "I had it kind a clean this summer. I did it the old-timey way and let the maggots work it."

It was all I could do not to gag. The body odor of the old man, the rotten wound, and now he was talking about maggots. It was about to get me. Doc touched his chin so I would close my mouth.

Doc said, "Iver, you might not have ever heard of using maggots to clean a wound. That's an old-time way that works well as long as the flies are buzzing. Flies eat the dead flesh and leave the living tissue. Battlefield medicine."

I was supposed to be talking but it was a challenge. I was having a time holding my biscuit down. "Mr. Munroe, how did you hurt your leg?"

"Back in July, I was stepping across the fence, like I belong to, and the fence post broke. It was a lightered post, and it splintered. A big piece stuck in my leg. I pulled it out. It didn't pain me much."

(A lightered post is a fence post made from the heart wood of a pine tree, preferably longleaf pine. The wood has a lot of resin, and it will not rot for a long time so it is good for fenceposts, but they will break.)

I counted on my fingers. He had that wound for five months.

Doc was pouring the steaming water over his legs, "Have you got much feeling in your legs?"

"No, Doc."

"How long have your feet been swollen?"

"Oh, they've been like that for a couple of years. My Ma's were like that. It runs in the family."

"Ma put moss in her shoes and soaked her feet in Mullen tea. They still stayed 'swolled' up. I just keep them propped. Was doing good 'til right lately."

I kind of caught a gag in my throat. Here was an old white man with swollen purple feet and a gash on his leg that smelled like rotten flesh. The smell was coming up with the steam. It was rotten, like roadkill.

Mr. Munroe started to shake a little. Doc asked him, "Do you need a little nip to calm the shake?"

I knew what that meant. I jumped up and stepped to the kitchen. I pulled out the first bottle I got to, Wild Turkey, and got a jelly glass. I was walking back in the room and heard Mr. Munroe say, "I didn't want y'all to smell liquor on me this early in the morning."

Doc said, "Don't try to do without when you come to see me. I don't judge anybody's habits. A man's got to do what a man's got to do."

I put the glass and the bottle on the desk. Doc turned and poured the glass full and handed it to Mr. Munroe. He downed it in one gulp. No gasp, no reaction, just a calm look in his eyes. It dawned on me that he was an alcoholic. He didn't want to be judged, so he came to Doc when he got concerned about his leg.

Mr. Munroe said, "I remember you when you were here years ago, Doc."

Doc said, "I don't think……"

"You came to my house when my wife couldn't have her baby."

Doc looked down and poured some water from the pan on his leg with a paper cup.

"I am sorry for your loss, Mr. Munroe. She was a beautiful woman and had a beautiful baby."

Mr. Munroe's eyes got watery looking. "I waited too long to come and get you. I just wasn't thinking." Doc's eyes were getting watery too.

"Stop right there. Mr. Munroe, things happen. I believe her heart would have stopped if she had been in a hospital in New York City. And we saved the baby, right?"

Mr. Munroe said, "Yes, she is a beautiful girl. I knew I couldn't take care of her."

Doc was nodding his head. "The Reynolds were so happy to get her, and she is a beautiful young girl. That was a good call."

Mr. Monroe was still holding the jelly glass, "I named her Celeste after her mother. I think they kept the name, but they call her Sissy. I check on her along."

Doc looked at me and said, "Don't you know Sissy?"

"Yes, Sir. I met her at the revival at the Pentecostal church."

Mr. Munroe said, "I went one night and listened from outside. I figured they were in there."

This was such a humble man; I couldn't help but like him. And I would never say a thing about Sissy to him or anyone else. I wouldn't break this old man's heart. It was in shambles as it was.

Doc said, "Let's see if we can clean this wound."

Mr. Munroe lifted his foot out of the bucket and I felt a gag coming up again. It was a green and gray and white mess coming out of the foot tub. I held on to the wall. Then the stench hit me.

"Iver, go get me a footstool from the front room."

I got the stool and put in front of Mr. Munroe. Doc put a few dish towels on the stool and put Mr. Munroe's foot on it. Then the tedious picking began. Doc got little pieces of scab to come off until there was a sore about the size of an Anacin bottle. The smell was overpowering, the wound and Mr.Munroe.

Doc called to Theola, "Could you get us some more hot water? Iver, pour this out in the backyard next to the oak tree."

I was relieved to get up and carry the foot tub out. Some fresh air did me good. Theola rinsed it out with Clorox this time. I carried it back in and Theola followed me with two pitchers of hot water.

Theola said, "I've got some knives sharpened, then boiled 'em about ten minutes, Doc. Just thinking ahead."

"Thank you, Theola."

"Mr. Munroe, I don't think you got all of that splinter out. I think that is what is causing part of this problem. Let's wash it off one more time."

Mr. Munroe said, "It didn't seem that it was that big when I did it. Peeled a good piece of flesh off, didn't I?"

Theola walked in with the pot with the knives in it. She had another handful of dishtowels.

"You read my mind, Theola. How about staying and helping me for a minute?"

"Are you ready for me to get this splinter out, Mr. Munroe? I need to open this up a little so I can get it out and it can drain some."

"Theola, could you hold Mr. Munroe's hands? And Iver, could you hold his knee? And I'm going to be fast."

With no more discussion, Doc reached in the pot, got a metal kitchen knife and split open the flesh. With the tip of the knife he flicked out a splinter about the size of a kitchen match.

"Mr. Munroe, I think this is part of the reason it wouldn't heal. Iver, take my car and go to the drug store. I'll call them and tell them what we need."

I was out of the office like a shot. The combination of the stinking wound and Mr. Munroe's body odor got the best of me. Fresh air can do amazing things. As I was driving, I was thinking about Mr. Munroe being Sissy's real father. He was a nice man. Her real name was Celeste and Doc delivered her. That stinking old man was the father of the prettiest girl I had ever seen and the first girl I kissed. Like the song on Walt Disney, "It's a Small, Small World." I was going to do something when I got off work that would probably make me an enemy for life. I was going to tell Sissy she needed to straighten up for all her parents' sake.

The girl at the counter at the drugstore had all the stuff Doc needed in a paper sack waiting for me. I pulled out my wallet and she said, "No charge. Dr. Edwards told us who it was for." The pharmacist knew Doc and Mr. Munroe. That's the way it is in a small town.

When I got back to the office with my bag of medicine there was another juice glass on the desk. Doc's was about half full and Mr. Munroe's was empty. I could tell that they stopped talking when I walked in. I guess they were talking about something I didn't need to hear.

Mr. Munroe's foot was back in the foot tub. It was fresh water because I could see the steam coming off of it. And smelled the Clorox. Doc said, "Thank you, Iver, for running to the store."

"Yes, thank you, son," said Mr. Munroe.

Doc painted around the wound with Iodine and shook Sulfur Powder in the raw meat. He wrapped the foot in gauze and then an Ace bandage fastened with a safety pin. The soaked foot was a light lavender. I guess the dirt kept the sun off of it.

Doc said, "Iver, go get my black bedroom slippers. I think Mr. Munroe can fit in them."

"I want to give you a pair of slippers for you to get home in. When the swelling goes down you need some soft shoes to protect your feet. When you get some slippers, you can bring mine back."

I got the slippers, but I kept thinking about that other dirty foot. I knew this was Doc's way of giving the old man some slippers.

"Now, Mr. Munroe, I want you to keep your foot elevated all you can. I want you to take this bottle of penicillin, three pills a day. And change the dressing on the foot. Sprinkle some sulfur on the wound. All the stuff you need is in the bag."

"Thank you, Doc."

"I want you to come back in a week if it isn't better, OK? Or better yet just come by for a visit."

"I'll come anyway. I'll get you a mess of collards. I've got some pretty ones."

I stepped in the kitchen to see Theola putting all the dish towels in the trash. "There is no way on Earth that I can bleach these towels enough to use them again. There is nothing nastier than old nasty men, white or colored. When I buy groceries tomorrow, I'll just buy another turn of dish towels".

I was sure about the nasty part, and he was pretty rank. But Theola was right about the towels. I took the garbage can out back and dumped it in the burn barrel. The little metal knife was in there too. And I added a little gasoline to the barrel to make sure it burned. When I walked back in the kitchen, Doc was sitting at the table.

"Theola, I didn't hire you to be a nurse. Thank you for stepping in."

Theola looked at Doc. "I remember when that child was born. It wasn't your fault that woman died. It was that old bastard's fault. I've never understood why grown men start drinking when their woman is in labor. He was too drunk to get a doctor and when he sobered up, she was about dead. It was too late for the momma and about too late for that baby. You did what you had to do."

Like an idiot, I blurted out, "What did you have to do?"

"I couldn't save the mother, so I cut the baby out right there on the bed. The baby lived but just barely. I carried the baby to the hospital in my car. She had a rough go for a week or so, but she survived."

"Munroe blames himself, as he should. I couldn't tell him it was his fault in the office. He already knows it and always will. I'm surprised he hasn't drunk himself to death before now. The whole situation just broke my heart. I did the best I could, but I couldn't save that woman. I was so upset that I closed my practice and went back to the circus. I made sure the little girl had a good home. The mother got buried in a decent manner.

"I wish I could help him let it go. Sometimes the past follows you like a shadow. The only time it's gone is when you are hiding. He hides in a bottle. It happens to many a person."

The three of us stood there in silence.

Doc said, "I wonder if he has any wood. He doesn't need to be chopping wood with that foot. Theola, do you know who I can hire to get a load of wood for him?"

Sure enough, next Monday morning Mr. Munroe was back with three of the biggest heads of collards I had ever seen. They were green as poison. "Doc, do you want to know the secret of my beautiful collards?", he asked.

"Well yes. I've never seen anything exactly like these."

"I empties my chamber pot around them every morning."

(A chamber pot is a container that people use to urinate or defecate in at night, so they don't have to go to the outhouse in the dark. Not everyone has an indoor toilet.)

Doc, Theola, nor I could say anything but, "Thank you."

Mr. Munroe left with Doc's slippers on.

Theola said, "I'm not cooking 'em."

I said, "I'm not eating 'em if you cook 'em."

Doc said, "Well, he is an honorable man. He promised collards and we got collards. We just got too much information. We didn't need to know Paul Harvey's 'Rest of the Story.'"

I took the collards to Momma's chickens. She said she wouldn't tell the chickens how Mr. Munroe fertilized his garden.

Chapter 16

Master of His Destiny

Tuesday was kind of slow and Doc got the idea that we needed to spruce up the Artificial Blood Circulation Machine. He said it needed to look more medical. My idea was to paint the bike red. My idea was rejected but I had to take a shot at it.

Doc liked to tinker with things. He wanted to add new red taillights that he got from the junkyard and wire up the little light bulbs. I kind of thought that one day the board was going to catch on fire.

"Iver, we need to make all of this more medical looking. I want you to paint the bicycle all white; it's going to take two coats. Let's leave the board black and the lights like they are, but I want to add some more toggle switches and a couple of blinkers. We can add some more identification plates with numbers under the switches. Let's see if all the lights burn."

"I can go to the store and get some Rust-o-leum paint. Daddy keeps some electrical stuff. I'll poke around and see what I can find."

"Don't forget to get a brush and some paint thinner. Go by the auto parts and see if there are some gauges, we can flush mount on the board, like on a hotrod."

"Doc, I can make some brass plates with numbers and stuff. You know, the tags Daddy stamps to put on dog collars?"

"That sounds good, Iver. Let me give you some money."

I had to give it to the old man; he liked the flashy stuff, his hair, his clothes, his car.

I went to the store, talked to everybody, gathered up what we needed, put the stuff in a box, including a Merita Spanish Bar Cake, wrote up the ticket, rang up the stuff, and sat down on the liar's bench with Daddy.

I said, "Well Daddy, I appreciate you and Mama going to the restaurant for me."

Daddy looked at me and said, "You're welcome. How did the date with Sissy go?"

"I don't think I am going out with her again."

"I'm sorry it worked out like that, Iver."

"Daddy, I learned a lot in a short time. Women pick us; we don't pick them."

"How do you figure that, son?"

"Sissy had already decided we were going to have sex. That girl is fast, and I didn't know it. I hadn't even considered doing that."

"Did you have sex with her?"

"No, Daddy! I don't want my name in the paper in a wedding announcement. I have heard how it can get out of hand. Sex one time and BANG! You're engaged."

"I'm proud of you son. Sex is really…"

"Whoa, Daddy. All you are going to do is make me want to dig a hole and bury myself."

"OK," Daddy said and laughed. "I'm sure Doc will give you the right advice."

"Daddy," I said with a somber voice, "You have no idea what that old man has told me."

I was back at the office by ten. I got the sheets spread out to protect the floor and started painting the Bone Cracker Bicycle. It was going to take two coats of paint. I turned the heater up so the paint would dry faster. Doc was fiddling with the board and the lights. He had a whole box of pieces and parts, a Craftsman electric drill, a tack hammer, screw drivers, a tool kit to do surgery on his board. He even had a circuit tester. Doc reminded me of a craftsman working. I guess doctors were craftsman at heart.

I stood up, moved to the other side of the bike, looked at Doc and said, "Doc, you are a real doctor, aren't you?"

Doc didn't stop painting. "Yes, why do you ask?"

"Why don't you advertise and treat sick people? You treated Mr. Munroe."

Doc said, "I could, but I don't want to treat sick bodies. I want people to be happier with their lives. We've talked about this before. The tonic gives them their dreams back. And the blood circulator doesn't do any harm, just gets them loosened up. Years from now doctors may use this for some kind of therapy. It may even be good for some people."

"But, Doc, there are a lot of sick people in the world."

"There are also a lot of sad people looking for happiness."

"Maybe you should be a psychiatrist."

"Well, I talk to all of my customers. I ask them about their lives."

"And another thing, Doc, why do you call them customers instead of patients?"

Doc said, "Because I am selling them something, not curing them. I sell dreams."

"That makes sense to me. Wonder what I can sell to make people happy."

"Well, son, I'll tell you what makes people happy: food, shelter, and sex. They want good food, a nice place to stay, and some companionship. Simple. By the way, Iver, how did the date with Sissy Reynolds work out?"

"Well, Doc, she was a little fast for me. She had the idea that we were going to have sex."

"Did you?"

"No, but I could have."

We both were quiet for a few minutes and then Doc said, "Why didn't you take the opportunity?"

"I guess I was scared. I kind of think of married people having sex, or if they are going to get married. And I can't see myself being married to Sissy. I don't think she is going to be the marrying type."

"Iver, you do know that people who are not married have sex don't you?"

"Of course, I know that. I just realized that there wasn't any attraction except sex. We would just be using each other. And I thought the first time would be very special. It would have just been sport sex."

"Sport sex. That is a good one, Iver. But you're right. Make it special because you'll never forget the first time. I remember the first time with all of my wives."

Oh, no. I'm going to hear something I don't want to know. Why am I telling my granddaddy this? Doc is going to think I am queer. Sex is all a boy my age thinks about. I had the perfect chance and turned it down. I didn't even feel a titty.

"Doc, you don't think I'm queer, do you?"

"No, son, you are not queer. You just think too much. You do know how it all works, don't you?"

"Of course, I do. I've seen the movies in the back of the sandwich shop."

"What movies, boy?"

"Rudolph told me that at the back of McFarland's Fish Camp on Friday nights you can watch dirty movies. You can see McFarland having sex with the woman that's his waitress."

Doc stopped working and looked at me. "What? That old fart?"

"He makes the movies. Do you know him? He has dyed-black hair."

"I know exactly who you are talking about. I've eaten in that restaurant."

"The girl that is the waitress is the girl in the movies."

"Damn."

"That's what I said when I saw her at church."

"Whoa, Iver. You don't know her circumstances. She might not have known any better. But I would have said the same thing."

Doc stood up and put the tack hammer down. He stood there like he was thinking, "That's something I would have thought would be in Atlanta or Richmond, not here. I guess we have made it into the 20th century."

Doc walked to the desk and took a drink of coffee. "So how much does he charge you to watch the movies?"

"It is a dollar to watch, and you can get a sandwich and a drink, but you have to pay for that extra. The only thing that really bothers me is that Mr. McFarland keeps his socks and shoes on. I wonder if he is ashamed of his feet. Maybe he thinks he isn't naked if he keeps his shoes and socks on."

"Are the movies color or black and white?"

"They are in color. And I think he must dye his body hair."

"What?"

"As old as he is, I'm pretty sure his hair isn't black all over."

"I wish you hadn't said that. Now I have a picture of him naked with socks and shoes, dying his privates."

"Doc, I kind of think it is funny."

"No, Iver. It's sad any way you look at it, from dying his hair to filming himself having sex. He is keeping his youth. He is proving to himself that he is still young."

"Doc, how old are you?"

"I'm old enough to sleep alone and young enough not to want to."

"I didn't mean to insult you."

"You didn't, boy. I like being old. I say what I want to say, do what I want to do, and McFarland proves we can still have sex."

I could not believe he said that. He knows I know that he and MaMariah are sparking.

"Iver, Mariah and I have been talking about getting married legally."

"Won't you need to get divorced several times?"

"No, officially I am a widower. My first wife died recently. Miss Judith saw it in The News and Observer and asked me if that wasn't her. Kind of hurt my feelings that our daughter didn't get up with me."

I looked at Doc. He had a sad look in his eyes.

"I get up with her on her birthday and at Christmas. I send a card with some money, and I always put a return address on the envelope. None of the cards have ever come back. I leave them alone. I have caused enough heartache. Sarah, that was my first wife, divorced me years ago and got remarried but I still thought of her as my wife."

"Doc, have you always thought of MaMariah as your wife?"

"Oh, yes! I have always loved her dearly and still do. It was just after Big Jack shot me and Mariah and Lauralee found out that life got complicated. It was just easier if I stayed away."

"So why did you come back?"

"I still love Mariah; I have always loved her. I didn't know Lauralee hated me so, but that is out of the way. And you boys are just icing on the cake. How do you think Lauralee will feel about us getting married? "

I guess I was shocked that Doc was talking to me about people's feelings, adult people's feelings. At heart, I still thought of myself as a child when anyone spoke of feelings. Grown people talk about feelings. Children are told about feelings. I was kind of taken aback when I realized Doc was asking my opinion. I suddenly perceived that Doc thought of me as an adult, maybe not an adult but grown enough to have some sense. I know Momma wants MaMariah to be happy. Why shouldn't she be happy? I want MaMariah to be happy, and I want Doc to be happy.

"Doc, I know Momma wants MaMariah to be happy. Every child wants their parents to be happy. Happy parents make life easy and if getting married would make her happy, I know Momma will be all for it." God knows I hoped so.

Doc was nodding his head.

"So, when y'all get married, where are you going to live? Are you going to move in with Momma, Daddy, Gene, Roy and MaMariah?"

"I haven't got that far. I know she doesn't need to move too far away from Miss Judith."

"Yes, sir, that is a fact. Bet cooks and MaMariah totes their lunch over to Big Judy's."

"What does Miss Judith do for supper?"

"She likes to eat supper alone. Her and Big Jack always ate supper together and listened to the news."

"So, Mariah carries enough for supper?"

" No, Bet cooks a plain pound cake every Monday and that is what Big Jack and Big Judy always ate for supper, buttermilk and pound cake. She says that if you eat the same thing every day you won't get sick. She says cows eat the same thing every day and they don't get sick."

"Well, she does have a point. Iver, what do you think about an Air Steam, beautiful camper trailers?"

"I don't want to hurt your feelings, Doc, but if y'all move in an Air Stream, MaMariah may have to cook, and I don't think that is a good idea. Big Jack said things improved greatly after Bet started cooking. He said the two of them together, MaMariah and Big Judy, could ruin boiled water. And MaMariah sits on the porch summer and winter. Maybe if you built a porch on the camper? I just don't know.

"Doc, I don't think your office is too far from Big Judy for MaMariah, and you will have Theola to cook supper."

"I don't know. Let me think. Mariah can drive to Big Judy's for lunch every day,"

There was a long pause in the conversation.

"Iver, you're right. I guess I was thinking about years ago in the circus. Those campers were so cozy. I liked living in them. In fact, Mariah and Lauralee traveled with me for a couple of years. We had a wonderful time, but it wasn't a place for little children. We just fell into the routine of me coming to stay a few weeks during the year. It worked out pretty well until the incident in Richmond. Your mama was fifteen when Big Jack shot me. Maybe it was for the best. Lauralee had always begged to come with me to the circus. I thought she needed to finish school. On the road I couldn't pay a lot of attention to either one of them. The last thing I wanted was something to happen to her. The circus is a different lifestyle. The relationships you make are kind of like the ones you make in school. Your best friend changes with the years."

"I wouldn't know about that. The only school friends I have ever had have been at Sunday school...."

"You have missed some things you don't even know about."

Maybe I should have not judged school so harshly.

"When we were on the road, the group we travelled with became a little society or a little town. There were people that came and went and some that stayed. I think it would be difficult for a child or maybe not. Looking back, I guess I could have had her with me a few weeks in the summer. I might have just not wanted the responsibility. Truth be known, I think I liked a part-time family."

"Doc, was that the way with all of your wives?"

"I guess so, Iver. I made enough money to send all of them money. The circus didn't travel all year, so I had time to visit all of them.

I think I told you my first wife divorced me in later years, after I had four wives."

"I hate to say this, Doc, but what were you thinking about getting married so many times? You knew it was against the law."

"Yes, I knew it was wrong. I just thought I was slick enough not to get caught. I had a wonderful system going until Big Jack shot me. And Iver, I'll just tell you---I just love women, all of them. I love the way they smell, the way their skin feels. I have always been a weak man when it comes to women. I love courting them, the wonder of the first kiss."

"Hold it, Doc. Don't tell too much. Don't forget you are my granddaddy."

"You're right, boy. I will tell you that I have always loved Mariah the most. I don't know why. Something about her, even after all these years. My other wives, I have loved them all, but Mariah......I just can't tell you why I have always been drawn to Mariah. After Big Jack shot me, I still kept up with Mariah and Lauralee and you boys when you came along. I even came to town once in a while and sat in a car in front of Mariah's house to get a glimpse of her."

"That sounds like something out of a trashy romance novel. Are you sure you're not making this up to spin me a tale?"

"No, it's all the truth. Ask Bet and Rudolph. I would stop at their house occasionally and get the news. I think I have gotten to the age where I want to enjoy Mariah; neither of us is getting any younger. I just swallowed my pride and became the 'master of my destiny' again. I have worked around and got my true love again. It wasn't as hard as I thought it would be.

"Lauralee was a tough nut to crack but I can understand why she felt the way she did. She was trying to protect her mother. She was justified. I hurt and embarrassed all of them. I wasn't who John and Judith had in mind for Mariah. I should have kept in closer touch during the years."

"Do you think you could have kept up with having all the wives if Big Jack hadn't caught you?"

"Oh, yes, I had everything scheduled and budgeted. But Destiny or Karma saw things differently."

"How many aunts and uncles do I have anyway?"

"My first wife, Sarah, and I had one little girl, Rose. My second wife, Eloise, and I have a boy named John Oliver and a girl named Mary Margaret. My third wife, Mae, and I have two sons, Robert Wallace and James Clark. My fourth wife is Mariah and we had Lauralee. My fifth wife, Marcia, and I don't have any children. I was in bed with her when Big Jack shot me. Kind of took the flame out of the marriage. So, I have two daughters and three sons, two dead wives, three that are still alive.

"As much as I love Mariah, I have no idea why I thought getting married again was a good idea. I've thought about it a lot of times. All I can come up with is the 'Thrill of the Hunt.' To be completely honest, travelling men don't need to be married. Soldiers don't need to be married either. Absence makes the heart lonely. A man gets to miss the warmth of a woman and there he goes on the Hunt again."

"What does MaMariah think about the other three that are alive? Have you asked her?"

"Well, I asked her what she thinks about us getting married again."

"What did MaMariah say?"

"She says she is still thinking about it."

"Doc, you have had a lot of experience with women, but you have got a problem. You think of all of these women as your wives. You aren't legally married to any of them, but your heart tells you something different."

Doc didn't say anything. He looked at me and I had to look away. I had said something I shouldn't have said. But MaMariah was my grandma. Doc didn't have any legal tie to her. It's bad to say but my grandmother had a bastard child by this man. He supported MaMariah and Momma, but it wasn't the same. And MaMariah still loved him. I should have just kept my mouth shut. I was sorry I said anything to begin with. The words came out of my mouth, and I couldn't take them back.

"Out of the mouths of babes," Doc said.

There was a long pause and Doc was just looking at me.

"I'm sorry I said anything, Doc. It just looks like the same pattern, the Thrill of the Hunt."

"No, Son. You called it. This relationship is complicated. The only difference is I just wanted to hunt Mariah again. I have always loved her the most."

Then I felt like a bolt of lightning had struck me, an epiphany, like in the Bible.

"Doc, MaMariah knows all of this, and she still wants to be with you. I don't think it's complicated. If she had a problem with these other wives, she wouldn't have anything to do with you."

"I believe you called it right, Iver. Maybe I will just let things ride along a while longer."

I was glad the conversation about MaMariah was over. Men should not talk with each other about things like this. We had probably broken some rule of the cosmos. A man talking about relationships is just wrong. In fact, the more I thought about it, the creepier it got.

Men hunt and protect the cave. Women cook and tidy up the cave. This is the way a man's world should be, none of this deep thinking about emotions. We may have tilted the universe.

Chapter 17

The Engagement

Life had gotten into a rhythm. I rode to work with Daddy on Monday morning. Doc drove me home on Saturday nights and ate supper at the house. I drove Doc's old Cadillac during the week for errands and Theola drove it, too. I liked to go home on Saturday night and go to church with Mama and Daddy. Big Judy let me drive her Cadillac on Sunday afternoons to ride around. I don't remember not going to church. Nobody said I had to go but it felt like I was supposed to. And Sunday School and church was where I could talk to the girls. I used to see some of the girls at the store in the afternoons but, by then, I was generally at the office with Doc in the afternoons. Now all the people I saw were old men that were stove up or wanted to buy a little bottle of Rooster Juice. I really kind of missed the afternoon girl watching.

I decided that working the other churches' Sunday Schools for girls was a little bit sacrilegious. I was just going to stick to the Presbyterian Church Sunday School. I was not but seventeen and I wasn't looking for a bride. I wanted a girlfriend, a regular one, not one so fast. Being honest with myself, Sissy scared me.

Besides Sunday School, the Dairy Queen was a good hunting ground. Saturday nights after supper and Sundays after church a lot of families went to the Dairy Queen for ice cream. It was a gathering spot for teenagers. Coveys of females and herds of males stood around looking at each other while trying to look like they were not paying any attention to the other. It was a complicated ritual. A male would break from the herd, walk over to the covey, and cut out a girl. The line usually used was 'Wanna talk?' Or a friend of a girl would flutter out of the covey and walk to the edge of the herd and say, 'My friend would like to talk to you. Would you like to talk to her?' Then the couple would walk over to his vehicle, lean on the fender and talk. Sometimes they would sit in the vehicle and talk; a really serious couple would get in his car and ride around and when they got back everyone would wonder if they had "done it". Sometimes the girl would laugh and flutter back to the covey to tell the other girls her secrets.

Once in a while this ritual would lead to the beginning of the dating ritual. My first experience with the dating ritual did not go so well. I had studied the subject extensively and I believed I knew the problem. I had not made friends with the girl (Sissy) before I went on a date. Doc was right. What were we going to talk about? I kissed her before I made friends with her, a big mistake. If I had talked a while, I would have realized that her beauty was only skin deep. An old saying, but it was absolutely true.

Fall had come and the tobacco market was closed, and hunting season was in full swing. Momma said that after tobacco season the wives were glad to get rid of their husbands for a while. That was really the reason wives let husbands go hunting. Daddy was happy; money was coming in instead of going out.

Daddy had a little tradition of putting on a chicken bog for all his customers or whoever wanted to come the Wednesday before Thanksgiving. Rudolph was in charge of cooking. He had his mother's old black wash pot that he used. The wash pot was set up beside the picnic shelter beside the store.

Daddy said the shelter had paid for itself by the increase in drinks, nabs and Vienna sales. The other canned meats, like oysters and mackerel sold well but little cans of Vienna sausages always sold the best.

The Lance brand of nabs sold the best, better than the Tom's brand. And Lance Toast Chez, the nabs with peanut better was my favorite.

Rudolph thought of himself as the "King Chicken Bog Chef" and I'll give it to him; it was good. He made what he called "South Carolina Style," with onions, smoked sausages, fat hens, long grain rice, black and red pepper, and boiled eggs. The Pepsi man left an extra ten cases of Pepsis and an extra ten cases of Mountain Dew. The Merita man left twenty extra loaves of light bread. There was something about the combination of chicken bog and light bread. I don't know what; but it was just right.

Rudolph started out the night before (or maybe Bet started the night before) and boiled 40 pounds of hens. And he had the fire just right. I guess he had fired a wash pot so many times he knew just how to do it. When he added the rice, the broth was just a little simmer. The pot never boiled over and the rice didn't stick. He had a bigger fire going for everybody to stand around and most everybody was thoughtful enough to throw their paper plates in the fire. I liked to stand and watch the plastic forks melt.

The interesting thing about the chicken bog was that everybody came, colored and white and some that go for Indian. It was like all of these men were friends. The next day they may go back to "help" and "boss man" but on that day they were just men swapping hunting stories and bragging about their children. Maybe one giant chicken bog would have solved all the problems of integration among other things.

That was our second Thanksgiving without Big Jack. That was his holiday. Big Jack and Big Judy moved beside us six years earlier, but we went back to the old house for Thanksgiving. I know they felt like this was their real home. Big Jack used to put on an oyster roast every year, Thanksgiving night. Big Judy would do some shrimp and flounder and sweet potatoes but the main thing was the oysters. He usually bought enough that we could pick out some for oyster soup. Big Judy made it with real cream and white potatoes.

Big Jack made a metal rack to cook the oysters. A low fire of oak embers under the rack and a wet burlap sack on top must be the way the angels cook oysters in heaven. Something about cold night air and eating oysters off the fire was just wonderful.

Momma said, "Big Jack loved his oyster roast. There is no reason we can't put it on in memory of him."

There wasn't any question of how to do an oyster roast. We were already trained. The only thing different was Gene, Roy, and I rode to Eagle Island to get the oysters instead of me and Big Jack. There was enough wood under the shed from last year and our oyster knives were in the kitchen drawer with our names scratched in the handles with a Bic pen. MaMariah got Doc his own oyster knife and scratched his name, Erastus, in it so he would not be left out.

We had eaten all the oysters we could hold, and we were picking out the oysters for the oyster stew. Doc said, "All of you come over here in a minute. I want to say something.'

We all walked over to where we could hear him. Doc said, "Mariah, please come over here and let me hold your hand."

I knew what was coming next.

MaMariah walked over and held out her hand. Doc got down on his knees; he couldn't do the one knee thing. He tried but just got on both knees. I couldn't take my eyes off of them. He was doing it like in the movies: with style. Gene and Roy came over and stood on either side of Doc. What was this? What were they going to do sing or something?

Doc says, "Mariah, will you be my wife?" and he kind of swept a glance over all of us and said, "If it is alright with all of you?"

Just like in the movies, he pulled a ring out of his coat pocket and put it on her finger. And just like in the movies, everybody said, "Awe."

MaMariah didn't say anything. She looked at him for a long time. She looked at him so long; Doc shifted his weight on his knees.

MaMariah said, "I'll marry you if you promise I am the one, the only, and the last wife."

Doc said, "I promise you, Mariah, and I promise all of you."

Now Gene and Roy's part kicked in. The boys were there to help Doc stand up. They had it planned out. I thought to myself, "What are grandsons for anyway?"

Daddy walked over to the smoke house, in the smoke house, walked out of the smoke house, walked to his truck, got a flashlight and a stack of paper cups, walked back to the smokehouse and came out with a dusty bottle of wine. "Roy, pass the cups around; you and Gene get one, too. We have got to toast the bride and groom."

Momma came out of the house with a corkscrew. Daddy was wiping the dust off with his handkerchief. We all got little cone-shaped paper cups of wine.

Daddy said, "Lauralee, you do the honors."

Mama said, "To Momma and Daddy getting married. I won't be a bastard anymore."

We all stood in silence. Momma downed her cup and laughed.

MaMariah said, "She's right. Congratulations, Lauralee."

I didn't know whether to be shocked or appalled. I was really happy MaMariah said yes, but what was Momma thinking when she said that? There was a hint of hatred in her voice. I know that all that resentment and anger didn't just disappear when Doc started coming to supper, but really, Momma, now?

I felt bad for Doc. Daddy put out his hand and shook Doc's hand and then he hugged MaMariah. The three of us boys did the same thing. Big Judy hugged Doc and hugged MaMariah.

Big Judy said, "I am so happy for my little Princess."

I had never heard Big Judy call her 'Little Princess.' It was kind of strange to think of my grandmother being a little girl and Big Judy being a young mother. Big Judy still loved her as she did when she was a little girl. I wondered if Momma would love me as a little boy when I was a grown man.

Then Big Judy caused the earth to rock on its axis. Big Judy walked up to Momma and slapped her across the face. Momma's mouth dropped open, and her hand went to her right cheek. Big Judy was left-handed. That slap left the whole side of her face red. She might have slapped the taste out of Momma's mouth.

Momma said, "Big Judy, what was that for? I've never been slapped in my life."

Big Judy said, "I should have done that a long time ago for your hateful attitude to your Momma and your Daddy."

Momma said, "Are you going senile?"

Big Judy said, "No, you act like you are the only person in the world that has ever had a problem. Your momma has a chance for a happy marriage with the man she has always loved, and you put a pall over the whole thing."

Momma had her mouth hung open and so did everybody else. This wasn't the sweet old lady that was my great grandma. I had never heard her say anything like that and surely not slap anything.

Momma started moving her jaw up and down but there wasn't any sound coming out.

Big Judy said, "You are a spoiled child that hasn't grown up. You still act like the world is spinning around you. And it doesn't spin around you. You are riding it like the rest of us."

Momma closed her mouth and tears were rolling down her cheeks.

Then Big Judy said, "On your birth certificate it says your parents are married and you had Erastus's last name. Don't come off with the bastard, poor little me shit. I wish Mariah and Erastus had more than you. Maybe you wouldn't have always been such a little pill."

Nobody said a thing. It was like the story of *"The Emperor Has No Clothes."* This was the most painful thing I had ever seen, but I was young. My mother, a grown woman, was being chastised in front of her family. And there must have been truth in it; Momma wasn't saying anything; her head was down, and her face had turned red.

Big Judy didn't say anything else. Momma didn't move from where she was standing for a long time. None of us had moved either.

Momma sucked in a big gulp of air and picked her head up. She walked over to Doc and MaMariah and stopped. She looked at them for a minute or so and said, "I am sorry for my comment. It was inappropriate. I am really happy that my momma and daddy are getting married."

Doc put his arm around Momma and said, "That's alright, LeeLee. We understand."

I had never heard Momma called LeeLee.

Ma Mariah put her arms around her, too. The three of them were standing there and Momma was sobbing. Doc and MaMariah looked like they had covered Mama with their bodies. Doc and MaMariah started crying, too.

Daddy, the twins, and I gathered up the kitchen stuff in the yard and carried it in the kitchen. Big Judy was sitting at the kitchen table with a bottle of wine and a tea glass. None of us said anything.

I looked out the back door and saw the three of them still standing together with their arms interlocked. They didn't look like they were crying anymore.

Daddy said, "Judith, do you want me to light the heater in your bedroom? I didn't know if you wanted to spend the night."

"Thank you, Walter. And will you light the heater in the living room?"

Big Judy got up and walked out in the yard. We were standing in the doorway watching but we couldn't hear what anybody was saying. She turned and waved for us to come outside.

Big Judy said, "Walter, carry your family home. Mariah, Erastus, Lauralee, come on inside."

We did just what she said. For some reason the image of the Matriarchal Elephant came to mind. Big Judy isn't big, but she told Momma the facts and told us what to do.

A painful drama had played out in front of me and as far as I know, I was not the cause of it, but I was young. An image comes to mind of the scene Doc told me about: the murder of his mother. He saw his father as a flawed human and I saw my mother as a flawed human. I was yet at another stage of maturity.

Neither Big Judy nor MaMariah nor Momma came home Thanksgiving night. Daddy drove me to the office and Doc wasn't there. Theola cooked me breakfast and I told her what happened at the farm. I needed to talk to Theola and tell her what happened. She was part of our family, too.

Theola said, "I'm sorry that you saw that. You have little brothers and you're a boy. Miss Mariah is an only child and an only daughter. Miss Lauralee is an only child and an only daughter. There is something about how mommas and their girls act to one another and when they are only children, life is just harder."

I said, "How can being an only child be bad? I would love it."

Theola said, "No, it is hard when you are an only child. Do you worry about being a failure?"

"Well, no."

"If you mess up your momma has got two more."

"Well, Momma isn't a failure."

"Have you ever thought of why she farms? She doesn't have to work. She is trying to prove her worth. Your daddy makes a good living at his store."

"I've never thought of this."

"And think about Miss Mariah. You know when Miss Judith found out about Dr. Edwards, she was disappointed. Her only child had messed up."

I was in wonder, "I didn't know this about only children."

"And Miss Lauralee probably blames Miss Mariah for not knowing about Dr. Edwards' other wives. I'm sorry you have seen the other side of people you love."

"I know its family history. I just hate to see them hurting."

I sat there at the table for a while. Theola sat down with her cup of coffee and said, "I feel sorry for Dr. Edwards."

I was nodding in agreement, "He is going to do the right thing and gets insulted. It just hurts, especially since it was Momma that did it."

Theola was holding her cup coffee in both hands, "Your momma will wish she could take those words back till the day she dies."

I couldn't talk about it anymore. I reached behind the kitchen door and got the outside broom and went to the front porch. I swept the front porch, the sidewalks, the steps, and the back porch. I dusted the porch furniture and sat down in the rocking chair with the broom across my knees.

Doc and MaMariah came up in his Cadillac and drove around behind the house. I walked through the house to the kitchen. MaMariah walked in the kitchen door with a big smile. Theola said, "I want to see your ring on your hand. You know I have already seen it, don't you? Doc had to show it to somebody."

MaMariah held out her hand and just smiled at Doc.

Doc poured himself a cup of coffee and walked into his office. Doc said, "Iver, come in here and close the door."

I walked in and closed the door behind me.

"Iver, the four of us worked all of this pain out. I know your Momma regrets what she said, but, son, she is our child, and we understand. I don't want you to worry. Families work things out."

I hung my head down.

"Doc, what about Momma and Big Judy?"

"I'm not sure how that is going to work out. Judith shouldn't have done what she did. There were many years of attitude that got slapped out of Lauralee. Judith had a lot of anger come out when she slapped Lauralee. We talked all night. Mariah and Judith got a lot of things out in the open."

"I can't see Big Judy apologizing to Momma. I know she thinks she is justified."

Doc said, "I think you are right. Judith doesn't regret the slap."

I realize that I am standing beside Doc with my hand on his shoulder.

Doc said, "This has been a stressful event, but, in the end, all of this will be for the best."

"Doc, I feel like I need to apologize for Momma and Big Judy."

"Iver, I know what you mean. I have felt like that about my daddy."

There was a knock at the door and in walked MaMariah. She said, "Iver, we have worked everything out, with your mother and, I think, with my mother."

"MaMariah, I am sorry for what Momma said to you and Doc."

"Iver, she is sorry she said it. It's past now. Erastus and I understand where it came from, and we forgive her."

Doc reached for MaMariah, "She may never get to the end of her hate for me. I can understand it. And I hope she forgives me for my shortcomings."

The Lord's Prayer came to my mind. "Forgive us our trespasses as we forgive those that trespass against us."

Doc and MaMariah are really getting married.

Everybody showed up for regular Saturday night supper after Thanksgiving. Doc and MaMariah kissed like teenagers. Gene and Roy couldn't stand it. They just groaned when the kisses happened. I was jealous that I didn't have a girl to kiss. Big Judy was nursing her bourbon and one ice cube. Momma and Daddy were late, which was not unusual. Daddy walked in and said, "I about had to run the customers out of the store with a gun. I'm hungry. Is Lauralee here yet?"

Bet already has the buffet line out.

MaMariah said, "At lunch she said to start supper without her. I don't know what she is doing."

Daddy asked, "Everybody got their hands washed?"

We were all standing around waiting for someone to say the blessing. Daddy said, "Dr. Erastus, will you return thanks?" Doc looked stunned. I hadn't thought of it, but I had never heard Doc pray out loud. He always bowed his head, and his lips moved before we ate. I do the same thing when he and I are together.

Doc prayed, "Lord, bless this food and bless us all. Keep us safe and never let us fall. Amen."

We all said "Amen."

Momma came in from the kitchen door drying her hands on a dishtowel as Roy brought up the end of the line. Roy turned around and said, "It's been blessed, Momma."

All of us sitting together felt just right. But I missed Big Jack.

Daddy said, "Well, Love Birds, when are you going to get married and (he hesitated) where are you getting married?"

Big Judy said, "Y'all got married last time at the courthouse in Charlotte. This time you are getting married by a preacher like you should have the first time."

All of us stopped eating and looked at Big Judy. That Matriarchal Elephant came to mind again.

She continues, "I am planning and paying for this wedding. I have made the decision that you are getting married at midnight on New Year's Eve. You are both old and I am old. We don't need a long engagement."

MaMariah said, "Where are we going to get married, Momma?"

Big Judy said, "We are going to have a party in the yard, and we are going to invite everybody we can think of." There were nods from everybody at the table. "We are going to start the invitations by announcing it at church tomorrow. I'll have it put in the bulletin next week."

Doc said, "Judith, we can have a quiet little wedding like, next weekend?"

Big Judy said, "No, this is something I have dreamed about since Jack shot you. It's going to be a classy affair. Y'all just show up with wedding clothes on."

Momma said, "What can we do to help?"

Big Judy said, "I want you to clean up our yards. And I want you to not ask a lot of questions. I want to do this and I am."

I knew what everybody was thinking: "Is this Big Judy's first bourbon or second?"

Everybody was eating kind of quietly like there was a lot of thinking going on.

Roy piped up and said, "Big Judy, Gene and I are going to help you and we can keep secrets."

Big Judy said, "Alright, the three of us."

I couldn't put my finger on it, but I got the feeling the three of them may have been talking about this before now.

Sure enough, Sunday morning during announcements, Big Judy not only stood up but went down to the front and made the announcement. She stood with both hands on her cane and her head tilted back and said, "I want to announce the marriage of my daughter Mariah

McLean to Dr. Erastus Rembrandt Edwards on December 31, 1969. All of you and your families are invited to my home for a New Year's Eve party and to witness a wedding."

I'm not sure, but I think it was Roy that started clapping and then the whole church erupted in applause. This was the first and one of the few times I had ever heard applause in the Presbyterian Church. The men got up and shook Doc's hand and the women hugged MaMariah and Big Judy. It was like the whole church was happy for them.

I sat in my spot watching everyone and it dawned on me that I was watching my family. I suddenly felt that the whole church was my family. I had the stark realization that these were other people that loved us, not just the Saturday night crowd. I should have known this already. Our family still loves us with our shortcomings and our church family loves us with our shortcomings.

I had heard Big Judy say, "You don't have to like what people do, but you do have to love them." It made perfect sense. I got up and hugged MaMariah and I hugged Doc for the first time. I felt like crying because I realized how much I missed Big Jack.

Chapter 18

Florida

It was the Monday after Thanksgiving and Doc wanted me to put up a Christmas tree. I had never heard of putting one up before the fifteenth of December. He wanted me to go to Roses or Western Auto or somewhere and get a tin-foil-looking Christmas tree, a rotating light, and all the colored Christmas balls I could find. And he wanted a lighted gold-foil star on the top. Doc handed me a hundred- dollar bill. He was serious about putting up this tree, for sure. The phone rang as I got to the door.

"Hold it, boy. Judith needs to talk to you." Big Judy had never telephoned me a single time in my lifetime. I thought the world must be coming to an end.

I picked up the phone, "Yes, ma'am. This is Iver." There were no other words needed except, "Goodbye."

"Doc, Big Judy wants to talk to you." All Doc said was a series of "Yes, ma'am's."

When he hung up, he said, "Iver, get the tree put up today. Y'all are going to Florida with Miss Judith tomorrow. You need to take Big Jack's Cadillac to the station and get it serviced today. When you finish with the tree, I'll run you over to get the car. You boys need to carry your bathing trunks."

And that was that.

Tuesday morning at 7 a.m. Gene and Roy were in the back seat of the Cadillac. I am driving and Big Judy was riding shotgun. When we got to I-95, we didn't see many North Carolina license plates. Most of the plates were from New York, Pennsylvania, and New Jersey. When we got to South of the Border we had to stop. The twins had seen the sheep jumping over the moon on the billboard for South of the Border. "All of your sheep are counted at South of the Border".

Around Florence I got the nerve up to say, "Big Judy, why are we going to Florida?"

"We are going to see some of my nephews and their families", she answered.

Roy said, "I didn't know we had any cousins from Florida."

"I haven't seen them for years. My brother Carl died about 20 years ago and I just haven't visited down there since. We write a couple times a year to keep up."

Roy said, "What did your brother do for a living?"

Big Judy said, "He trained elephants."

Well, folks, I just about drove Big Jack's Cadillac off of I-95. Big Judy's family was in the circus business, too. Well, that makes sense.

Roy piped up from the back seat, "So, that's how MaMariah got up with Doc?"

"Yes, Ralph, my brother, was in Charlotte with the circus and Mariah and I went to stay with him for a couple of weeks. By the time the show was over in Charlotte, Doc and Mariah were married."

Gene said, "Why didn't you tell us you knew about the circus?"

"I didn't want you to run away and join the circus like Carl did. When he got it in his blood, he stayed with it until he couldn't travel anymore. His sons work one of the circuses now, Raleigh and Roscoe. One works with elephants and the other with horses."

Gene said, "This is unbelievable. Are we going to see the elephants?"

Roy said, "I can't believe this. Elephants.".

Big Judy was laughing, "I'll make sure you get to ride them some. I used to love to ride one and wear a costume." My great-grandmother had just gotten more wonderful.

From Donahoe Creek to Sarasota, Florida, is about six hundred and fifty miles. We had to stop for stretch breaks about every hour and a half. Big Judy got stiff if she sat too long. When we crossed the South Carolina-Georgia line, I could tell Big Judy was tired.

Big Judy said, "Be on the lookout for a Holiday Inn or a Howard Johnson's. We'll stop and eat supper and get a fresh start in the morning."

We found a Holiday Inn with an indoor pool and a restaurant. This was big stuff. We got a room with two double beds and rented a roll away cot. I got to sleep on the cot. We played in the pool until 8 o'clock and got room service to bring our supper. That was living.

Big Judy was up and dressed before any of us had stirred. She turned on the television and was drinking a cup of coffee when I woke up. We packed up, checked out, and ate breakfast in the hotel restaurant. Big Judy knew how to travel.

Driving across Georgia was pretty uneventful but when we hit Florida it was like we were driving through Paradise. There were tourist attractions everywhere.

Big Judy said, "The first place we are going to stop is the Fountain of Youth in St. Augustine. Iver, watch for the signs."

When we stopped, Big Judy got a half-gallon orange juice bottle out of the trunk. We paid to get in, looked at the plants, all took a big drink, got a jug of water and hit the road again. The jug was held upright between the suitcases.

Big Judy said, "I want to stop and see somebody wrestle an alligator. We've got to get us a camera. Nobody will believe what we are seeing. Stop at the next drug store we see. I know they have them. And a couple of extra rolls of film."

Gene, Roy and (I'll admit) I were about to come out of our skins. The signs said, "Alligator Wrestlers." The place we stopped had real Seminole Indians putting on the show. We got our picture made with the 'gators.

Big Judy said, "We have got to stop and see the mermaids. They are beautiful girls. I want you boys to see them." All right, Grandma.

We finally made it to Sarasota and got a room at Howard Johnson's. We lived big again.

When we got up Thursday morning, I said, "Are we going to meet the cousins today?"

Big Judy said, "Yes, they are looking for us when we get there."

When Big Judy checked out, she had the clerk call a taxicab. Roy said, "Are we going to ride in a taxicab?"

Big Judy said, "You can ride with him if you want to. Iver and I are going to follow him to Raleigh's"

When the cab showed up, Big Judy handed him a card with an address. She walked back to the car and said, "Follow that cab." She was the smartest woman I have ever known.

While we were driving to Cousin Raleigh's my perspective on the world changed. I felt like I had gone to a place in a dream. Every time the cab made a turn, I saw something I wanted to stop and look at. And when we got to Cousin Raleigh's, I felt like I belonged there, just like I was at home.

There were three young cousins waiting for us: Marcus, Troy and Virgil.

Marcus welcomed us. "We've been waiting for you. Come on."

Cousin Raleigh said, "Wait a minute. I'm going to get a golf cart so Aunt Judy can drive around with us. We can walk." The man had a golf cart!

We spent the morning walking, with Big Judy riding, around the circus neighborhood where they lived. There were neighbors that had bears in cages, some with lions and tigers. There were elephants and horses that did tricks. There were people practicing walking on stilts and tight ropes. There were midgets and dwarfs and giants. If I had died right there, I would have gone to heaven happy.

We made it back to their house about 1 o'clock for lunch. Cousin Ralph said, "We want you to spend the night here with us and we can go to the Circus Museum tomorrow. Then you can get an early start Saturday morning to go home."

Big Judy hemmed and hawed. She said we were planning to stay in a hotel that night and leave for home in the morning. "I am afraid that if I stay too long, I won't be able to get these boys back to North Carolina. This is not what I had in mind, but plans can change."

The six of us boys kissed her on the cheek.

That afternoon Big Judy, Raleigh and Roscoe, the horse man, drove off in the Cadillac. The three of us country boys were in paradise. Our three new circus cousins were acrobats or tumblers and they tried to teach us how, but it was obvious they had been doing all that since they were babies. We were so jealous in one way but in awe in another way. I then knew why people ran off and joined the circus.

Friday morning, we went to the Circus Museum. We had to buy more film. Friday night, Raleigh and Roscoe's neighbors came for a cookout. We couldn't get enough of the stories about the circus.

Saturday morning came and we didn't want to leave. I knew we needed to go home, but this place had a magic spell on me. I was possessed. It made me kind of crazy in the head. I wanted to go on an adventure with these people.

But soon I was driving back north, and I said to Big Judy, "Don't we need to be planning the wedding?"

Big Judy said, "No problem, we've got it in the bag."

I didn't know what bag she was talking about. I hadn't seen any decorations for New Year's or a wedding. Maybe she had forgotten we needed decorations.

I asked, "Don't we need some decorations? Get a cake? All that frou-frou stuff you see at a wedding?"

"Boys, should we let him in on our plans?" Big Judy turned around in her seat to look at the boys. Both were nodding "Yes."

Big Judy said, "I have hired a circus to come to us. The circus is a small family, one-ring circus: horses, motorcycles, and an elephant. The tent is going to be put up in the yard. There is enough room."

I was stunned. And I was silent. I couldn't believe this. "We need some gas."

I pulled in the first gas station I saw. The attendant pumped the gas, washed the windshield, checked the oil and Big Judy handed him the money out the window.

I still didn't say anything. Big Judy said, "They are going to bring the popcorn stand and the cotton candy stand. Our preacher is going to perform the wedding in the ring at midnight. What do you think, Iver?"

"I think this is the damnedest thing I have ever heard."

"Raleigh and Roscoe are under contract so they can't bring their animals. We rode to some friends of theirs and made a deal. They are going to bring the circus, everything, for four thousand dollars. One show, one night. Iver, you are going to have to move this car. You are blocking the man's pumps."

I forgot I was driving.

Roy said, "We are not going to tell anybody. They are just going to show up, right, Big Judy?"

Gene said, "We are just going to invite everybody to a New Year's Eve party and wedding."

I am driving with tears rolling down my cheeks.

Big Judy said, "What's wrong, Iver?"

"Big Jack would have loved this whole plan." Then all of us were crying. The sniffing dried up by the time we got about halfway to Georgia.

One thing I could always say about Big Judy was that when she did something, it was really big. We stopped every hour and half on the way home for Big Judy to walk around a little. I think we got a snack and went to the bathroom at every stop.

We got home at one o'clock Sunday morning. I drove the car across the yard to Big Judy's back door. But instead of unloading, she said, "You boys drive the car on over to your house. I'll get my stuff tomorrow."

Mama and Daddy were still up when we went in. We stayed up till three o'clock in the morning telling them about the trip.

Mama said, "Your great-grandma is a tough old bird to take you boys to Florida. I want you boys to think of something special to do for her."

I laid in bed thinking. I never thought my life could be such an adventure. Then I remembered I was almost eighteen and the draft was waiting for me. I kept up with the paper about Viet Nam. In my heart I just didn't want Viet Nam to be my adventure, but I knew I was going to be drafted. Maybe I could hide in the circus or go to Canada.

Dreams of a child.

Chapter 19

The Wedding

Gene and Roy and I were about to bust, but we kept the secret.

Monday morning arrived and Momma and Bet were getting our house decorated and Big Judy's decorated. It was a little early for them to decorate for Christmas, but they were not going to be outdone by Doc. Big Judy said she was staying in bed until Tuesday. She could do whatever she wanted. I knew she was just an angel in disguise.

Monday morning at work I was on top of the world. I told Doc and Theola all about the trip except the part about hiring the circus. Theola said that she knew the Florida Indians were crazy; wrestling alligators just proved it. Doc asked a lot of questions about the mermaids. "I can see you really studied the mermaids," he said with a grin. I never mentioned the words "hired circus" once. It was hard but I did it.

At lunch Doc said I needed to carry the Cadillac to get it serviced again. "Doc, will it be OK if I take a few minutes and carry our film to the drug store?" I ordered double prints of everything.

When I got back from the gas station, we had two 'ritus customers so we were busy the rest of the afternoon.

"Doc, may I use your car to go to the house for a few minutes?"

"No, but you and I can go see Mariah," he answered with a big smile.

I slipped over to Big Judy's. She was sitting in the kitchen eating pound cake and buttermilk.

"Big Judy, are the cousins from Florida coming for the wedding?" I asked.

"As far as I know, they're coming. Did I tell you that Roscoe and Raleigh juggle together? They said they would bring their Indian clubs so you boys could try them out."

"No, you didn't! This is getting better and better."

Big Judy laughed, "Yep, it's going to be something for all of us to remember."

"Are we going to have a wedding cake?"

"I haven't planned to, but we can get one."

"I think you should get a pink wedding cake, Big Judy." I don't know where I got the idea for a pink wedding cake. That was a girl thing.

"Alright, I know a lady at the Methodist church that makes wedding cakes and I have the perfect thing for a topper." She paused and said, "We need to order a really big one."

Big Judy got up and went to her dresser and came back with a porcelain figurine. It was a carriage with a princess and prince being pulled by two white horses.

"Big Judy, is this the wedding you wanted for MaMariah?"

She laughed, "Maybe not a circus. But, yes, I wanted my Little Princess to have a beautiful wedding."

"It is kind of strange to hear you call MaMariah your Little Princess." Big Judy just smiled and nodded.

Christmas came and went. New shotguns for the boys, new pistols for Momma and Daddy, bracelets for Big Judy and MaMariah, new pipe and tobacco for Doc. Cash for Theola, Rudolph, Betsy and Henry. I kind of knew that Rudolph was going to spend some time in Abadaba Land, stoned on marijuana. He said he was going to buy a new suit. Theola and Bet are going to shop for new hats, dresses and shoes. Henry was going to Rhode Island to visit for a few weeks.

New Year's Eve morning and we boys were ready to get the show on the road. I don't know what more we could do to get ready. I even made the beds up in the extra bedrooms at Doc's office. Doc had the office open Wednesday and had a few customers. Theola and I said that if he didn't close the office on New Year's Eve, we were going to strike all of January. He was quarreling about being closed on a Thursday, but it was his wedding day.

Doc had come over to the house to visit. He said as old as they were, seeing the bride on their wedding day was not going to be bad luck.

At nine o'clock we heard horns blowing on the road in front of the house. We about fell over each other trying to get out of the front door. There was an elephant standing in our yard with a woman in sequins riding on its back and there was a Roman soldier on a white horse beside the elephant.

The Roman soldier leaped off his horse and strode up to the porch and said, "Best wishes to the bride and groom. I am Maximus and I have brought my circus to entertain you."

We just stood there and looked at him, the elephant, the pretty woman, and the line of trucks. The Roman Soldier, Maximus, stood there holding the bridle of his white steed and said, "Show me where to build my arena."

Big Judy walked down the front steps with her cane. Maximus gave her a low bow. She took her cane and waved it around the yard. She said, "I think it will fit here."

Maximus said, "Yes, madam," and gave another low bow.

Momma said, "I'm going to call Walter. He needs to close the store and come home. Then I'm calling everybody I know."

It was on then. Those folks had done this before. There must have been twenty-five people spreading stuff out. They even used the elephant to stand the tent up. We sat on the porch and watched. Bet brought us a plate of sandwiches, so we didn't have to go inside to eat. People just kept on coming to watch. Big Judy waved me over. "I want you to walk around and invite these people to come tonight to the show. Tell them everything is free including the refreshments. The show starts at nine o'clock."

This wasn't a gift to just Doc and MaMariah; it was a gift to the community. We watched all day. The cousins from Florida drove up about two o'clock and wanted to see the farm. We rode out and checked the chickens and livestock. When we got back, Bet had us collards, black eyed peas and cracklin' cornbread. She said we needed to eat it on New Year's Eve and New Year's Day just to make sure the luck sticks. I thought she just liked collards and peas.

At eight-thirty the tent was full. There was a special box seat for MaMariah, Doc and Big Judy. Everybody was in awe. The elephant danced and Momma rode it around the ring. Maximus rode two white horses round the ring Roman style, one foot on each horse. There were a bunch that did tricks on unicycles. There was a lion that did tricks like a dog. There were motorcycles that did everything but crash.

Raleigh and Roscoe appeared juggling swords and dressed like genies. They even had turbans on. The lady that rode the elephant swung around by her hair on a cable. There were two midget clowns that drove a little car around with Gene and Roy, complete with makeup and wigs and riding in the backseat. Maximus stopped a horse in front of me and had me get on. As we (me and the horse) were galloping around the ring, Maximus jumped on the back of the horse, did a flip and ended up in front of me.

All of the time the show was on, a man walked through the bleachers handing out popcorn, cotton candy and soft drinks.

At eleven-thirty the parade started. All the performers walked in the parade including us. Daddy had on a red coat and top hat and came in on a carriage, pulled by two white horses. He stopped in front of the box seat and got MaMariah, Doc and Big Judy. Everybody applauded. I didn't know Daddy could drive horses. They rode around the ring a couple of times waving at the crowd. Then Daddy and Maximus stopped the carriage in the center of the ring, and everybody got out. Our preacher came out of the shadows dressed in his robe and stole. Everybody looked at their watches. It was eleven-fifty-three. We all got in our places. Momma handed MaMariah her bridal bouquet. The preacher finished at exactly midnight and Doc and MaMariah kissed. The whole tent erupted. The elephant shook her head, the lion roared and the horses stood on their back legs. Then the two midgets drove a little truck in the ring with the wedding cake on the back. They pulled the plates and forks out of the cab. Doc and Ma Mariah cut the cake and fed each other a piece of cake. It was official. The marriage was complete.

All the pink wedding cake got eaten. Even the elephant got a piece. The photographer made sure he got a picture of that.

The circus was packed up and gone by noon the next morning. Gene, Roy and I watched the whole process. Marcus, Troy and Romeo had seen it all before, except a wedding in a circus.

It was the most wonderful wedding that anyone could have had. My thoughts sounded like a girl-- again.

Daddy, Raleigh, and Roscoe had gone to the store. Doc and MaMariah had come by to tell us goodbye before they left.

Momma said, "Let me carry Big Judy her lunch."

MaMariah said, "I'll walk with you so I can tell her goodbye."

Momma paused and said, "Mother, Father, I am so happy for you." That was the first time I had ever heard her call them such formal names. It was nice.

Both hugged Momma. MaMariah and Momma walked out the back door with Big Judy's lunch. In just a few minutes they both walked back in the door.

I said, "Big Judy is dead, isn't she?" I don't know why I said that.

Everybody was silent. Momma was holding a piece of pink paper. She handed it to Doc.

"'My little princess is married. My prayer is answered.'"

And life goes on.

Amy Stephens lives at the end of the dirt road in Carver's Creek, Bladen County, North Carolina, the Center of the Known Universe. She is a farmer, wife, mother, grandmother, collector of stories and useless ephemera. NCSU 1980, Animal Science, not English.